MASTER OF KAYOS

THE HOUNDS OF ZEUS MC
BOOK 6

BY FAITH GIBSON

Copyright © 2022 by Faith Gibson

Published by: Bramblerose Press LLC

Editor: Candice Royer

Proofreader: KDL Editing

First edition: June 2022

Cover design: Jay Aheer, Simply Defined Art

Cover photography: © Wander Aguiar Photography

Cover model: Clayton Wells

ISBN: 978-1736890042

DEDICATION

This one is for you, the reader. It's been a fast eight years since I began this writing journey, and if it weren't for every single one of you, I wouldn't be where I am. You are the reason I do this.

PROLOGUE

QUINN FELT UNEASY walking down the semi-dark hallway, but she really had to pee. When she reached for the doorknob to the women's restroom, a hand covered her mouth. Quinn struggled, but whoever was at her back was stronger. The back door of the convenience store opened, and she was shoved through. Quinn struggled with all her strength. Goddess, why hadn't she waited for someone to go with her?

"Grab her feet," the man behind her demanded, and the other did as instructed. Quinn squirmed in their grip, moving her legs back and forth until she was able to break one foot free. She kicked out, hitting the one holding her legs in the nose. He dropped her other leg to cover his bleeding face. With her lower body now free, Quinn used the momentum of her legs falling to carry her forward, flipping the man behind her over her back. As soon as she was out of his clutches, Quinn ran.

The store backed up to dense woods, and Quinn headed that direction instead of circling the building where humans wouldn't react well to seeing wolves. The vegetation was thick, but Quinn bullied her way through the branches and undergrowth. Snarls and

1

snapping of jaws sounded close behind, so Quinn urged her body to go faster. The trees opened up slightly, and Quinn had a moment of hope until she caught sight of more wolves. These weren't your garden variety timber wolves either. These were massive with silver fur covering their backs and black on their bellies and legs. She was no match for six dire wolves, but that didn't mean she wouldn't fight like hell before they finally took her down.

Quinn fought with everything she had, but it didn't take long before they had her incapacitated and in the back of a vehicle, driving away from the store. Once they subdued Quinn, they bragged about how their father would reward them for finally bringing Quinn to him, which meant they were both her uncles. But how the hell had they known she was there at the store? Or in New Mexico for that matter? Fuck. Someone had betrayed her, and when Quinn found out who, she would add them to the list of people who needed to die.

"What the fuck is that?" Henry, the driver of the SUV, was intent on something in the rearview mirror. Quinn turned to look out the back window. A large eagle grabbed one of the bikers and tossed him off his motorcycle.

"Shoot that fucking bird," Henry instructed his brother.

Quinn lunged for the male sitting in the passenger seat when he aimed a pistol out the window. Henry swerved before regaining control of the SUV. Bradley cursed as he turned the gun on her. "That was a mistake." No, the mistake had been leaving her guard behind. She didn't respond. Instead, she glared at Bradley who was snarling at her. Knowing her guard wouldn't stop until he found her, Quinn needed to be smart. Do whatever it took to stay alive, and that meant she couldn't attack her uncles. Not when one of them kept his weapon trained on her.

When they neared her grandfather's home, Quinn was expecting living arrangements like a subdivision of similar houses. Instead, small cabins dotted the tree line, and those didn't appear to be in top condition. Henry pulled to a stop in front of a massive structure reminiscent of a lodge, and she guessed that's where all the pack's money went.

With the pistol aimed at her chest, Bradley opened the back door. "Get out. And if you try anything stupid, I *will* shoot you, niece or not."

CHAPTER ONE

Kayos

"YOU KNOW YOU want me."

At the sultry voice of one of his subs, Kyllian's head snapped around, and he not-so-silently cursed the young man making a scene. Kyllian was leaning against a booth at Dominion, the BDSM club where he was one of the Masters, chatting with Spyder, Hawk, and their two females. Brandon, the sub, was leaning across the bar, his bubble butt encased in tight pants. If Kyllian swung that way, he would have already gotten balls deep in the man. Kyllian pushed off the booth and stalked across the floor. He didn't say a word to the bratty sub. One look was all it took for Brandon to duck his head and follow. When they reached the back hall where private rooms lined both walls, Kyllian entered the first door of an unoccupied space. When Brandon was inside, he immediately dropped to his knees.

"I'm sorry, Master."

"Did I give you permission to speak?" Being a Gryphon, Kyllian had to be careful. He had the ability

4

to voice others. The mind manipulation was a gift from Zeus to ensure the wrong people didn't find out about shifters. The Hounds also used the ability in their family mercenary business to gain information. It was not to be used on bratty subs who couldn't obey the rules.

Brandon shook his head. Kyllian, being a shifter, also had to be careful in his particular skillset. Too much wrist action and he could damage his human partners. Brandon Agnew was a young man trying to outrun an abusive homelife. When Kyllian first got into the lifestyle, he found it odd that people who were abused outside the club wished for pain to remove their grief. Justin, the owner of the club and the male who had taught Kyllian how to use the various implements in his particular kink, explained the psychology behind pain. What a whip or cane offered was an escape from reality. The pain they produced took the sub to a place outside themselves where they could forget about life for a while.

"What happened?" Kyllian asked. Brandon coming into the club and mouthing off to the bartender was a cry for help.

Speaking of crying, Brandon's voice trembled. "He found me."

Kyllian didn't have to ask who Brandon was referring to. The young man had been in an abusive relationship for the last two years. When Brandon asked Ted to spank him, Ted gave him what he wanted at first. When Brandon asked for Ted to spank him harder, something inside the other man flipped, and he began whipping Brandon with a belt. He took

Brandon's need for pain as permission to abuse the young man. Brandon had come to Kyllian a broken soul, and with patience and a steady hand, Kyllian gave the sub what he needed without harming him. Theirs wasn't a sexual arrangement. That wasn't to say Brandon didn't get off on being whipped; he did. But Kyllian never touched the man in a sexual fashion. The orgasms were a byproduct of the cane. The aftercare where Kyllian tended to the marks on Brandon's body as well as giving him cuddles weren't of a sexual nature either. They were nurturing. Caring.

His family rarely saw that side of Kyllian. He was the broody brother. He and his oldest brother, Ryker, had that in common. Now that Ryker had found a mate in Rhiannon, he was less broody and smiled a hell of a lot more often than before. Kyllian laughed and cut up with his brothers, Hayden especially, but when he wasn't around family, he rarely smiled. Didn't really have a reason to.

"Did you go to the police?" Kyllian asked. He had convinced Brandon to get a restraining order against Ted. Kyllian helped Brandon move out of the apartment the two men were sharing. Since Brandon was a successful CPA, his name had been on the lease. He paid the majority of the bills, so when he broke the lease and moved to a neighboring town, he had left Ted without a home or a boyfriend.

"Yes, but they said since he didn't actually threaten me, there was nothing they could do."

Kyllian should have handled Ted before now, but he had wrongly assumed the restraining order would do the job. Stepping into Brandon's space, Kyllian ran his fingers through the man's dark curls. He didn't often show his softer side to his subs, but sometimes a gentle touch worked better than a heavy hand.

"I'll take care of it. But Brandon? The next time you come into Dominion and cause a scene like you did with Frankie, the punishment will be harsh. You get me?"

"Yes, Master K."

"Good boy. Here's what I want you to do. First, go out there and apologize to Frankie. While you do that, I'm going to talk to Justin. He and Silas are here tonight. I'm going to ask them to keep you company until I have a talk with Ted. When I give them the all-clear, they'll take you home." Kyllian put enough of his Gryphon's influence into his voice so Brandon obeyed without question.

"Thank you, Master K."

Kyllian offered his hand, and the young man took it. Once they were in the hallway, Kyllian said, "Go into the bathroom and wash your face." He waited outside while Brandon got himself together. When he exited the washroom, he gave Kyllian a hesitant smile. Kyllian ruffled his hair, then strode out into the main room with his sub following. Brandon headed to the bar, and Kyllian turned to go to the office. Before he got two steps in, a familiar voice called out.

"Kayos, wait up."

Kyllian's heart pounded steadily. If Ryker was in Dominion, something was wrong. He grabbed his oldest brother's shoulders. "What the hell are you doing here? What happened? Is it Rory? Pop?"

"Calm down. They're both fine. Is there

7

somewhere private we can talk?"

"For fuck's sake. Just tell me."

"It's about a job."

Kyllian narrowed his eyes. "You came all the way out here to talk to me about a job?"

Ryker jutted his chin. "You weren't answering your phone."

"Because I was working. Jesus." Kyllian grabbed Ryker's forearm and pulled his brother away from the floor. He led Ryker to the same room he had used to talk to Brandon. "Wait here."

"Wait—?"

"Yes, wait. I was in the middle of something when you intercepted me." Kyllian didn't give Ryker time to argue. He made his way to Silas's office and told him and his mate, Justin, what happened with Brandon and Kyllian's plan to get rid of Ted. He wouldn't kill him, but he would encourage him to get out of town and stay there. "If you wouldn't mind keeping watch over him, I would appreciate it." They both readily agreed, and Kyllian returned to his brother, closing the door behind him. Ryker was livid, but Kyllian couldn't find it in himself to care.

"Now, what's so fucking important you had to come disrupt me here?"

Ryker straightened to his full height, but he didn't intimidate Kyllian. Only his parents could do that. "Your loyalty to our family comes before sex."

"Oh, for the love of… You have no idea what goes on here, so get off your fucking high horse. Either tell me about this job, or get the fuck out." Kyllian hated when people got their feathers ruffled about things they didn't try to understand. Spyder had recounted the conversation he and Hawk had with Ryker regarding the lifestyle a few months back. Ryker hadn't approached Kyllian to ask questions. If he had, Kyllian would have explained what he did and why.

"It's Quinn. She's being threatened."

"And? We're mercenaries, not bodyguards."

"No, but in this case, she needs someone to watch her back, and Pop asked for you specifically since you're single."

"Me? Why? I do have responsibilities."

"What? This place?" Ryker scoffed.

Kyllian's Gryphon was close to the surface. He had never hit his brother in anger, but he was close to doing so. "Yes, this place. If you would bother to ask about my life instead of judging based on everything you do not know, you would understand what I do here is important. It's not about sex, Ryot. It's about giving my subs something they need to get through their shitty lives."

Ryker cocked his head to the side, his posture still stiff. "You're right. I don't understand, and I haven't asked because I honestly don't want to know what you do in your personal time." Relaxing a fraction, he offered, "I'll try to do better in the future."

"Thank you. So again, what does being single have to do with the job?"

"I don't know how long it will take. I need someone to not only watch over Quinn but help her find out who is behind the threats. I didn't realize you came here to do a service to others. I'll find someone else."

9

"I didn't say I wouldn't do it, Ryot. I'll take the job, but first, I have to call in a friend to cover my shifts here." Kyllian hadn't spoken to Gunnar in a few months, but the male owed Kyllian a favor.

"These people you help, they're okay with someone else doing whatever it is you do to them?"

"Yes. They know I would never hand them over to another Master who wasn't as skilled or as caring as I am."

"Master? Like, they're your slaves?"

"There are different types of Masters. Yes, some have slaves, but Master or Mistress is also someone who is the best in their particular kink. Someone the owner of the club trusts with each and every person who walks through those doors."

"But you're only thirty-two. If you're a Master, I take it you've been doing this a while?"

"I have." Kyllian had no intention of telling Ryker just how long he'd been into the scene. "Listen, there's something I need to take care of, so how about you go home, and as soon as I'm finished, I'll meet you there? You can fill me in on everything related to watching over Quinn."

Ryker looked around the room. There was nothing related to what Kyllian did in his kink, so he wasn't sure what his brother was looking for. "Okay. And Kyllian? I am sorry for being judgmental. I'll try to do better."

Kyllian lifted his chin. He wasn't going to let Ryker off the hook that easily. Only time would tell.

It wasn't often Kyllian got involved in his subs' personal lives outside the club, but his instincts told him Ted wasn't going to go away easily, and he'd been right. He'd be going away now, though. Kyllian stopped by the private Masters' lounge where he changed out of his tight leather pants into jeans and a hoodie. He then left via the employee entrance instead of walking through the club.

Kyllian was glad he'd already had Bishop track Ted's movements when Brandon left the man. The address to Ted's apartment was closer to Brandon's new place than Kyllian liked, especially with a restraining order. The drive to the apartment took half an hour, and when Kyllian reached the fourth-floor door, he didn't bother knocking. Waking up the neighbors so late, even on the weekend, wasn't a good idea. Having gotten the man's phone number from Bishop, Kyllian called once he reached the parking lot and voiced the man to be waiting for him. Ted stood in his doorway, clearly confused. Kyllian pushed Ted backward until he was far enough inside the room to close the door behind him.

"Who are you?" Ted asked.

Ignoring the question, Kyllian let his Gryphon come to the forefront. "You're ready for a change of scenery. You no longer like the cold weather, so you're going to move south. You will pack all your belongings and be on the road no later than tomorrow evening. Once on the road, you'll call your boss and tell him you have a family emergency that requires you to leave immediately. You will not return to New York. And you will never contact Brandon again."

Ted's eyes glazed over. "I need a change of scenery. I need to start packing." He turned around and started gathering the few items he had lying around. Kyllian slipped out of the apartment and quietly made his way down the stairs. Before he got in his own vehicle, he placed a tracker on Ted's car. The compulsion never failed, but Kyllian wouldn't take a chance with Brandon's well-being. Once inside his car, he texted Silas and told him the coast was clear for Brandon to go home.

The drive to New Troy took longer than normal since Ted lived in the opposite direction from the club. Kyllian took the time to think about giving up his time to watch over Quinn Shepherd. He had never met the woman as it was Ryker who oversaw their mercenary work. Kyllian knew nothing about the female other than she was the daughter of one of Sutton's friends. When Ryker first informed the Hounds they would be working with the father-daughter duo, Havyk asked if she was hot, and Ryker said she wasn't bad, but she was older and way too serious for Hayden. Older than his youngest brother could mean anywhere from thirty upward. Kyllian understood a serious demeanor, especially for someone who oversaw the type of business she ran. Quinn might not be the one to pull the trigger or use a claw to end someone's life, but she dealt in death on a daily basis. That had to take a toll on her psyche.

When Kyllian pulled into Ryker's driveway, his brother was waiting for him outside. As shifters, they were impervious to the cold March weather, so finding Ryker enjoying the peacefulness of the early morning wasn't surprising.

Kyllian joined Ryker on the front porch. "What do

we know?"

"Not a lot. It was Trenton who called Pop, not Quinn. He said she's not taking the threats serious enough."

"Does that mean I'm going to have a pissed off female on my hands?"

"Probably. It's one of the reasons Pop wants you for this job. He said you have the best temperament to handle Quinn."

"And the other reasons?"

Ryker blew out a breath. "He didn't share those with me. In fact, he didn't share much at all. I get the feeling he's hiding something."

"And that's supposed to help me guard the woman?" Kyllian huffed in frustration, but he knew their father. If Sutton Lazlo was withholding information, he had a good reason.

"I would say call him, but I doubt he'll tell you any more than he did me."

"Why would they ask us to a do job without giving us the necessary details to do it properly?" Fuck. Kyllian wished he hadn't agreed to the job. Then again, he would never tell his pop no. "What *can* you tell me?"

Ryker pulled a folded piece of paper from his back pocket. "This is the address. Trenton is expecting you. He'll meet you in the morning and tell you what he can before he introduces you to Quinn. That's both their home and office. When you pull up to the gate, roll down your window and look at the camera. I've already sent Trenton your photo."

Kyllian took the paper. "You're assuming I'll drive

13

instead of ride my bike."

"Like I said before, I have no idea how long this will take. If you want to pack enough clothes for a month on the back of your bike, that's up to you."

"A month? Damnit, Ryot. I—"

"Have responsibilities. I get that. If Pop hadn't requested you specifically, I would ask Ace or Judge to do it." The front door opened, and Rhiannon stuck her head out.

"Everything okay?" she asked.

"Just work stuff, Angel. Go back to bed. I'll be there in a few minutes."

Rhiannon gave Kyllian a wave and Ryker a brilliant, sleepy smile before closing the door. Ryker's face was soft, and Kyllian mentally shook his head. Seeing his oldest brother in love was both wonderful and strange. After the loss of his pregnant wife twenty years ago, Ryker became hard and unmovable. Finding out his baby girl had lived went a long way in softening Ryker's heart, but it wasn't until he rescued a little witch from a cult that his heart completely melted.

"Since you can't give me any more information, I'll let you get back to your female." Kyllian pocketed the address and gave his brother a two-fingered salute. Ryker was already in the house with the living room lights off by the time Kyllian got in his car. Scrubbing a hand down his face, Kyllian stared at the house. Inside were not only Ryker and Rhi, but also Ryker's daughter, Mac, and her boyfriend, Elijah. The three newcomers to the Lazlo family had all endured pain at the hands of The Ministry. Josiah Talbert, leader of one of the compounds, was in the wind, but it was only a matter of time before they tracked the bastard down. His parents would have to do so without his help because Kyllian had a handler to babysit.

Arriving home less than fifteen minutes later, Kyllian went inside and called Gunnar while he packed his duffel. Being a biker used to limited storage space in his bag, he could arrange clothes so quite a few garments fit easily. As a Gryphon, he didn't have an arsenal to carry to Quinn's. He did have the handgun Ryker insisted the Hounds carry on their merc jobs, but it fit in the holster he could hide beneath his leather jacket. Kyllian took a long shower, then slid beneath the cool sheets, cradling his head on a bent arm. Normally, after a night at Dominion, Kyllian was relaxed after a scene or two with his subs, but he and Hawk had monitored the floor while Spyder and his mate did a Shibari scene. Instead of being relaxed, Kyllian was restless. Both from not inflicting pain, but also from thinking about being away for who knew how long.

Quinn

QUINN SCOWLED AT her father. "You did what?"

"I called Sutton." Trenton turned from staring out the window, his face lined with worry. Sutton Lazlo was one of Trenton's oldest friends, father to five sons,

15

six daughters, and former President of The Hounds of Zeus. The Hounds were more than a motorcycle club. Some of the members worked with Sutton and his wife, Rory, searching for The Ministry, a cult responsible for the near apocalypse some thirty years prior. Some had jobs as doctors, lawyers, and other "normal" positions in society. Then there were those who Quinn called on to take out the trash.

"Dad—"

"No, Quinn. This is serious, and you aren't taking it that way. I know how capable you are, but we don't know who we're up against. And goddess knows I can't help you."

Quinn did know. Trenton was former military and could shoot the wings off a fly at a thousand yards in the right conditions with the right equipment, but this wasn't a stationary target. This wasn't a known enemy in a secluded area with his army buddies watching his six.

"And you think one of Sutton's Hounds will be able to help?"

Trenton ran a hand over his gray hair. Her father was normally put together. Always clean-shaven. His clothes pressed and unwrinkled. His hair kept military short. He was none of that now. It was one thing for Quinn to lose sleep, but her father couldn't afford to go many nights without rest. Not with his heart condition. Her situation wasn't doing him any favors.

"Yes. We discussed the situation at length, and he's sending Kyllian."

Quinn mentally ran through what she knew of Sutton's second-youngest son. Age thirty-two. Six-foot

16

three. Dark hair and eyes. A shit-ton of ink.

"When you say at length?"

Trenton's grey eyes bore into her blue ones. "Yes, I told him everything. I had to."

"And he believed you?" Quinn was stunned. The truth was something they'd kept hidden for years. It was why they had moved from New Mexico to Upstate New York. It was why Trenton started the mercenary company in the first place.

"Let's just say he's seen things in his life that allow him to believe the unbelievable."

What the hell did that mean? Seen what things? Before Quinn could ask, the motion detector from the gate beeped. Quinn studied the biker on the camera. It was March, which meant the temperature outside was a balmy twelve degrees, yet Kyllian Lazlo wore a leather jacket over a T-shirt. He had on fingerless riding gloves. How the hell was he not cold?

"I'll go meet him," Trenton said. Quinn was fine with that. It gave her a few minutes to slip into the half-bath and make sure she was presentable. Before her father reached the door, he looked back. "Sutton didn't share what I told him with Kyllian." Quinn nodded. She didn't know if that was good or not. The man needed to know what he was up against. What *they* were up against.

When Quinn returned from the small bathroom located next to her office, she checked the monitor. Her father and Kyllian were no longer at the gate. The sound of a large motorcycle rumbled up the long driveway. Quinn's office had once been the parlor in the large house she and Trenton resided in. They didn't need a formal office somewhere in the city. Not for what they did. The mercenary business was conducted online for the most part. Trenton met with any assassin they hired after Quinn vetted them through the internet. Then she contacted them through encrypted messages via secure phones she mailed to the assassins.

Ryker Lazlo was the only employee she'd ever met face-to-face, and that only happened since Trenton and Sutton went way back. She had sensed something "other" about the male, and when she mentioned it to her father, he wouldn't tell her anything. Quinn walked through the foyer to greet Kyllian. If they were going to be in close contact for any length of time, maybe she would figure out what that "other" was.

CHAPTER TWO

Kayos

SLEEP WAS A long time coming, and when Kyllian woke after only two hours rest, he was grumpier than usual. He liked having time to eat a big breakfast and down a pot of coffee, but he didn't want to show up late at the Shepherds' place. Opting for toast and one cup of joe, he ate standing at the counter. Afterward, he went back upstairs where he slid into a pair of comfortable jeans, a white T-shirt, and his well-worn boots. Kyllian nor any of his brothers had ever acted as bodyguards, but he didn't figure he needed to dress nice to protect their handler. After strapping the holster over his tee, he checked the safety on his pistol and inserted it into the nylon holder nestled against his left side. Even though it was winter, he didn't need the leather jacket to stay warm, but it was necessary to hide the weapon.

The ride to New Utica was uneventful, and when he pulled up to the gate, he removed his helmet and waited. Ryker said they would know he was there, so he didn't bother with the security box. As he waited, Kyllian studied his surroundings. What he could see of the property was gorgeous. Lots of trees backed up to the iron fence set around the perimeter. Footsteps sounded, and Kyllian turned his gaze up the driveway where an older man was walking toward him.

"Kyllian, thank you for coming." Trenton Shepherd pressed a button on a hand-held device, and the gate rolled open. Trenton continued through, holding out his hand.

Kyllian shook it and replied, "Tell me what you know."

"The first thing is that Quinn believes I'm being paranoid." The desperation showed in the man's eyes. "She's all I have left in this world, and I'd rather be safe than lose her."

"I can understand that. Let's say you're right. What makes you believe someone is after your daughter?"

Trenton looked in the direction of the house. "I think we should continue our conversation inside. I'll introduce you to Quinn, and the two of you can talk further. She can explain what's going on."

Kyllian took a calming breath. He needed more information if he was going to protect Quinn, but if someone were after the handler, it wasn't safe to stand close to the road. "Would you like a ride?"

"No, I need the exercise." Trenton took a step back, and Kyllian put his helmet back on before driving toward the house. He glanced in his side mirror, and Trenton waited until the gate was fully closed before beginning the trek back. Kyllian angled off his Harley, and while he waited, he studied the large two-story house. The porch stretched the whole width, but there were no chairs or swing where someone would enjoy the night air. Landscaping was a minimum with only trees surrounding the place. There were no flower beds, only low bushes that had grown dormant in the winter months. Kyllian turned when Trenton's footsteps sounded behind him. The human appeared to be fit for his age, but there was a weariness in his gaze.

Not human.

Kyllian reached out with his senses. His beast was right. Trenton Shepherd was *other*, and wasn't that interesting? Trenton opened the door, gesturing for Kyllian to proceed. As soon as Kyllian stepped across the threshold, he took in the pretty female. She was tall and fit with her dark hair pulled back in a ponytail. Kyllian took a step forward to greet the woman. Instead of offering her hand, she honest-to-Zeus growled. Within seconds, Quinn shifted into the largest wolf Kyllian had ever seen. Not that he'd seen many up close and personal like this, but still. The fur on her back was silver, her underbelly and snout were black, as was the tip of her tail. It was her eyes that stood out the most. They were a brilliant copper. If she hadn't been growling low in her throat, he might have taken a closer look at the other colors swirling in her gaze.

Trenton shouted, "Quinn, no!" but it had no effect.

When she bared her sharp teeth, Kyllian reacted without thinking. "Stop," he commanded in his Gryphon voice.

The wolf – Quinn – whined and dropped down onto her belly.

"What the fuck?" Kyllian turned to Trenton who had his back pressed to the wall.

"She must be reacting to your..." Trenton trailed off, not spilling Kyllian's secret.

Kyllian squatted so he was closer to Quinn's level. Holding out his hand, he said, "I won't hurt you." Instead of coming to him like he hoped, Quinn found her paws and ran toward the back of the house. Kyllian stood and turned to Trenton. "She doesn't know?"

"Not exactly. Meeting Ryker didn't have this effect." Trenton sighed and pushed off the wall. "She recognized he was different, but I didn't tell her what he was. Sutton agreed it would be best if you told her the truth if it came up."

"Are you a shifter too?" Kyllian asked.

Trenton's silver eyes blinked several times before meeting Kyllian's. "I'm half wolf, half human. I can shift, but it's nowhere near as impressive as Quinn. Her mother was all wolf."

"Why don't you go talk to her? I'll wait outside until she's calmed down." Kyllian needed a few minutes to himself.

Trenton nodded and headed toward the back of the house where Quinn had disappeared. Kyllian let himself out the front door and leaned against the porch rail. He knew there was more than one kind of shifter out there, but this was unexpected. Kyllian figured Sutton knew, considering Trenton was one of his closest friends. He wondered again why his pop chose him to watch over Quinn. Was this it? No. All the Hounds would keep her secret. It had to be something else, and Kyllian would ask the next time he talked to him. Now that the shock of seeing Quinn turn into a wolf was over, he had time to think about what it meant. His Gryphon had already thought about it.

Mate.

You know that after five seconds?
Yes, and you do too.

No, Kyllian didn't know that. Gryphons didn't have fated mates, and it was obvious by Quinn's reaction, he wasn't hers. She wouldn't have run if he were. If her Wolf reacted that strongly to his Gryphon, neither he nor the other Hounds would be able to watch over her.

She didn't have this reaction to Ryker.

Then it was Kyllian she was opposed to for whatever reason. All he could do was wait until she was once again in her skin to find out why.

Quinn

THE FRONT DOOR opened, and the hair on Quinn's arms stood on end. Before she could stop it, her Wolf took over. Bones snapped and morphed. The shift was no longer painful. It was as natural as breathing. Just as she prepared to lunge, the imposing, tatted male said, "Stop." It was a command she couldn't disobey. The air changed. It swirled with a heaviness unlike anything Quinn had ever felt. Her Wolf whined and dropped to its belly. This was more than the voice of an Alpha. It was powerful and brooked no argument. Kyllian squatted and held out his hand. Her Wolf ached to crawl toward the man. No, Kyllian Lazlo was no man. But he wasn't wolfkind either. Her father knew that. Knew what Kyllian was. It was probably the reason he felt Kyllian could protect Quinn.

It took every ounce of energy she could muster, but instead of giving into her Wolf's wants, Quinn jumped to her feet and ran the other way. When she reached the back door, Quinn shifted into her skin and strode outside to catch her breath. Her Wolf demanded they go back inside and present their neck to Kyllian. This was bad. This was so very bad. She had thought by keeping herself locked away inside her home she would never come across her true mate. What were the odds the one Hound sent to watch over her would be that to her? He might not be able to or even want to mate with her since he wasn't a wolf. Quinn didn't want to be bonded to another lifeforce. Not since—

"Quinn?" Trenton reached out for her when he followed her outside, but she took a step back.

"What is he?"

"Kyllian will need to tell you himself. I'm sorry I couldn't warn you. I assumed your Wolf would recognize him as something other than human the same way you did Ryker, but I didn't think it would react so strongly."

"I want him out of here."

"Quinn, you need someone watching over you."

"I'm not arguing about that. I'm saying it can't be him."

"All the Hounds—"

"Aren't my mate," Quinn hissed. Trenton's eyes widened, then his face softened, but she couldn't have her father getting any ideas of what that meant. It meant nothing. "No, Dad."

24

"At least talk to him. He's already here, and Sutton sent him in particular for a reason. You don't have to get close to him to let him protect you. Please, Quinnlyn." It was rare her father used her full name. It alluded to just how tired he was. She wouldn't risk his health any more than she already was with the perceived threat looming. Reaching out, she pulled him into a tight hug. "Okay. I'll talk to him." Quinn kissed him on the cheek. When she pulled back, she placed a hand on his shoulder. "This isn't going to end up like you want it to."

Trenton gripped her wrist. "The only thing I want is for you to be safe"

Quinn gave her dad a brief nod before heading inside. She stopped off in the half-bath to check her reflection. Her lupine magic allowed her to shift without shredding her clothes, so that was one thing she didn't have to worry about. Her ponytail was askew, so after fixing it, she inhaled deeply, steeling her resolve. She found Kyllian standing in her office, his arms crossed over his chest. Why the hell did he have to be so sexy?

"Would you like something to drink?" Quinn motioned to the chair in front of her desk, and Kyllian took a seat.

"I'm good. Why don't you explain to me why you need a bodyguard?" Kyllian was relaxed. Maybe it was his size, or maybe it was whatever he was, but the male wasn't threatened. Quinn didn't know how to feel about that.

Quinn moved to her own chair, the desk offering a barrier between them. She leaned forward, clasping her hands on the desk. Kyllian made her nervous, but she knew better than to bare her neck to any unknown entity. His dark eyes narrowed on her, waiting. They needed to address the elephant in the room. "What *are* you?" she blurted.

Kyllian's eyebrows shot up, and his body tensed. Quinn sat back, eyeing the male. If this was going to work, she had to trust Kyllian. Maybe if she offered her truth, he would do the same. "Trenton thinks my old pack is sniffing around." If Kyllian was surprised by her admittance, he didn't show it.

"Our kind doesn't have packs, so you'll need to explain to me how that works."

"And your kind is what?" she asked instead of explaining pack dynamics. She would get to that, but first, Quinn wanted to know what Kyllian hid beneath his human façade.

Kyllian narrowed his eyes, shifting in his seat. When she merely stared at him waiting, he blew out a breath. "I'm a Gryphon."

It was Quinn's turn to frown. She had read about the mythological beasts, but she never thought they were anything other than a fairy tale. "Like half lion and half eagle?"

"Yes. I can shift into a full Gryphon or take the form of either animal. Now that we have that out of the way, tell me about how a pack works and why you think your old one is after you."

Quinn didn't normally drink so early in the day, but this wasn't something she wanted to talk about without a little liquid courage. It had been many years since Trenton stole her away from her mother's pack.

Standing, she walked over to the cabinet where she kept the liquor and poured a glass of bourbon, not caring she didn't have any ice. Holding up the glass, she asked, "You sure you don't want a drink?"

"I'm sure."

Quinn took a sip as she leaned her hip against the cabinet. "I can't speak for all packs, but the one my mom was born into, the River Canyon pack, didn't believe in mating with humans or wolves that were half breeds. They didn't want there to be anything other than dire wolf in the pack."

"A dire... I thought those were extinct."

"Almost. That's the reason Dennis and all Prime Alphas before him intended to keep the bloodline pure. As far as I know, the River Canyon pack are the only ones left. Anyway, my mother was promised to an alpha, but she met and fell in love with Trenton. When she got pregnant with me, she couldn't hide the fact since other wolves can sense a second heartbeat. Instead of admitting who the father was, my mom lied and said it was a wolf from a rival pack."

When Quinn paused to take another sip, Kyllian asked, "River Canyon, where is that exactly?"

"New Mexico. Just outside San Rito. Dad never hid that from me when he told me about how he and my mom met."

"Where's your mother now?"

"Dead." Returning to her seat, Quinn placed the drink on a coaster but kept both hands wrapped around the glass. "The lie she told started a pack war. The alpha she accused of getting her pregnant was already mated. Back then, it wasn't uncommon for alphas to take more than one female, at least in her pack. The more females an alpha acquired, the more offspring. The more offspring, the bigger the pack. If Mom had accused one of our alphas of being the father, it wouldn't have caused such an uproar. The pup – me – would have been an added number. With Trenton being half human, there was no way he would be accepted. Mom knew if they were found out, Dad would be killed, so during a pack run, she claimed she wasn't feeling well. With most everyone away from the lodge, she took a chance and ran."

Kyllian canted his head. "I take it since you're alive, she managed to get away?"

"For a while. The gestation period for our kind is typically around three months. She and my father made plans as soon as she knew she was pregnant. He left a car with friends of his. He didn't share Mom's true nature with Mack and Carmen. He only said she was in a bad situation, and they agreed to help. What none of them planned on was my grandfather coming after them with his enforcers."

"Your grandfather?"

"Yes. Dennis, her pack Alpha, was my mom's sire. She made her way to the car and took off to meet Trenton. They then headed east, putting as much distance between themselves and River Canyon as possible. Not only was my grandfather Alpha, he was an excellent tracker. He followed Mom's scent to Mack's house. Neither he nor Carmen knew where my parents were, but that didn't stop my grandfather. His enforcers were able to get Trenton's name from Mack's phone. Dennis had a lot of people, human and wolfkind, in his pocket. He paid someone to trace Trenton's phone. Dad was smart enough to ditch it quickly, but by that time, Dennis knew which direction they were headed."

Quinn hated thinking about the next part, but Kyllian needed the whole story. "My parents didn't know my grandfather found Mack and Carmen. They had agreed to no contact after my mother retrieved the car, so they didn't think anything of it when they didn't hear from Mack. It wasn't until after I was born that Dad reached out to them. When he called, the phone was no longer in service. Dad found out about his friends' brutal death online. Dad was ex-military and had a few connections of his own. They managed to stay off-grid, moving every couple of months. I was three when they felt enough time had passed and they could relax." Quinn closed her eyes, bringing up the image of her beautiful mother. She didn't remember her exactly, but Trenton kept photos of Finola upstairs in an album.

"Long story short, they let their guard down, but Dennis never stopped searching. Mom had gone to the grocery store when one of the pack's trackers found her. When she didn't come home, Dad knew. Even after three years, they texted constantly, checking in. He put me in the car and drove to the next town over. He parked at the mall in a designated area and waited. After an hour, he got on the road again. When Mom didn't reach out to him, he kept going. Trenton went back to moving every month or so, zigzagging across the country. I lived in twenty states by the time I was seven."

"How long ago was that?" Kyllian asked when Quinn downed the last of her bourbon.

"Thirty-three years."

"So why now? Why wait all this time to come after you?"

"That's the million-dollar question. Maybe it took this long for them to locate us, or hell, it could be any number of reasons, if it is even them."

"Who else could it be?"

There was one other explanation, but Quinn didn't want to think about it. Instead, she shrugged. "Other mercenary groups? Ours isn't the only one out there; you know that. Maybe Nexus didn't appreciate me taking the Hounds away from them."

"Have there been threats? Dead cats on your porch? How do you know someone's after you?"

If Quinn were a weaker female, she wouldn't appreciate the cat remark. Being a shifter, she was far from squeamish. "Several bikers have shown up in town, and they aren't from any of the local MCs." When Kyllian narrowed his eyes, she said, "I didn't mention the pack is also one of the largest MCs in New Mexico. At least they were when Mom was there."

"Random bikers shouldn't be cause for concern. The Hounds travel all over as do any number of other clubs. Are these visiting bikers wearing your pack's kuttes?"

"That's just it. They aren't wearing any colors, at least none Trenton has seen."

"I'm guessing he didn't recognize any of them." Quinn shook her head. "And you haven't seen them for yourself?"

Quinn leaned back in her chair. "No. I don't leave the property."

"But you're a shifter. That can't be good for your Wolf," Kyllian argued.

"I didn't say I don't leave the house. It's why we own so much land. When I was younger and we moved around often, I went a long time without being able to let the wolf out to run. It took its toll on me and, in turn, my dad." Quinn hated thinking about those years. She had been a girl without a mother and a wolf without a pack. She wasn't meant to live a solitary existence. Puppy pile wasn't some cute term. Wolves were tactile creatures, needing the comfort of others of their kind. It was why—

"Back to these bikers," Kyllian said, interrupting her maudlin thoughts. "Have they caused trouble in town?"

"Not that we know of."

"I'll reach out to the president of the Savage Sons. See if these newcomers have introduced themselves. They could be rogues looking for a new club."

Quinn's stomach rumbled, and she felt her face blushing. "Sorry, but I skipped breakfast. Are you hungry?"

"I could eat."

"Why don't you grab your things, and I'll show you to your room. While you unpack, I'll make lunch."

Kyllian gracefully rose to his feet. "Sounds good." He didn't wait on her to show him out. Quinn couldn't stop herself from admiring the way his faded jeans hugged his ass and thick thighs. It had been too long since she had been with anyone, wolf or human. Quinn

31

mentally chastised herself. Kyllian might be a god in a leather jacket, but he was there to protect her. Nothing more.

After showing Kyllian to the guest room, Quinn made her way to the kitchen where her dad was sitting at the table cradling a cup of tea. His color had been off ever since he noticed the bikers when he went to the store a week ago. Quinn had brushed his worry off, but Trenton wouldn't let it go. Figuring Kyllian's Gryphon had exceptional hearing, she didn't get into their conversation with her dad. Instead, she set about making lunch for the three of them.

By the time Kyllian returned downstairs, Quinn had lunch ready. Salad with grilled chicken for her dad, and sandwiches for her and her new bodyguard. "I hope grilled chicken's okay," she said. "We try to eat healthy."

"I'm not picky," Kyllian responded, taking the seat next to Trenton. Quinn did her best to ignore the way his T-shirt stretched over his muscles. She also tried to ignore all the ink coloring his arms and neck. Bad boys were her kryptonite, and Kyllian Lazlo fit the image perfectly. She handed him a beer and grabbed water for her dad and herself.

Kyllian ate with gusto, only stopping when he'd finished his first sandwich. After chugging half his beer, he wiped his mouth with the napkin Quinn had provided. "So, you and Sutton go back a ways?" he asked Trenton.

"We do." Trenton set his fork aside, having only eaten half his salad. "Your dad is one of the best men I know. He had my back more than once in the trenches.

When we both left the military, I tried to convince him to start a security company with me, but he had other ideas of how to protect civilians."

"He became a cop."

"Yes, and it was during his time on the force he was introduced to cults. It didn't take long for him to shift his focus. When he left the force and began searching, he didn't have a name to go with the largest cult in the States. Sutton and your mom came across a young man who had escaped from what we now know was a conversion camp. Disbanding that group led to the two of them seeking out others like it, and that led them to The Ministry. Knowing the good he was doing, I couldn't resent him not working with me."

"Where does all this come in with you meeting Quinn's mom?"

Trenton smiled, but it was weak. "I met Finola on my last leave before I retired from the army. I had already put in my discharge papers, so she and I were separated for a month. My family and I didn't see eye to eye on most things. They came from old money. My father and his before him were high-powered attorneys. I was expected to follow in their footsteps. When I announced I was joining the army, it didn't go well. If it weren't for my grandmother on my mother's side, I'd have come home with a small savings account. My gran set up a trust fund for me, one my parents couldn't touch. Anyway, when I walked off base for the last time, I began seeing Finola."

Trenton took a sip of water, clearing his throat. "As soon as I met her, I recognized the shifter inside, but I had no idea her pack was different than most. She admitted the truth when she told me she was pregnant. Since I grew up with the females in my family being wolves, I didn't understand why I was never allowed to see where Finola lived." Trenton got a far-off look in his eyes, and Quinn figured he was thinking about her mother.

"I told Kyllian the rest of it." Quinn didn't want her dad to focus on Finola's death. "Well, everything except you starting the company."

Trenton leaned back in his chair. "With the threat of the pack, I decided to start a mercenary business instead of private security. I would still be protecting civilians from the worst of society, but I would also have men at my disposal to help watch after Quinn if the need arose."

"Makes sense. Like I told Quinn earlier, I'll reach out to the president of the Savage Sons and see if these bikers have made contact."

"What would that matter?" Trenton asked.

"It's courtesy to inform the locals why you're in their territory. Some clubs are made up of cops and firemen. Local church groups banding together to do good for the community. Others, like the Sons, aren't as altruistic. If rogue bikers are hanging around without stating their intentions, it would be seen as encroachment. Either the newcomers are looking to join, or they're scoping out the area. Looking for chinks in the armor, so to speak."

"Or," Trenton said, "they're looking for a way to hang around without causing suspicion."

"Or that. Either way, I'll find out."

"And then what?" Quinn asked. The sooner the

threat was dealt with, the sooner she could get Kyllian Lazlo out of her home. He could go back to being an employee and nothing more.

CHAPTER THREE

Kayos

"AND THEN I'LL assess the situation. Call in reinforcements if required. If these bikers are from your old pack, it doesn't mean they aren't armed just because they're wolves. I might be a Gryphon, but I'm not impervious to a bullet." Kyllian stood, grabbing his empty plate and bottle. His Gryphon insisted he take his sweet time in dealing with the threat, even though Quinn's demeanor was not welcoming. Ever since she came back inside, she had been stiff and not exactly friendly. He had no doubt her Wolf felt threatened with a bigger baddie in the house.

"Leave those," Trenton said.

Kyllian ignored him and tossed the bottle in the recycling bin before putting his plate in the dishwasher. He turned to his hosts. "No time like the present. Where did you see these bikers, and how many are there?" Kyllian asked Trenton.

"I've seen ten at the same time, but there could be more. I noticed them several places. Mamo's Diner during lunch Monday. Camino Mexican restaurant for lunch on Wednesday, and Hank's Tavern last Tuesday and Thursday evenings."

"Did they notice you?"

"Not that I know of. I was in my car each time I saw them. I drove around every day after that, but I couldn't find where they were staying."

"Did you check the local campground?" Kyllian knew there was one nearby because he had stayed there several times with Hayden.

Trenton shook his head. "No. I didn't want to risk it. Even if they aren't pack, I would still be outnumbered if they stopped me. I'm not as young as I used to be." There was defeat in Trenton's voice. His Gryphon picked up something else. Trenton's hands were shaking. The male sitting at the table wasn't well. Kyllian wondered if Sutton was aware his friend was sick. He walked over to Trenton and gripped his shoulder, squeezing once before letting go.

"That was smart. I'm going to grab my kutte and go see the Sons. Let them know I'm in the area. While I'm gone, I'll scope out the campground from the air. Trenton, I need your phone number in case I run into trouble and want to let you know I'm not returning straight away." They exchanged numbers, and Kyllian pocketed his phone. "If nothing goes awry, I will see you both in a couple hours."

Kyllian went upstairs and changed into a long-sleeved Henley before putting his vest on. His hosts were still in the kitchen when he came back downstairs, but Kyllian didn't feel the need to say goodbye. He let himself out the front door and got on his bike. When he reached the end of the driveway, the large gate opened automatically. Backtracking the way he'd come, Kyllian rode toward town. The Savage Sons' compound was located on the west side of the city, but Kyllian didn't head directly there. Instead, he passed by all the establishments where Trenton had noticed the bikers. Not catching sight of them, he ventured on.

The Sons' compound was as different from the Hounds' as it could be. It sat off the road behind a tall chain-link fence. At the entrance, two of their members guarded the gate. Kyllian pulled to a stop, turned his bike off, and removed his helmet.

"Kayos? That you?"

Kyllian placed his helmet on the handlebar after climbing off his bike. Smiling, he held out his hand. "Yeah, it's me. How you doing, Viper?" Kyllian might not agree with the illegal things the MC did, but they were honorable for the most part. They didn't involve kids or women in their dealings.

"Can't complain." Viper was a grizzled older man. His long, gray hair had yellowed with age, and his stomach stuck out from under his kutte. The Vice President patch was new. He gripped Kyllian's outstretched hand with a toothy grin. When he released the shake, Viper pointed a thumb at the other male. "This here's our newest prospect, Demon." Demon gave Kyllian a chin lift but remained where he was seated. Viper tossed the cigarette he'd been smoking to the ground and stomped it out with his worn black boot. "What brings you our way?"

Kyllian didn't know Demon, nor did he trust the man. When Viper caught Kyllian's gaze aimed at the prospect, Viper told the kid to scram. Only when he was out of earshot did Kyllian speak. "Two things. First, I wanted to let you know I'll be in the area for probably a couple weeks. And second, I was wondering if you've seen any rogue bikers hanging around."

Viper crossed his arms over his ample belly. "Thanks for the check-in. As for these bikers, yeah, we've seen 'em. They did a check-in when they first rolled into town. Said they're looking for someone. Said the man they're looking for stole something from them. When Judas asked what the man stole, they said it was one of their old ladies. Kidnapped her out from under their noses."

Kyllian kept his face blank. While they had spoken the truth, it wasn't the whole truth. "How did Judas respond?"

"Told 'em if they didn't find the woman soon, they needed to move on."

If Trenton was right, the wolves had been there at least a week. If he could keep Quinn safe for another seven days, they should be golden.

"You know anything about this woman?" Viper asked.

It wouldn't do to lie to the Sons, so Kyllian nodded. "Yeah, I do. And these bikers didn't tell the truth about the situation. She isn't someone's old lady, and she wasn't kidnapped recently. She wasn't kidnapped at all." He couldn't admit to Quinn being shifter, so he hedged his own truth. "Her grandfather was president of their MC back when she was born. Her mother met and fell in love with someone outside the club, and the two of them left town. The grandfather hunted them down, had the mother killed when they found her by herself. The woman and her dad have been hiding out ever since."

"Damn, Kayos. I know there's some crazy fuckers out there, but killing your own kid? If this woman was a baby when all this shit went down, why the hell are they still after her? You sure her parents didn't take something else that didn't belong to 'em?"

"Pretty damn sure. You know how some people hang onto grudges when they feel slighted. I guess the grandfather just can't let it go." But that did bring up a good question. Why were they still after Quinn all these years later? He had a feeling there was more to the story than she'd told Kyllian.

"I take it she's under your protection?" Viper asked.

"She is." Kyllian slid into his Gryphon voice. "I'd appreciate it if the Sons didn't help these rogues in any way."

Viper thumped his chest with a fist. "You have my word, I'll talk to Judas and relay this information."

"Much appreciated." Kyllian turned to head back to his bike, but Viper stopped him.

"Kayos? It might not mean anything, but there was a woman riding with them. On the outside, she was a real looker. But the vibe I got from her didn't sit well. Her eyes were dark, and I don't mean brown. They were ominous, like she could peer into your soul."

"Did she say anything?"

"Nah. Just listened and watched."

Kyllian inclined his head. "Thanks for the heads up." Straddling his Harley, he headed toward the campground to have a look around. He parked well away from the entrance and walked to the edge of the woods, where he removed his clothes, then shifted into his Eagle. Flying over the whole campground didn't take long, and when he didn't see any bikes, he flew back to his own motorcycle. Kyllian did another loop through town but still didn't catch sight of the newcomers, so he rode back to the Shepherds' home, making sure he wasn't followed. He wouldn't put it past the Sons to follow him. The gate opened after a couple seconds, and Kyllian rolled his bike to the front of the house. He needed to ask about parking in the garage. He didn't like leaving his bike to the elements of Upstate New York.

Trenton met Kyllian at the front door. "Did you see them?"

Kyllian ran a hand through his dark hair. "No, but you were right. They introduced themselves to the Sons. Told them they were looking for one of their old ladies who'd been kidnapped. I set the story straight and told them the female they were looking for was under my protection."

"Do you think that was a good idea? What if the Sons decide to betray you?"

"They won't." Kyllian didn't elaborate. Instead, he opened his senses for Quinn. She wasn't in the house, so that meant she was somewhere outside. "If I'm going to protect your daughter, she and I need to have another chat."

"Whatever you need to do. I can't lose her, Kyllian."

Kyllian clapped Trenton on the shoulder as he

passed him on the way to the back door. As soon as he stepped outside, the hair on his arms bristled. His Gryphon was pushing to be turned loose, but Kyllian pushed back. He wouldn't show Quinn his full shifter. Not yet. He didn't have to search for the female. His body was already in tune with hers. Kyllian strode toward the trees, veering right when he came to two diverging paths. Her scent was embedded in his brain, and his Eagle's keen vision allowed him to track her movements even though she was a good hundred yards away. He padded on silent feet toward the large wolf, admiring her coloring and size. Were all wolf shifters that large? It would make sense considering both his Lion and Eagle were larger than their animal counterparts.

Quinn froze and turned her dark muzzle his direction, her copper eyes focused on him. Her forelegs bent, and she shoved off, running away from him. Kyllian didn't need to shift to be fast, but if she wanted a chase, a chase she would get. Stripping down, Kyllian called forth his Lion, then bounded down the trail. If Quinn had been honest, she wouldn't leave the property, so he didn't worry about her going too far. That didn't mean the rogue wolves weren't out there, on the perimeter, searching. Using their wolf's enhanced vision to track her movements.

Leaves crunched and sticks snapped behind him. Kyllian waited until the last second to leap into the air, dropping back down behind Quinn. She slid to a stop, rounding on him. With fangs bared, she lowered her head, ready to pounce. Kyllian growled low, shaking out his massive mane. When she first shifted back in the house, her Wolf whined, but he didn't know if that was from wanting to submit or from his Gryphon's dominance. Maybe it was a bit of both. Kyllian stood his ground while his Lion swished its tail behind them. He wouldn't cow down to his She-Wolf. He couldn't. It wasn't in his nature. Patience, however, was. Being a Master in the kink world, Kyllian had learned to read cues. To study his subs words as well as their silence. Studying Quinn, Kyllian got the impression she was fighting her Wolf. It wanted to submit, but her human didn't.

Quinn's beast huffed, and within seconds, she was back to two legs. With her clothes intact. That wasn't fair at all. If he wanted to talk to the female, he could shift and stand naked in front of her, or he could run back to where he left his clothes. Neither was the right scenario, so he opted to shift and cover his dick with his hands. When he was back to his human form, Quinn's eyes tracked his body, and he let her look her fill.

"Where are your clothes?" she asked.

"At the edge of the trees. I don't have the ability to shift without shredding them."

"Huh. Not that I'm opposed to you being naked, but I think it would be easier to talk if you were dressed," she admitted. The fact that she wanted to talk instead of run from him was a good sign.

"Meet me back at the house?" he suggested.

Quinn nodded, her eyes on his chest. Kyllian knew he looked good. He didn't consider himself handsome. Not like his brothers. But he was fit, and being a Gryphon, it didn't take much work staying that way.

43

Instead of walking back through the woods with his junk dangling, Kyllian shifted to his Eagle, both to get through the trees faster and to let Quinn see his other animal. He was dressed and waiting by the time she reached the house.

"Both your animals are impressive. I can't wait to see your Gryphon," she said as she reached his side.

"So is your Wolf. She's larger than I would have imagined," Kyllian admitted.

"That's the dire gene."

"But Trenton isn't a pure blood, which means you aren't either. Why come after you if they want a pure bloodline?"

Quinn folded her arms over her chest and looked up at the sky. Whatever she was thinking wasn't pleasant. "The dire wolf gene is prominent. Even if we mate with a human, the offspring will be a shifter. Anyone with dire blood comes from the River Canyon pack, and Dennis demands they remain on pack land. If I were to go back and mate with a pure blood, my child would then be closer to pure. When they mate with a pure blood, their child then becomes closer to pure and so on down the line."

"Well, that's shitty. I guess the stories about wolves having one mate are wrong."

Quinn returned her gaze to him. "They're not wrong. It's why Mom's accusation about my father was caused so much trouble. The alpha already found his destined mate, and as such, there was no way he would've cheated on her. It's not possible. The wolf would rather kill itself than take someone else as a lover. That's why Dennis doesn't allow those pairings unless your fated mate is one of their pack."

"Your grandfather sounds like a dick."

"That he is, but it's the way things have always been." Quinn swallowed hard. "My mother wrote everything about the dire wolves in some journals for me since everything was different than normal packs. Dad didn't give it to me until... When I shifted for the first time, I knew what to expect. Dad had talked about my animal side ever since I can remember, preparing me. With him being half human, the need to shift and run isn't as strong. He either didn't understand how much I would need to be in my fur, or he'd forgotten what it was like for Mom. Moving around as we did, Dad was more focused on keeping us safe and off the pack's radar. We never settled anywhere I could shift and run freely. He did take me a few times to some wooded areas, but it was only long enough for me to run about ten minutes."

Quinn took a deep breath and blew it out. "Dad was doing his best to keep his business going while on the move, and he had an unruly teenager to deal with on top of that. It finally got to be too much for my Wolf, and I took off." Quinn turned and looked at the house, tilting her head to the side. When she returned her gaze to Kyllian, her eyes were haunted.

Kyllian's phone rang, interrupting Quinn's story. He apologized as he pulled it out of his pocket. "Sorry, I need to take this. Hello, Luce. Everything okay?" His niece was in New Atlanta with her mate, and she didn't usually call Kyllian.

"I'm not sure. I called Ryker about this, and he said you're with your handler. Can you ask Quinn if she's

45

received any contracts on Rafael Stone or his family?"

"You mean like a hit?" Kyllian glanced at Quinn who was frowning. Being a shifter, she could hear Lucy's side of the conversation. Quinn shook her head.

"Yes," Lucy said. "Rafael and two of his brothers were targeted this morning. Since the men went after them with rifles, they weren't aware—"

"Quinn said the contracts didn't come through her." Kyllian cut Lucy off so Quinn wouldn't hear the part about the Stone brothers being Gargoyles.

"But you didn't ask her," Lucy argued.

"She heard your question." Kyllian tapped a button and put Lucy on speaker, hoping she wouldn't catch him in the lie. "Sorry, but I had you on speaker. Let me talk to Quinn and call you back."

"Yeah, okay." Lucy hung up on him.

"What was that about?" Quinn asked. Kyllian squeezed the bridge of his nose. Keeping secrets was necessary, but sometimes it was hard.

"Three of my niece's mate's family were targeted this morning." Kyllian didn't want to explain Lucy's mate wasn't a Gryphon.

"Let's go to my office. If there was a contract and it didn't come to me, maybe I can figure out who took it."

Kyllian followed Quinn. When she sat down behind her desk, he took the chair opposite and crossed his ankle on his knee. While she tapped away at her laptop, he studied the female, thinking back to when Ryker told the Hounds about their new handler. Havyk asked if Quinn was hot, and Ryker had responded, *She's not bad, but she's older than you and way too serious.*" Meeting Quinn for himself, Kyllian

46

could understand the sentiment. Well, the second, because the female was so much more than not bad. To him, she was gorgeous, even if she never smiled. Knowing what little he did about her, Kyllian didn't imagine Quinn had much to smile about. How long had it been since she'd interacted with someone other than her father? Kyllian only knew about wolves in the wild, and they were pack animals, not solitary creatures. Did she have friends who came to visit? Or were she and Trenton too paranoid to allow anyone into their home?

As much as Kyllian loved Sutton and Rory, he'd go nuts if he only had the two of them in his life. He loved his brothers. He adored the twins. Kyllian was enjoying getting to know little Mateo and watching him come out of his shell the longer he was around the others. Quinn didn't have siblings to hang out with. To get into trouble with. Cause chaos with. She only had her father, and to Kyllian, that was a sad existence. Not that he found fault with Trenton; the male was solid. But spending twenty-four seven with a parent was completely different than having a brother or sister to confide in.

"I'm not finding anything," Quinn muttered as she continued typing. Kyllian's beast rumbled in his head. Kyllian had been ignoring his Gryphon's insistence that she was their mate. He didn't deny she was beautiful. Or fierce. Seeing as how they didn't have fated mates, he wondered why his beast was so adamant.

Her Wolf calls to me.
Literally?

Yes. She says you are her destined mate, but Quinn is against claiming you for some reason.

Probably because we're not wolf kind.

I think it goes deeper than that. I feel so much sadness.

Someone hurt her. But if she never leaves…

This level of heartache is long reaching.

Quinn had been explaining her past to him before his phone interrupted them. It was possible whatever she had yet to tell him was related to that pain. Kyllian couldn't imagine something so bad to keep someone holed up, especially a shifter. The need to let the animal out was like needing air to breathe. The Hounds were lucky in that they could shift into their Eagle and take to the sky.

"I'm not finding any chatter," Quinn said. "But that's not unusual. Most people who hire mercenaries keep their business private. Are you sure these men didn't deserve the contract?"

"I'm sure."

"Then tell me what you're hiding. If they were targeted and still alive, these assassins aren't very good at their job unless there's something else at play. I can see one shooter missing, but three?" When Kyllian didn't respond, Quinn sat back in her chair with a huff. "I get it. Keeping secrets, that is. Not your story to tell or something like that, right? Look. I don't want my true nature spread to strangers either, so don't worry about it."

"Until about a year ago, I thought Gryphons were the only shifters out there. I won't tell you what the others are, but I will tell you these are the good guys.

48

They've been around as long as Gryphons have, which is since the beginning of time."

"You said they are your niece's mate's family, so I guess mating between the species isn't frowned upon?"

"Unlike Gryphons, these others have fated mates. Lucy was welcomed with open arms."

Quinn chewed her bottom lip, looking across the room. When she turned her gaze back to Kyllian, she asked, "If Gryphons don't have fated mates, how do you choose who to spend your life with?"

"From what I've been told, those who have found their other half say they just know. Or at least the beast does. Maveryck lived with his girlfriend but didn't feel strongly enough to claim her. Since she was human and wanted the ring he wasn't offering, she left. Four years later, she showed up with twins and just handed them off to our family and walked away. Soon after, Mav was on a merc job, pitted against a female assassin. When they met face-to-face, they didn't kill each other. This little Russian spitfire grabbed his heart as well as those of his twins. Now they're a happy family."

Quinn tilted her head a fraction. "And that makes you smile."

"I want all my family to be happy, but the twins make me smile, yes. Those two little boys light up the world."

Quinn frowned harder. "And do you want that? The mate and kids?"

Kyllian could feel the turmoil in her question. He really needed to find out what happened in her past to cause such sadness. "It's complicated." Best to get this

49

conversation over with sooner rather than later. "I would love to find the other half of my soul, but she's going to have to be understanding with my lifestyle." Kyllian uncrossed his legs and stood, walking over to the cabinet where the liquor was stored. He helped himself to some whiskey before answering. "Not many people are aware of this, so if you would keep it to yourself, I would appreciate it. I am a Dom at a BDSM club. My specialty is pain. It doesn't have to be sexual, and most often it isn't." A low growl sounded from Quinn's throat, and Kyllian's Gryphon rumbled in his head. It liked the jealousy. "If I were to find my mate, all sexual encounters outside our relationship would cease immediately, but I enjoy the service I provide. I'm good at it. Some people need a different type of therapy."

"Would you give up being a Dom if your mate asked you to?"

"Being a Dom is as much a part of me as my Gryphon. Unless my mate liked a good flogging to allow me that release, then probably not. I'm not saying I wouldn't compromise. I would give up doing private sessions that were sexual in nature. But to me, the perfect mate allows you to be your true self. They don't ask you to temper the parts of you they might not understand. They accept you completely. Like with my brothers and their mates. The females might not like that they're mated to mercenaries, but they not once asked them to give up the job because it went against what they believe. They understand the job is providing a service to humanity – taking out the trash. What if you found your mate and they asked you to give up being a handler? Or leave the solitude of your home?"

Quinn picked up an ink pen and twirled it between her fingers. "I would tell them to go fuck themselves," Quinn muttered just as her computer pinged. With Quinn focused on the screen, Kyllian relaxed. He might be her true mate, but if her reaction to him being a Dom was any indication, things between them wouldn't work.

She just needs time. She'll come around.
Maybe.

CHAPTER FOUR

Quinn

THE NOTIFICATION ON Quinn's laptop was from the dark web where she received requests for hits. She was thankful for the interruption. She needed time to think about Kyllian being a Dom. She had never thought about the lifestyle other than what she read in a romance book. She had imagined being spanked, but it held no appeal. Being a shifter, Quinn could endure a bit of pain, but that didn't mean she liked it.

"We need to pause our conversation. I have a contract I need to vet."

"No problem. I'll go find Trenton."

Kyllian headed toward the door, and Quinn couldn't help from admiring her mate. Yes, she would admit that was what he was to her, but she wouldn't act on it. "If he isn't downstairs, please don't go looking for him." Her dad had begun taking naps lately. His human half had been diagnosed with heart disease, and Quinn was scared. He was the only constant in her life, and she couldn't lose him. After her troubles as a teen, they agreed she would remain close to home. What started off as acquiescence to her father's wishes became the norm. Having been duped by so-called friends had Quinn gun-shy from meeting new people and accepting their words as truth. The longer she remained behind the protective shield of their home, the easier it was to be alone. At least until Kyllian walked in the front door. Now her Wolf was demanding she not only open her heart to another person but to also submit to his Gryphon.

Kyllian agreed and left Quinn alone in her office. As soon as he closed the door, she blew out a deep breath. Her Wolf wouldn't allow her to refuse their mate for long, but she needed time to think about what giving herself to another person – again – would entail. She had been young and uninformed during her time away from Trenton. He hadn't shared her mother's journals outlining the truth of dire wolves, and being naïve, she believed what her new friends had told her. Quinn now knew the truth, and that was she couldn't resist Kyllian, not without causing irreparable damage to her Wolf. It needed their mate, but how was she supposed to be okay with a male who was a Dom?

He said he would compromise. You have to do the same.

But at what cost? Especially now that other wolves are sniffing around.

Maybe it's time to meet the past head-on. Mate with Kyllian, and your pack won't have any hold on you. You'll become part of his pack.

Quinn hadn't thought of it that way. Not that Gryphons had packs, but if she were to accept a bonding with him, she would have a clan. A family of mighty warriors at her back. She had yet to see him shift into his full beast, but it had to be impressive if the pictures she'd seen on the internet were any indication. Surely an eight-foot eagle/lion hybrid could overtake a wolf. Even a dire wolf would be no match for such an imposing foe. Kyllian had stopped her attack with one word. She had no idea if it was because he was her mate or if there was some other ability Gryphons had that put so much power behind one command. Either way, she wasn't sure she liked him having that much power over her.

He's our mate. He would never abuse that power with us.

Quinn wanted to believe her Wolf. It had never steered her wrong. Even as a runaway teen, her Wolf had tried to tell her she was making a mistake, but Quinn hadn't listened. Maybe she should now. Then again, since Gryphons didn't have fated mates, why would he want someone broken?

You're not broken, just stubborn. We are strong; you have forgotten this about us.

Quinn didn't feel strong. Hadn't since— Her computer pinged again, reminding her she had a job to do. Turning her attention to the screen, she read the request and rolled her eyes. The thing about running a mercenary company was the responsibility of weeding through legitimate hits and those that made her roll her eyes. More often than not, the person requesting her services was the one who needed to be taken out. Quinn had been a handler for a lot of years, giving her insight into the person on the other end of the request, which gave her pause when she thought about Lucy's family. If someone put a hit out on the good guys, then the person requesting the hit was the one who had something to hide. And that meant the handler for those hits either didn't do their job in vetting the hits or they themselves were dirty.

Instead of focusing on the email she just received, Quinn decided to do a little digging. Kyllian's family broke their ties with Nexus, a large mercenary group. She had heard of the company over the years, but until she met with Ryker, she'd thought they were aboveboard. When she didn't immediately find anything out of the ordinary, Quinn set up an alert on the dark web that allowed any chatter about the group to come to her automatically. Once that was taken care of, she stretched, then settled back into her chair and focused on the request that interrupted her talk with Kyllian. Before she further contemplated mating with the male, she would need to come clean about her past, and she wasn't ready to do that.

Knowing her dad would keep Kyllian company, Quinn remained in her office the rest of the day. She vetted the hit, spending hours looking into the man being accused of raping a child. These deep dives left their marks on Quinn's soul. Even studying psychology to better understand the working of a person's mind left her no closer to answers. Some people were just evil. When she first began helping her father, Quinn would rush from the room and vomit. She tried to scrub the images from her mind with scalding showers. She began drinking. Nothing worked. Quinn never became fully immune to the darkness that hit her computer screen, but she no longer threw up. At the end of the day, she sent the hit off to Ryker for him to choose which Hound would go after the mark. She found her father in the kitchen chopping vegetables.

"Where's Kyllian?"

"Patrolling. Since we don't have cameras surrounding the property, he said his time was better spent outside keeping watch. I also think he's giving you space."

"I appreciate that."

Trenton set the knife down and lowered his chin to his chest. Quinn crossed the kitchen and rubbed his neck. "I'm thinking about it, okay? It's just... There are things that happened when I was with the Ozark pack, things I'm not ready to talk about. Let's just say those things skewed my opinion of mates and leave it at that. Kyllian is a good male, and my Wolf is ripping me a new one for not claiming him already. I need time, Dad. There's more to being mates than a bite on the neck. There are logistics. Personalities. Lifestyle differences. I need to work through all these before I give in."

Trenton nodded, then went back to fixing dinner. She left him to it and went upstairs for a shower. In her bedroom, she crossed to the window and opened the blinds, searching for the male who was never far from her thoughts. She caught sight of his Eagle and couldn't help but wonder why his wings were blue. It was another thing she didn't know about her mate. Instead of joining them for dinner, Kyllian remained outside until after Quinn went to bed. Her lupine hearing allowed her to follow every step he made from the back door opening to him pulling his plate out of the fridge and reheating it in the microwave. He didn't linger over the meal. He ate in record time before he rinsed his plate and put it in the dishwasher. The back door opened again, and by the time she fell asleep, he hadn't returned.

The next morning, Kyllian was already out the door by the time Quinn woke and met Trenton in the kitchen for breakfast. Her dad attempted to make small talk, but it was strained. He wanted what was best for her, but Quinn didn't know if that was Kyllian or not. After helping him clean up, she kissed him on the temple as she retreated to her office. Kyllian came in for lunch. The two males chatted while they ate, then Kyllian was gone again. Quinn appreciated him giving her space, but she needed to spend time with him to know if they could make things work. For the next six days, Kyllian made himself scarce, and Quinn was getting tired of it. She was barely maintaining control of her Wolf. It demanded they find Kyllian and spend time with him. The animal rumbled in her head often, but it wasn't conversing with Quinn.

Kyllian had been there a week before she saw him again. She was in her office having received another request for a job. Just as she was typing the intended mark's name into her search engine, the gate alarm sounded. Quinn turned to the monitor to find a woman standing at the gate. Trenton was adamant that he be the one to respond to anyone who pushed the button, so Quinn ignored the woman, stood, and went to wake her father if he were sleeping. When she opened the office door, Trenton and Kyllian were moving her way from the kitchen.

"Who is at the gate?" her father asked.

"Some woman, and she's on foot."

Trenton froze, and Kyllian looked between them. "I take it that's unusual?"

"Unless her car broke down somewhere nearby, then yes." Trenton went to the intercom and stared at the screen. "I don't recognize her," he said before pressing the button. "Can I help you?"

"I need to talk to Quinn. It's about her daughter."

Quinn gasped, unable to help herself. Trenton glared at her while telling the woman, "You have the wrong house."

Quinn couldn't face her father, and when she turned, Kyllian's eyebrows were raised. She couldn't face him either. She blinked back the tears threatening to fall. After all this time—

"I'm at the right house. Tell Quinn her daughter's in trouble. I'll wait."

"Quinn?" Trenton grabbed her arms and turned her toward him. "Tell me this woman is lying." The tears did fall then. She couldn't lie to her dad. Not now.

"Quinnlyn, how? When?" Trenton grabbed his chest, his knees buckling.

"Dad!" Quinn reached out for him, but Kyllian was faster. He gently lowered Trenton to the floor, and Quinn squatted next to him.

"Call an ambulance," Kyllian instructed.

"No. I'm fine," Trenton argued. "Well, not fine, but it's not a heart attack."

"You don't know that. We can't take the risk. I'm calling for help."

Trenton grabbed her wrist. "No, you're not. You're

going to tell me what the hell she's talking about."

Kyllian brushed a tear off Quinn's cheek. "Would you like some privacy?"

Quinn shook her head. "No. You need to hear this too. Let's get Dad off the floor first."

Kyllian scooped Trenton up like he weighed nothing and carried him into the living room, settling him on the sofa. Trenton reached out a hand, but Quinn wrapped her arms around her waist, keeping distance between them. She didn't deserve his love or comfort.

"I didn't tell you the whole truth about what happened when I ran away." Looking at Kyllian, she explained, "As I told you earlier, we moved around a lot when I was young. Being a dire wolf, I needed to shift. To run. To be with others of my kind. We had just moved again, this time landing in Arkansas. We were near the Ozarks, and my animal was clawing to get out. One night, I snuck out and took off in my fur. I ran into a pack, and it was like coming home. I lied to them, telling them I had lost my family, and the Alpha, Stewart, welcomed me into theirs. I didn't know anything about pack dynamics or fated mates. I hadn't read my mother's journals, so I believed what they told me. What I didn't know was they also lied to me. I knew I was different because in shifted form, I was larger and had different coloring. They recognized me as a dire wolf, and..." Quinn closed her eyes and took a deep breath. "The Alpha's heir, Blake was his name, claimed I was his mate. Promised to take care of me. My Wolf fought with me. Refused to allow Blake to claim me. I wanted what they promised – a family, a pack, somewhere to belong – so my beast and I compromised. Long story short, Blake and I... we, uh..."

"You had sex," Trenton said.

"I was so stupid. They didn't want me; they wanted my dire genes. It wasn't until after Nikita was born that I found out the truth. Blake took Nikita while I was asleep. When I woke, Stewart told me Blake and his true mate had taken Nikita to raise as their own, and while I was welcome to stay with the pack, I would never see my child again. I immediately shifted and attacked Stewart. Even though he was Alpha, I tore his throat out, and with his blood dripping off my jaw, I challenged every other member of their pack. My Wolf knew what it was doing even though I didn't. All I knew was I'd had my child taken away from me and I needed to find her. Each and every member bared their necks to me. Everyone except Karen, Stewart's mate. She ran. I didn't realize I should have chased after her. I was caught up in the emotions of losing my child and killing the Alpha."

Quinn sat down in one of the chairs opposite her father. "In that moment, I became Alpha of a pack I didn't want. When I shifted back, I asked them where Blake had taken Nikita, but no one could tell me. One of the females, Mercy, admitted they were aware of Blake's plan to seduce me because of my dire genes, but she said they didn't realize he was going to take Nikita and leave. I shifted into my fur and took off in the direction Karen had gone. I eventually lost her scent, but I kept searching the area. After a month, I gave up and came back to the apartment."

"Oh, Quinn." Trenton rose from the sofa and knelt beside her, gripping her hands in his. "Why wouldn't you tell me? I knew something happened because you shut yourself off from me, but this? You should have told me so I could help you." Trenton bent his head and placed it against her stomach. Quinn released his hands and cupped his head.

"I was scared. Until I read Mom's journals, I had no idea I had become the Alpha. I just thought I'd killed someone."

"That's why you've been hiding all this time?" Kyllian asked.

Quinn looked at him through watery eyes. "Yes. By the time I figured out shifter laws were different, I was already used to the solitude. Even if I had known what killing Stewart meant, I wouldn't have wanted the title. I was just a kid, and I was only able to take him down because I surprised him. I wouldn't want to live every day not knowing if that was the day someone would challenge me."

"What do you want to do about the woman at the gate? If you want, I can get rid of her, or I can compel her to tell the truth," Kyllian offered.

"How?" Quinn asked, stroking Trenton's hair.

"It's a Gryphon gift."

Trenton raised his head and kissed Quinn's cheek. "Let's hear what she has to say. If my granddaughter is in trouble, we need to help her."

Quinn had always known her father was a good man, but she had never loved him more than in that moment. "Okay."

61

Kayos

KYLLIAN WAS SHOCKED at Quinn's story, but it explained the despair his Gryphon recognized from the female. Being a mercenary, he had killed before, but never out of anger. He didn't fault Quinn for her actions. She was a young mother whose pup had been stolen. Just a teen trying to find her place in a pack. Kyllian didn't fault Trenton for keeping her from others of her kind. Both had been dealt with so much grief. Kyllian would do everything in his power to help them.

It was Quinn who let the woman know they would meet her at the gate. Trenton was still pale from shock, and Kyllian kept one eye on the male to make sure they didn't need to call an ambulance after all. Instead of walking, they took Trenton's SUV.

"Mercy," Quinn muttered when they reached the end of the driveway. She opened the door, and Kyllian hurried out with her. Instead of opening the gate, Quinn strode to the metal barrier. "How did you find me?" she asked the other woman.

"I've always known where you were. When you took off, Jeremy and I followed you. With Stewart dead and you running, the pack was in disarray for a while, but eventually Blake returned and claimed Alpha status. We didn't agree with what happened to you, so Jeremy and I vowed to watch over Nikita while keeping tabs on you."

"Who's Jeremy? Your mate?" Kyllian asked.

"No, my brother."

"You said Nikita's in trouble. What happened?" Quinn asked.

Mercy glanced at Kyllian before answering. He uncrossed his arms, trying to look less imposing.

"Nikita always knew she was different. She has your size and coloring. When she asked why, Blake told her that she took after her ancestors and left it at that, but the whole pack knows her story, and one of her friends mentioned her real mom was a dire wolf. That caused a shitstorm, and Nikita demanded to know about you. Blake lied to her. Said you didn't want her, left her with him and Bethany, then took off. Since the pack knows better, Tarryn, her best friend, told her it was a lie. Blake banished Tarryn and her parents from the pack, and Nikita ran off the night after they packed up and left. All the best trackers went after her, but we lost her scent in Texas."

"Why didn't you call instead of coming here?" Quinn demanded.

"I wasn't sure you'd believe who I was without seeing me face-to-face."

"Was Nikita aware Quinn's original pack is in New Mexico?" Kyllian asked.

Mercy nodded. "It's possible. Quinn admitted that's where her family's pack was from when she first arrived, so it wasn't a secret."

"Shit. If Dennis gets his hands on her, we'll never get her back," Quinn said. She turned to Kyllian. "Is she telling the truth?"

Kyllian had no reason to doubt Mercy's story, but to be sure, he used his Gryphon voice and asked, "Is everything you've told us the truth?"

Mercy gripped the bars of the gate, no doubt fighting the compulsion. "It is."

"How long since you lost Nikita's scent?" Kyllian asked.

"Two days. I left Jeremy there to keep trying to track her, and I came here."

"Does Blake know you're tracking her?" Quinn asked.

"Yes. He doesn't want the River Canyon pack to get their hands on her."

Kyllian thought about the rogue bikers in the area. "We might be too late." When Quinn grabbed his hand, he threaded their fingers, hoping to ground her. "The rogue bikers."

Quinn inhaled deeply, her eyes widening. "But if it is them, how did they know where I am?"

"What rogue bikers?" Mercy asked.

"There are some bikers in town asking about Quinn. At least we assume it's her because of the description they gave." Kyllian squeezed her hand as he asked Mercy, "Who else knows Quinn's location?"

"Just me, Jeremy, and his mate. When Blake came back, he made it clear if Quinn ever showed up, he'd take her down."

"He could try, but I don't want to be Alpha any more now than I did back then." Quinn released Kyllian's hand, and he missed the connection. He missed being around her these last seven days, but he vowed to keep his distance so she had time to decide whether or not she wanted him. "Let's assume these bikers are from my old pack. Someone had to have told them where I am. Are you sure Jeremy's mate didn't tell anyone else where I am? Or maybe someone followed without you knowing? Even if Nikita made it all the way to New Mexico, these bikers have been hanging out in town for a few weeks. The timeline doesn't fit."

Trenton, who had been quiet up to that point, asked, "Why would Nikita run to New Mexico?"

Mercy shrugged. "We don't know that's where she's headed. We only assumed so because she went south."

"Is it possible Nikita found out where Tarryn's family planned to go? Maybe she was following them instead," Trenton offered.

"I don't think so. Blake restricted Nikita to their home until after Tarryn's family was gone. That doesn't mean she isn't out looking for them. They did have cell phones, and Tarryn could have contacted her before they left."

Kyllian felt the first tinge of hope. "Have you tried tracing Nikita's phone?"

Mercy shook her head. "She didn't take it with her."

"Do you know her number? I can have one of my people see if she and Tarryn swapped information."

Mercy narrowed her eyes at Kyllian. "Blake destroyed her phone when he found it before realizing it could be useful."

"Still, the information might be on the cloud. Give me the number," Kyllian demanded, putting a little

Gryphon voice into his command. Mercy immediately rattled off the digits, and Kyllian sent the number to Bishop, requesting he try to recover any messages. He was glad the Hounds had another computer expert now that Lucy was busy working on a formula with Jonas Montague, the scientist who cloned the first baby some thirty years ago. That clone who happened to be Lucy's mate, Tamian.

After receiving a response from Bishop, Kyllian said, "Bishop will see what he can find. Until then, we need a plan. Quinn, I can call in other Hounds to go search for Nikita while I stay here with you and Trenton, or vice versa."

Trenton fisted his hands at his side. "I'm not staying here while my granddaughter is out there somewhere."

"Dad, no. I need you here. Safe. I'll go. She's my daughter, and it sounds like I need to set the record straight once we find her. Kyllian, call in as many Hounds as you can. Send two here and the rest can come with us to New Mexico."

"Quinn—"

"Dad, please." Quinn grabbed Trenton's shoulders and squeezed. If that were his father, Kyllian would feel the same. The male might be part wolf, but he wasn't strong enough to go up against a dire wolf much less a whole pack, especially with a heart condition.

"Fine. But you have to promise to call and keep me updated. I can't lose you too," he whispered.

"I promise." Turning to Mercy, Quinn asked, "Where are we going?"

"New Amarillo is where we lost her scent."

"I have family in New Laredo," Kyllian said. "I'll call and have anyone available to meet us there."

"Is Daniel still in Texas?" Trenton asked.

"You know Daniel?" Daniel was mated to Kyllian's sister Poppy. All six sisters, three sets of twins, lived in Texas still.

"He was in the army with Sutton and me."

"Yes, he's still there." Turning to Mercy, Kyllian asked, "Where in Amarillo should we meet your brother?"

"There's an old campground – the Durango – that never reopened after the world fell. That's where we've set up camp for a meeting place."

"Call him and tell him to expect several Hounds of Zeus bikers. Not sure how quick we can get a flight out. Quinn, you work on that while I make some calls of my own."

"On it." Quinn pulled her phone from her back pocket and tapped at the screen.

Instead of calling his brother-in-law, Kyllian reached out to Daniel's son, Devon, who was Pres of the Hounds MC in Laredo. Devon and his son, Jericho, had helped Hayden when he had a job taking down a Mexican drug cartel. It was on that job where Hayden found his mate, Sadie. Kyllian jogged up the driveway to put distance between himself and Mercy. Being lupine, she would have enhanced hearing.

"Kayos?" Devon answered. "What's up?"

"Hey, Devil. I'm on protection detail for our handler, and her daughter is missing." Kyllian explained about Nikita's situation, trusting Devon with

67

the truth of the wolves. "She was last scented in Amarillo, and I'd like to enlist your help in tracking her down."

"Of course. Just let me know how many of us you need when and where, and we'll be there."

"The old Durango campground is where they've set up camp. I haven't yet shared with Mercy that we're not human, but I will voice her not to share that information if I do tell her."

"Understood. I'll grab Jericho and some of the others, and we'll get headed that way."

"Thanks, Devil."

"No thanks needed, Uncle. It's what the Hounds do."

After they disconnected, Kyllian called Ryker and filled him in, requesting someone to come watch over Trenton.

"More wolves? Makes me wonder how many other shifter species we don't know about."

"More? As in you know of other wolves?"

"Yes, Wynter is also a she-wolf."

"Hawk's Wynter?"

"I'm not sure Hawk has claimed her, but yes. When Spyder and Charlie were attacked at her floral shop, Wynter shifted and took a bullet meant for Charlie. Ace was there, and he happens to be free at the moment, so I'll get him and Ripper headed that direction."

"Thanks, Brother. Get them on the road ASAP."

"Will do. Be careful, Kayos. If what you said about this Dennis Alpha is true, he's not going to let Nikita go without a fight if he gets his hands on her before you do."

"I'm not worried about him. I'm a Gryphon."
Kyllian said his goodbyes, but instead of heading
toward the gate, he waited on the porch since he could
hear Trenton's SUV. Trenton stopped and let the
females out before driving on to the garage.

"I've got the three of us on the 6:20 flight. It
connects in New Baltimore," Quinn announced.
Kyllian didn't have to be her mate to feel her
trepidation.

Reaching out, he took her hand. "Are you going to
be okay?"

"I have to be, don't I? This is my daughter. I didn't
abandon her, Kyllian. She was stolen from me. And I
guess I should have gone looking for her when I was
older, but I didn't want to disrupt her life. If I had
known..." Quinn looked up, blinking back tears.
Kyllian pulled her into his arms, wrapping her in a
tight embrace.

"Shh. None of that. We'll find her, then you can tell
her the truth of what really happened." Kyllian pressed
his lips to Quinn's temple, inhaling her scent. His
Gryphon rumbled with appreciation.

"What are you?" Mercy asked Kyllian as soon as
Quinn stepped back so she could wipe her eyes.

Kyllian didn't want to tell the female about
Gryphons. Not yet. She had been truthful up to that
point, but he didn't know her. The sound of motorcycle
engines had the four of them turning toward the
sound. "Are you sure you weren't followed?"

"I wasn't. I swear," Mercy vowed.

"Trenton, take the females inside. Quinn, go pack

whatever you're taking." Kyllian urged. He waited until the three of them were in the house before jogging toward the gate. Stepping into the cover of trees, Kyllian quickly stripped, shifted to his Eagle, and took to his wings.

CHAPTER FIVE

Kayos

SOARING ABOVE THE estate, Kyllian caught sight of the bikes and followed as they drove past the gate and down the road to where a car was parked. He assumed it was Mercy's car. Three males parked their bikes, and one of them strode over to the car, peering inside when he found the door locked. He then lifted his face and sniffed the air.

"It's a rental, but I can smell the wolf," he told the other two. "She has to be around here somewhere."

"We need to hide the bikes and search for her on foot," one of the others stated.

Shit. Mercy had been followed. Kyllian scanned the area for other vehicles traveling down the road. When he didn't see anyone, he dropped down in front of the males, shifting as he landed.

"Who are you and what are you doing here?" he demanded, using his Gryphon voice.

The one who was searching the car answered, "River Canyon Wolves, and we're looking for a rogue wolf. Dude, what the fuck are you?"

Kyllian ignored the question and asked one of his

own, "Why are you searching for the wolf?"

"Our Alpha wants his granddaughter back," the third male answered.

"How do you know where she is?"

"We were told to follow the wolf named Mercy. They said she knew where Quinn was."

"Who is they?"

Male number one clenched his fists, probably trying to fight the compulsion, but he couldn't. "Alpha didn't say. Just gave us our orders."

"Tell your Alpha she isn't here. The female you're looking for is in Oregon. Are there more than three of you?"

"Yes. Seven more and Sting's mate."

"You're going to go get your pack mates and tell them you need to head west. Tell them you found Mercy and forced her to give up Quinn's location, then all of you will get on the road and head that direction."

Male number one returned to his bike, and the three wolves took off without speaking. Kyllian shifted into his Eagle and followed them until they arrived at the campsite. He didn't wait to make sure they left town. He needed to get back to Quinn and get her the hell out of New York. He hoped Ace and Ripper got there quickly to watch over Trenton.

After landing and getting dressed, Kyllian ran to the house. Trenton and Mercy were in a stare-off in the living room, but Quinn was nowhere to be seen. Reaching out with this shifter senses, he found her upstairs, and something was wrong. Kyllian rushed up the stairs, following his nose to the door at the end of the hallway. Quinn was sitting on the bed with her

72

head between her knees.

Dropping down in front of her, Kyllian gripped her hands. "Breathe, Quinn. Come on, Pretty Lady. Take a deep breath in." Quinn raised her head, wide-eyed, but did as instructed. "Good. Hold it, now let it out." Kyllian dealt with Brandon's panic attacks and had learned how to handle them. After a couple minutes, Quinn was breathing normally.

"Goddess, what is wrong with me?" she asked, searching his face.

"You haven't left your home in quite a while. You're not only stepping foot off the property for the first time in forever, but you're getting on a plane, headed to the one place you shouldn't be going." Kyllian squeezed her hands. "If you need to stay here, I'll go with Mercy and find Nikita. If you decide to go, I vow to you on Zeus that I won't let anything happen to you."

Quinn shocked the shit out of Kyllian when she leaned forward and pressed her lips to his. When she started to retreat, he wrapped her ponytail in his fist and kept her mouth on his, licking at her lips until she opened for him. That was a mistake because his Quinn tasted like everything right in the world. Using her shifter strength, Quinn pushed Kyllian's shoulder, knocking him on his ass. He waited for a fist to the jaw, but instead, he got a lap full of his female. Straddling his legs, Quinn grabbed Kyllian's hair and surged back in for another earth-shattering melding of their mouths and tongues. His dick hardened behind his jeans, pressing painfully against the zipper. Quinn rubbed against his erection, moaning sinfully into his mouth.

"Quinn, are you— Oh, uh. Never mind," Trenton huffed, retreating from the door.

Quinn broke the kiss and pressed her fingers to her lips. "Sorry. I don't know what came over me," she muttered as she scrambled off his lap.

Pulling one knee to his chest, Kyllian remained on the floor, trying to get his beast under control. They had more pressing matters than dealing with what just happened. "Don't apologize. We have bigger problems at the moment."

Quinn fisted her hands on her hips, scowling. "You think kissing me is a problem?"

Kyllian popped to his feet and gestured toward his still hard dick. "When we're not where we have privacy to take things further? Yes." He grabbed her around the waist, pulling her flush to his chest. Pressing his mouth to her ear, he whispered, "Let's get one thing straight. I want you. My beast wants you. It's demanding I claim you here and now. I don't think that's what you want, but if it is? We'll have to wait until we find Nikita until we do something about it, because Quinn? If you say the word, if you tell me you want me? It's game on." Kyllian nuzzled her neck before releasing her. Kyllian pushed his erection to the side of his jeans trying to relieve the pressure from the zipper.

"I'm sorry," Quinn said again.

"Unless you're apologizing for giving me blue balls, there's nothing to be sorry about. We need to talk to Mercy. She was followed."

Quinn's pupils were dilated. She briefly closed her eyes, taking a deep breath. When she looked at Kyllian, she said, "Lead the way."

Rory would kick his ass if he wasn't a gentleman. At least in this instance. He stepped into the hallway and gestured for her to go ahead of him. "Ladies first."

When they reached the living room, Mercy was pacing alone. "Where's my dad?" Quinn asked.

"I'm in here," Trenton said, coming from the kitchen. "I was going to suggest dinner before you leave."

Kyllian appreciated Trenton's thoughtfulness, but they would have to pass. "We'll grab something at the airport. Mercy, those bikers knew who you are. They followed you here. They also know you've been watching Quinn. They said someone told their Alpha, so if you and Jeremy only confided in his mate—"

"No." Mercy sliced her hand through the air. "Kinsley would never betray us that way."

"Someone did. You're wolves. You have enhanced hearing."

"But why not tell Blake instead? Why go to Quinn's original pack?"

"That's something we'll have to ask when we find out who shared with them."

"What did you do to the bikers?" Quinn asked.

"I voiced them. Told them you could be found in Oregon, to gather the others in their group, and head that way."

"Voiced them?" Mercy asked.

"Yes. Something you need to know about me is I have the ability to make you tell the truth. I also have the ability to coerce you into doing whatever I wish. It's a gift of my species, and since I can also wipe your

75

memories, I'll let you know I'm a Gryphon, which means if you betray me by sharing my species, I'm strong enough to take out your whole pack, so don't fucking betray me."

Mercy trembled, taking a step back. "I w-won't. I pr-promise."

"Quinn, do you have any idea where the River Canyon pack is located?"

"I know exactly where they are." Quinn's tone was filled with malice, but that wasn't shocking considering the pack had killed her mother. "In Mom's journals, she described the area as well as drew a rough map, and with technology such that it is, I homed in using Google Earth."

"Excellent. We need to get going. I want to make sure nobody follows us to the airport. We'll take Mercy's rental so Trenton won't be without a vehicle. Quinn, go grab you bag while I retrieve Mercy's car." Kyllian held out his hand, and Mercy dug in her pocket for the key. Kyllian took off down the driveway at a jog, vaulting over the gate. Once inside the rental, Kyllian checked it for weapons and Mercy's phone. When he didn't find either, he drove back to the gate. It opened immediately, and he continued on to the house. Trenton and the females were waiting outside.

"Ace and Ripper are on their way. They should be here soon," Kyllian told Trenton.

"I'll be fine until they arrive." Trenton gripped Kyllian's shoulder. "Keep her safe."

"You have my word." Kyllian took Quinn's bag and loaded it into the trunk before sliding into the driver's seat with Quinn sitting next to him. Mercy didn't protest about being relegated to the back seat. It wouldn't have done her any good. Kyllian needed Quinn close. He kept his eyes peeled for anyone following, taking a circuitous route to the airport. On the way, Quinn peppered Mercy with questions about Nikita.

"She's smart. Feisty. She looks just like you did at her age. Nikita is top in her graduating class, but I'm not sure what will happen if she doesn't finish out the year. It really sucks that Blake banished Tarryn's family. The girl is set to graduate in a few months as well, so it would make sense her parents wouldn't take her too far. I know I wouldn't if she were my kid. I'd hang around long enough for her to finish out her senior year."

Kyllian still didn't know enough about pack life, so he asked, "How are packs different from human communities other than having an Alpha?"

Quinn shifted in her seat. She had turned to look at Mercy, but now she focused on Kyllian. "I only know about the River Canyon pack from what my mom wrote in her journals. It was completely different than the Ozark pack. When I was in the Ozarks, they basically live in the same community. Like a large rural neighborhood with a pack house where everyone gathers for meetings and such. Stewart's house was larger than everyone else's. The adults work outside the pack and pay into the pack's central account. That way if one family is ever in need of something they can't afford, money is there for emergencies. With the River Canyon pack, everyone lived on pack land. Dennis has his Alpha house, and everyone else lives in small cabins throughout the land. It's more of an insular community."

"How do they make money?"

"Some have jobs outside the pack too, but all the money goes back into the pack. They hunt for meat and grow their vegetables. The kids aren't sent to local schools. Instead, they're homeschooled," Quinn explained.

"Like a cult?" Kyllian asked because that sounded a lot like how The Ministry operated.

"I guess you would see it that way, but it's how things have been done since the beginning of time," Mercy answered before Quinn could. "Our pack started off that way, but Stewart's father, Grady, changed things up in the nineteen hundreds. Technology had a lot to do with it as did his mate. Stana was a brilliant woman, and she wanted to be a doctor, not just a healer. She begged Grady to be allowed to go to college and then medical school. Grady would have pulled down the moon for Stana if he could, so he said yes. That set the precedent for everyone after. The pack lands were changed over the years, and instead of being a compound like what Quinn described with her old pack, it was developed into a modern community. Like this huge neighborhood. They still own all the land, but if anyone outside the pack wanders into the area, it just looks like any other human neighborhood."

"And what about the kids going to school? Isn't the Alpha afraid the kids will shift accidentally, outing the wolves?"

"They have to wait until after they reach puberty

and have their shifting under control before they're allowed to go to public school, generally in high school. Some choose to not go, but most do. Unlike Quinn's old pack, we aren't separated from humans our whole lives. We are taught we are different and that we must keep our wolf kind secret. Our pack has been interacting with humans for quite a while, ever since Stana decided to go to college."

Kyllian turned to Quinn. "If your mom's pack was insular like you said, how did she meet your dad?"

"Finola hated her life. The pack isn't without utilities or technology, so when she began seeing what life on the outside was like from watching TV, she wanted to see somewhere other than New Mexico. Women in their pack are allowed to work because not all are cut out for being gardeners, bakers, cooks, and homemakers. She met Trenton at the café where she was a waitress. They both recognized the animal inside each other, and from what he says, they recognized each other as mates immediately. It was difficult for them to talk and make plans, but somehow, they managed."

Kyllian knew the rest of the story. His phone buzzed, but since he was in the rental, he hadn't set it to connect to Bluetooth. Keeping one eye on the road, Kyllian answered and put it on speaker. "Hey, Bishop. You got something for us?"

"It's not much, but the last text Nikita sent was to Tarryn. She asked Tarryn to take notes in their classes, and she would get them from her when she got back. Everything before that was just teenage girls talking about the boy Tarryn was dating and things like graduation."

"Back from where?" Quinn asked.

"It didn't say, but that text was sent, then deleted almost a week ago."

"So she had already planned on leaving?" Quinn asked softly. Kyllian reached over and took her hand.

"I'm sorry I don't have more for you," Bishop said.

"No, Brother. You can't recapture what isn't there. If she had taken her phone with her... Can you tap into Tarryn's phone? See if she has texts from an unknown number? It's possible Nikita snagged a burner phone somewhere."

"I'll give it a try, and I'll let you know if I come up with anything."

"Thanks, Bishop. We're pulling into the airport now, so if I don't answer right away it's because we're in the air."

"Ten-four."

After returning the rental, they entered the terminal. They were early, so Kyllian suggested they grab something to eat. Quinn picked at her food while Mercy told them more about Nikita's life. He couldn't imagine how Quinn felt hearing about her child from someone else's point of view. It wasn't like she'd given her baby up for adoption willingly so the child could have a better life. Nikita had been taken from her.

"You need to eat." Kyllian put just enough Gryphon voice into his words that she wouldn't realize it wasn't a suggestion. Quinn obeyed, but he could tell she wasn't enjoying the flavors, merely eating for sustenance. By the time they finished their meals, their flight was being called. Since they had tickets in first class, the three of them boarded before everyone else. He and Quinn sat together with Mercy across the aisle. Quinn was quiet, which Kyllian expected. What he didn't expect was for her to thread their fingers together and settle their hands in her lap and keep them there throughout the first flight. They had an hour and a half layover in New Baltimore, and once they offboarded, Quinn pulled Kyllian into a bar along the concourse with Mercy following. After ordering drinks, his female peppered Mercy with more questions about the pack, leaving out the words wolf, mate, and pack. She wanted to know about Nikita's life with her father and stepmother.

When they were seated on the plane to Oklahoma City, Quinn immediately took Kyllian's hand. After about an hour, Quinn leaned her head on his shoulder. Kyllian pressed a kiss to her hair, letting her know silently he was there for her. She wasn't shaking near as badly as she had been when they first left New York, and for that, Kyllian was proud of her.

During the flight, she asked about his family, so Kyllian told her about his brothers and sisters, the kids, and his parents. The only one he didn't speak about was Lucy. He trusted Quinn, but unless they were true mates and she was in his life for the long haul, Kyllian wouldn't share about the Gargoyles or the serum Lucy was working on. Only their immediate family was aware of the journal Lucy's adoptive father left in his home detailing genetic testing. Lucy was working with Jonas Montague to perfect a formula using Gargoyle DNA that would prolong human lives. When Gargoyles mated, whatever was in their saliva extended the life of their human mate. Gryphons didn't have that ability. Nor did they live a thousand years as the Goyles did.

Kyllian's Gryphon rumbled, but it wasn't to Kyllian. He figured it was talking to Quinn's Wolf, but he didn't want to interrupt to ask. He'd never known his beast to truly be separate from him. Didn't know it was possible. Even around his family, he'd never felt the Gryphon conversing with another. It was odd, but at the same time, it was soothing. Quinn might not want Kyllian as a mate, but her Wolf did. Kyllian trusted the two animals to somehow work things out, and wasn't that a kick to the balls? Before meeting Quinn, Kyllian was content with his life. Sure, he had been slightly sad when Bonnie decided to end their contract, but that was more from not having a regular sex partner. The woman was smart and funny and the perfect sub. The sex was good. Kyllian could bed almost anyone he wanted, but now? Now he didn't want anyone other than the female sitting beside him. Now he understood what his brothers meant when they said once you meet your other half, you didn't want anyone else.

He had no idea how things would work between them. They led separate lives. Quinn never left her property; except she had left to go find her daughter. Maybe after they got Nikita back, Quinn wouldn't feel the need to hole up at home, hiding from her old pack. With Kyllian as a mate, he would guard her with his life. When they met up with her mother's pack – and he had no doubt they would at some point – he wouldn't allow Dennis to keep her with their pack just

82

because she was a dire wolf. Kyllian wasn't kidding when he said the River Canyon pack sounded like a cult, keeping to themselves and not allowing the wolves to mate with anyone who wasn't also a dire wolf. And he would raze the pack to the ground to keep both her and her daughter safe.

Kyllian had a message from Bishop when they landed in Oklahoma City.

Bishop: *Good news. I was able to get into Tarryn's phone. Nikita sent her a message saying she was going to try and find her mother. She sent several more messages with pings of her locations. The last was at a bus station in New Santa Rosa, New Mexico. That was this morning at 10:15. I'll update you if she sends another text.*

Mercy shrugged the strap of her duffel higher on her shoulder. "I don't understand. How does Nikita know where to look for your old pa— family? Even Jeremy and I weren't made aware where they're located other than New Mexico, and that's a lot of ground to cover."

Quinn stopped in the middle of the concourse. Numerous travelers had to walk around the trio, some of them voicing their irritation. "The only ones I ever told were Stewart and Karen. We know Stewart didn't tell her, so that leaves Karen."

"But why would she tell Nikita? For all intents and purposes, Karen is her grandmother."

Kyllian tugged on Quinn's hand. "Let's continue this conversation in the car." He didn't want one of them to slip up talking about packs where humans could overhear. Once they secured a rental and were on the road to New Amarillo, he looked at Mercy in the

83

rearview. "Do Blake and Bethany have more kids?"

"Yes. Nathan is seventeen, Carrie is fifteen, and Jake is twelve. Why?"

"How do the others get along with Nikita? Is she first in line to take over the pack after Blake? Or does that fall to Nathan since he's male?"

"In our pack it's the firstborn alpha who is next in line, and that would be Nathan."

"What happens if there isn't an alpha offspring?"

"If the current Prime Alpha has an alpha sibling, they could take over, or if the sibling is an omega and has an alpha child, that child would take over."

Kyllian was glad Gryphons didn't have such convoluted hierarchy. "And it stays in the family? What if that family isn't what's best for the pack?"

"Someone can always challenge the Alpha. Technically, it's what Quinn did when she took down Stewart."

"Since you said Nathan is the firstborn alpha, that makes Nikita what? An omega?"

"No, she's a beta. At least that's what Blake says. Honestly, she feels more like an alpha to me."

"How do you know she isn't? Do you just take Blake's word for it?"

"It's a scent thing. Wolves can sense what every other wolf is. Blake said because Nikita's a dire wolf, she smells different."

"Jesus fuck. Okay, I'll try to wrap my head around that later. What's the difference in alphas, betas, and omegas?"

"Only alphas can rule. Betas are used as trackers and enforcers, and omegas bear the offspring."

"So betas can't get pregnant? You can't have kids? That doesn't make sense. Quinn is an alpha and she had Nikita."

"Quinn's not a…" Mercy leaned forward and sniffed Quinn. "Holy shit. Quinn's an alpha. How is that possible?"

Quinn turned sideways so she could see Mercy. "Did you forget I took down Stewart? I only know what my mom wrote in her journals about my old pack, but the hierarchy was the same, except only males are allowed to lead. At least that's how it was thirty-six years ago."

"No, I didn't forget. We just assumed it was because you're a dire wolf and stronger than the average lupine."

"Back to Nikita. If your nose is correct, she could be an alpha, and someone doesn't want her to know it. How does she get along with her siblings? Do they know she is their half-sister?"

"They all get along as well as any other siblings. Sure, they squabble, but no more than other kids. As far as I know, the others are aware Nikita isn't biologically Bethany's. That would be impossible to hide because of her coloring when she's in her fur."

Kyllian's head was spinning. "Is there anyone she doesn't get along with? Someone who feels threatened because she is a dire wolf?"

Mercy stared out the side window. "Not that I'm aware of, but I'm not around her twenty-four seven. Nor do I know everyone's heart. People can put on an act when deep down they feel something different." Her voice held a note of melancholy as though she

85

were speaking from experience.

"You got that shit right." Quinn rubbed her jean-clad thigh with her free hand. Kyllian assumed she was thinking about Blake and how he duped Quinn into thinking he cared for her.

Kyllian tugged at the hand he was holding. "How are you going to handle seeing Blake again?"

When Kyllian turned for her answer, Quinn's eyes were glacial. "I'm going to rip his fucking throat out."

CHAPTER SIX

Quinn

FLYING FOR THE first time was an experience. One Quinn didn't want to encounter again anytime soon. Her Wolf was antsy being cooped up in a flying tin can, so it reached out to Kyllian's Gryphon. She could sense her animal talking, but she didn't know what it was saying. It worried her, the not knowing. She didn't doubt it was conspiring against her. They both knew Kyllian was their mate, but Quinn wasn't ready to accept it.

Kyllian isn't like that sonofabitch.

Oh, now you want to talk to me? And who said anything about Blake?

I know you. You vowed to never allow anyone close again after what he did to you.

Quinn didn't respond. She latched onto Kyllian's hand for comfort against her better judgment. She had to admit the connection was nice. And when he kissed her hair? She felt wanted for the first time in forever. Blake had been charming, and Quinn had been too young and naïve to know she was being played. Even though she hadn't dated anyone, hadn't been around men other than her father, she liked to think she was a better judge of character at thirty-six than she'd been as a teen. Staying away from others, Quinn spent her free time devouring forums on male behavior. She majored in psychology at the university she attended online. Some of her classes required her to participate via video chat, so it wasn't as though Quinn never interacted with anyone. She just didn't do it in person.

She also had to consider who Kyllian was. He was the son of one of her dad's oldest and dearest friends. Her father *was* a good judge of character. According to Trenton, Sutton Lazlo was the best male he knew. Sutton wouldn't have sent Kyllian to watch over Quinn if he, too, weren't a good male. When Kyllian spoke of being a pain master, it was more of the service he provided instead of the sexual aspect. If she were to give in to her Wolf's desire to mate with the male, she didn't know if she could give him what he needed. Quinn had been with only one male in her life. They had been two horny kids going at it, or so she thought. Blake made her first time memorable. He hadn't taken her against her wishes. She admitted to being a virgin, and he took care with her. Once she was pregnant, he didn't touch her again. Everything that came after – him taking Nikita – tainted the experience. Kyllian was sex personified. He said he would compromise and keep his sexual encounters to his mate only, but would she be enough to keep him satisfied?

True mates don't want anyone else.

Gryphons don't have true mates. One of his brothers has kids with someone who isn't his mate.

Like you said, the mother wasn't his mate.

88

What if I'm not Kyllian's mate? What if I give myself to him and he tosses me aside? I can't go through that again.

We are their mate. They feel it.

I need to focus on Nikita.

Kyllian tugged on her hand, bringing Quinn back to the conversation. "How are you going to handle seeing Blake again?"

Quinn narrowed her eyes. "I'm going to rip his fucking throat out. He used me, then stole my child. Lied about me, turning my daughter against me."

Mercy gasped in the backseat. "He's a powerful alpha."

Quinn turned her anger to the female. "So am I. Plus I'm a dire wolf. I might not have fought anyone since Stewart, but Blake doesn't scare me."

"Plus she has me." Kyllian squeezed Quinn's hand again, returning her focus to him. "Don't forget though, if you put Blake down, you'll be Alpha. Again. You said you don't want that."

Quinn leaned back in her seat. No, she didn't want that. "No. I don't want a pack who allows males like Blake and his father to lead."

"Then I guess I wasted a lot of fucking years keeping tabs on you." Mercy's anger was palpable.

Quinn turned to look at the female again. "Why would you want me to be Alpha?"

"Because it's like you said; we should have a leader who's honorable."

Huh. "I don't know anything about leading. Except for the few months I was with the Ozark pack, I've lived a sheltered life. If you've watched me closely, you know I don't get out. I don't associate with others.

89

Every interaction I've had since returning to my father all those years ago has been online."

"Why did you give up looking for Nikita?" Mercy asked.

"I was a kid. I searched for over a month, but I was alone, tired, and scared. I needed my dad."

"Why didn't you tell him what happened? Wouldn't he have helped you search for your daughter? He is a wolf after all. Did you think he wouldn't understand?" Mercy's tone wasn't judgmental, only curious.

"I tried to tell him so many times, but I didn't want him disappointed. He would have helped, but our lives were crazy enough, moving from town to town. The more we moved, the farther away from your pack we got. After a while, it became easier to believe my baby was where she was supposed to be, as was I. Did you tell Blake you were coming to get me?"

"No, because then I'd have to tell him how I knew where you were all this time. He would consider it treason against the pack. Jeremy and I made a vow to one another to keep you a secret until we couldn't. Kinsley's family is also part of the Ozark pack, and if Blake made us leave, Kinsley wouldn't take it well. That's the biggest reason I know she didn't betray us."

Mercy's phone rang, and Quinn faced forward again, taking in the scenery. She had never been in this part of the country, not that she remembered anyway. Trenton had zigzagged all over but had stayed away from New Mexico.

"Jeremy, did you find something?" Mercy answered. With shifter hearing, Quinn didn't have trouble listening in.

"Hey, Sis. No, we're still at the campground. I just wanted to let you know Blake is headed back to Arkansas."

"That's probably a good thing. Quinn's threatened to rip his throat out."

"Now *that* would be a good thing. I fucking hate that prick."

Quinn was surprised at the loathing in Jeremy's voice. She wondered how bad of an Alpha Blake was. Kyllian must have heard Jeremy's response, too, because he glanced over at Quinn, his eyebrows dipping between his dark eyes. Her ma— Kyllian wasn't classically handsome, but he was stunning in his own bad boy way. She'd always had a thing for ink, and Kyllian had plenty of it.

"We both do, but for now, we need to focus on Nikita. Once we find her, we can decide what happens next."

"Yeah. I'm gonna shift and go for a run."

"Claws down, head up," Mercy said before disconnecting. That phrase sparked a memory, and Quinn shook her head trying to dispel it.

"You okay?" Kyllian asked.

"I'm fine. I was thinking about Blake giving up on the search," Quinn lied. "But I did the same thing."

"It's not the same at all. You were just a kid on your own." Kyllian rubbed his thumb back and forth across the top of her hand, soothing her frazzled nerves. And Quinn was nervous. What if Nikita didn't believe Quinn's truth? Kyllian didn't push the conversation. Instead, he allowed Quinn to have time to think on what he said. Both he and her father said the same thing; she had been a kid back then. If only Quinn had been brave enough to share what happened with Trenton. Her dad understood packs and how they were run. It was possible he could have helped her get her daughter back. But hindsight and all that, she hadn't shared with him, so now she would have to see things through on her own.

No. You have a mate to help.

He's not our mate.

Not yet.

The sun had set by the time they pulled into the campground. Three Harleys were parked beside a couple cars, and Quinn counted six men. She recognized Jeremy and Scott from the Ozark pack. The other wolf was a stranger. The three males wearing biker gear were the ones Kyllian called. As they stepped out of the rental, one of the bikers jogged up to Kyllian, and that's when Quinn lost it. The shift was quick, and her large beast stood between Kyllian and the stranger.

Kyllian knelt beside Quinn, resting his hand on her scruff. "It's okay, Quinn. No one here is going to hurt you. I won't let them. You're safe, Pretty Lady." Quinn's copper eyes met his as she released a low whine. "You're safe, Baby," he whispered. "I promise, you're safe." If she hadn't shifted back, Kyllian could have voiced her, but his words must have reached her Wolf. Within seconds, Quinn was back in her skin. Kyllian stood and gripped her nape, gently squeezing. The gesture settled both her and her animal.

Quinn apologized. "Sorry about that. It's been a

while since I was around so many shifters."

The biker she had tried to protect Kyllian from pointed at her. "How do you shift with your clothes intact?"

"Goddess magic," Quinn explained.

"Well, it's cool as fuck if not a little unfair. Now, is it safe to hug my uncle?"

Quinn stepped aside, her face heating. "Yes. My Wolf isn't used to new people."

The biker side-eyed her as he stepped up to Kyllian and wrapped him in a bear hug.

"Devil." Kyllian's voice was soft and fond.

"Kayos, it's been too long, Uncle." When Devil stepped back, one of the other's took his place. Quinn figured him to be Devil's brother, as they looked so similar.

"Hey, Joker." As Kyllian hugged his relative, he asked, "How's my sister?"

"Gramma's great. She said to tell you she'll beat your ass if you didn't come see her what with you being so close." If Quinn remembered correctly, Devil was Devon, who was married to Nora, and that made Joker their son, Jericho, even though he didn't look that much younger. Kyllian's sister Poppy was Devon's mother. It made Quinn dizzy thinking about having ten siblings, all of whom had mates and kids. That was a bunch of Lazlos.

Joker stepped back and gestured to the third male. "Kayos, do you remember Storm?"

Kyllian reached out a fist, and Storm bumped knuckles. "Yeah. It's been a few years. How are you?"

Storm kept an eye on Quinn as he responded with

a hint of Texas twang, "If I was any better, I'd be twins."

Kayos

KYLLIAN WAS PROUD of Quinn for holding her shit together. He couldn't imagine being agoraphobic – a term he used, not Quinn. But that's basically what she was, not having left her home in almost twenty years. She clung to his hand almost constantly, and that made his Gryphon preen. It made Kyllian sad. As soon as she stepped outside the car though, she shifted. The silver hair on her back bristled like an angry dog. Everyone took a step back. The wolves of Mercy's pack were wide-eyed and nervous around the dire wolf, most likely remembering how she'd taken down their Alpha when she was still a kid. The Gryphons? They stood their ground, and Joker muttered a "wow".

Kyllian knelt beside his dire wolf and promised she was safe. His Gryphon soothed her beast, and soon, Quinn shifted back and apologized. "Sorry about that. It's been a while since I was around so many shifters." She probably didn't realize she had outed the Gryphons without stating what exactly they were, but he let it go. She was already under enough stress without him making her feel worse.

After introductions were made, Kyllian filled everyone in on the messages from Bishop and how

Nikita's last known ping was from a bus stop in New Santa Rosa. That gave them a direction. "It's late. Is anyone ready to stop for the night?" A chorus of "no" and "let's keep going" rang out. "Okay. Instead of all of us going to one location, I think we need to split up. One group go to the bus terminal and another group ride on ahead to the pack and try to intercept Nikita before she gets there."

"How about the three of us head toward River Canyon pack land?" Devon suggested, gesturing at himself, Joker, and Storm. "Just a few bikers out for a ride. Since we aren't wolves, if we do come across some of the RC Pack, it won't look like we're there to challenge Dennis, if he is still the Alpha." The River Canyon, or RC pack, as they'd begun calling them, was an unknown entity. Kyllian had been in a hurry to get back to Quinn when he questioned the wolves outside her home, and he'd neglected to ask if Dennis was still in charge. Thirty-six years was nothing in the lives of Gryphons, and according to Quinn, wolves lived just as long. Dire wolves even longer.

"You're not just going into biker territory," Jeremy said. "These are wolves, and dire wolves at that."

"We can handle them," Joker assured the wolf.

Mercy gripped her brother's arm. "Trust me; they can."

Jeremy looked from his sister back to Joker. "If you're not wolves, what are you?"

Joker winked. "Something much larger and stronger. If we get Nikita back, maybe we'll show you."

"*When* we get her back." Kyllian had every faith

they would find Quinn's daughter. It might not be before she reached the RC pack, but four Gryphons were mighty enough to take on a whole pack of wolves. When no one else objected, Kyllian told the Hounds to head on out. He thought splitting up made sense, but he would rather be going with them. He preferred riding his bike to driving a cage. Still, he wouldn't want to leave Quinn alone with Mercy and the other wolves. Mercy said they were on Quinn's side, but he didn't know these wolves. Hell, he didn't know Quinn that well either, but she was his responsibility. When no one objected, Kyllian gave his nephews and Storm knuckle bumps. The three Hounds straddled their bikes and rode west.

When Mercy opted to ride with her brother, Kyllian and Jeremy traded phone numbers. Kyllian trusted Mercy to keep his secret having threatened her earlier. After loading up in their respective vehicles, Kyllian took lead and followed the directions on the GPS. After a few miles, Quinn placed her arm on the center console, palm up. Kyllian took the invitation and laced their fingers. Quinn let out a quiet sigh, but he heard it.

"Devon and Jericho look more like brothers than father and son."

"It's a Gryphon thing. The aging process eventually stops. It's the reason my pop moved from Texas to New York. He was too well-known to remain any longer without causing suspicion. Mom had to introduce all the girls as her sisters instead of daughters."

"Tell me about your mom."

"Aurora Rose Lazlo, or Rory to friends and family, is a force to be reckoned with. She's the kindest, most loving woman I've ever met, but if you cross anyone she loves, the Lioness will come out. She's opinionated without being judgmental, and she always let us make our mistakes. If she thought we were doing something stupid, she would say so, but she would step back and wait. If she turned out to be right, she'd just hug us better. All except War. She stopped talking to him for years when he let his mate's aunt and uncle adopt Lucy when her mother was killed. Rory was furious. Said Lucy belonged with our family."

"But Lucy's in your lives now."

"She is, but only because both of her adopted parents passed away. Vera, her adopted mother, left Lucy clues as to where she came from. Lucy became part of our family before she and War patched things up. He basically cut all ties with us when Harlow died. Harlow's own mother was killed by a group of bikers, and in turn, she hated anyone who rode two wheels. Since she was his mate, War did whatever Harlow wanted, including giving up riding. When she died, he gave Lucy to Lucius and Vera, then continued on the path he'd set out on with his mate. He became a professor. It wasn't until Lucy came back into our lives that he decided long enough had passed doing what his dead mate wanted. Rory was glad to have her son back, but it was rough in the beginning."

"How did Sutton feel about all that?"

"He wasn't any happier than Mom, but he's always let us carve our own paths. He says it isn't for him to decide how we live any more than it was for his father to dictate how Pop lived. The hardest part for Sutton was watching Rory ignore War for so long."

"Warryck is Maveryck's twin, right?" Kyllian nodded. "And Mav is the one with the two little boys."

"That's right."

"I can't believe Mercedes turned out to be Hayden's mate. And I hate that I didn't delve further into her life before I put the contract out. If anything, that taught me to be more cautious when taking on jobs."

"Do you like being a handler?"

Quinn's thumb that was stroking Kyllian's knuckles paused. He glanced over at her, but she was looking out the side window. She must have felt his eyes on her because she turned to look at him, her brow furrowed.

"Honestly? No. Especially after what almost happened with Mercedes. It's a lot of responsibility. Besides that, I have to delve into the lives of the marks. These are the worst kinds of humans, and I can't unsee the evil they do."

"Then why do it?"

"I owe my father everything. After what happened in the Ozarks, I was a mess, but he never gave up on me. Kids aren't supposed to live with their parents after a certain age. They're supposed to go out and find their own way, but I didn't. I couldn't. He paid for my education while I contributed little to his life other than cooking and cleaning. I said I studied psychology in college to try and understand those people I have to investigate, but honestly? It was to help myself more than anything. You can read all about the mind and conditions like PTSD. You can learn how to deal with trauma. I did learn how to deal with my own issues, but putting those practices to use are harder when it's yourself. The longer I stayed holed up in our home, the easier it was to ignore my condition. I couldn't very well get a job as a psychologist when I couldn't help myself, so I started working with Dad for something to do as well as to help him.

"Having a mercenary company is so much more than taking a contract and pushing it out to the assassins. There's a lot of deep diving into the mark. It was interesting at first because he taught me how to access the dark web. You know the kind of contracts that come through. The types of people we're targeting. My degree in psychology had already introduced me to how complex minds are. I was still freaked out about rapists and child molesters, but before I would run to the bathroom and throw up, I would take each one and study the person. Try to figure out why they did what they did. In doing that, I was also helping alleviate all the time Dad spent researching the person."

The GPS instructed them they were less than a mile from the bus terminal, so Kyllian took the opportunity to tell Quinn what he hadn't while Mercy was with them. "I'm proud of you, Quinn. I know leaving the house was next to impossible for you, but you did it."

Quinn laughed, but it wasn't a happy one. "That has nothing to do with me and everything to do with you. Don't get me wrong. I was freaking out on the inside, but I feel safe with you."

Kyllian lifted their joined hands and kissed her knuckles. "You are safe with me." It was in that moment he knew he would do everything in his power to win over this female. Yes, their lives were different, but so had his brothers and their mates been, and they had worked things out to be together. He didn't want to give up being a Master, but if that's what it took to have Quinn in his life, he'd do it.

CHAPTER SEVEN

Quinn

QUINN WASN'T LYING when she told Kyllian he made her feel safe. If she'd learned anything about the mate bond from reading her mom's journals, it was that a true mate was your safe haven. The one being you would do anything for. Be anything for. She was still shaking on the inside from leaving her home for the first time, but it was only because she was with Kyllian she'd been able to do so without having a panic attack. It had been touch-and-go when they first pulled out of the driveway, but she'd used her breathing exercises while listening to Mercy talk about Nikita. The more she learned about her daughter, the easier it was to breathe until she'd been surrounded by all the shifters and taken to her fur. Not her finest moment, but again, Kyllian talked her off the ledge. She had smelled the fear coming off the wolves, and the Gryphons? They'd just looked upon her with awe.

Kyllian parked in a restaurant lot down the street from the bus terminal, and the two other vehicles followed with Jeremy pulled into the space beside them. Jeremy rolled the window down, and Quinn did the same.

"We think Kyllian should go in and ask the ticket agent about Nikita while the rest of us sniff around outside." Quinn didn't want to wait in the car by herself, but she was no help to the other wolves since she didn't know what her own daughter smelled like. Not anymore. Quinn might be able to recall what color Nikita's newborn eyes had been, how her downy hair stuck up like a Mohawk, and the way she scrunched her forehead when she was about to cry, but her scent had vanished from Quinn's senses over time.

Kyllian agreed and cut the engine. "Do you want to come with me or stay in the car? Your choice."

Quinn was anxious about being around strangers, but she'd done well at the campground. If she were going to stop hiding at home, she had to become accustomed to others. Taking a deep breath, she opened her door. "I'll go with you."

Kyllian met her at the front of the car and held out his hand. Quinn grabbed onto it like the lifeline it was. She wasn't sure what she expected, but the inside of the terminal was clean. Several people sat in chairs much like they had in the airport while waiting on their ride. Kyllian strode to the ticket window where an older Black woman sat working a crossword puzzle.

"Where to?" she asked when she looked up.

Kyllian slid the photo of Nikita through the narrow window in the plexiglass. "Hello, ma'am. We don't need a ticket. We're looking for our daughter and were hoping you might have seen her." Quinn's Wolf perked up at Kyllian claiming Nikita for his own.

The ticket agent *tsk*ed. "Such a shame. All the kids

that come through here." She studied the photo for only a few seconds before glancing up at Quinn. "No doubt this one's yours. Looks like you spit her out, for sure. And yes, she came through here earlier, but she didn't get a ticket. She did ask if I had any ones since the bill changer over there's broke. She got her money, bought herself some snacks, and took a seat while she ate 'em. I try to keep an eye out on the young ones. Too many creeps these days preying on the runaways. Anyway, after she finished her snack, she went to the restroom, and when she came out, she sat down and played on her phone. After about fifteen minutes, she tucked it into her pocket and walked out the front door." The agent slid the photo back to Kyllian. "Your daughter didn't look distressed. She seemed like she was waiting on her ride to pick her up. I take it that's not the case."

"No, ma'am. Well, not that we know of. Nikita's best friend moved recently, and it's possible she was the one our daughter was texting. Please take my number down. I doubt she comes back through, but if you happen to see her, give me a call." The agent jotted Kyllian's number down, and they wished her a good day. Silently, they headed back to the vehicles. The wolves weren't back, so when Kyllian leaned against the rental, Quinn stepped close so they could talk freely. Kyllian pulled Quinn into his side, wrapping an arm around her waist.

"I feel so useless," Quinn admitted.

"Me too. For now. But that'll change once we find her. If she happens to make it all the way to the pack, I won't hesitate to do whatever's necessary to get her away from Dennis."

"What if she doesn't want to come with us?" Quinn turned and rested her head on Kyllian's chest, taking advantage of the closeness to inhale his scent.

"That's always a possibility. She's young and impressionable. She'll be with others of her kind, but we'll offer her another option."

Quinn looked up at him. "What's that?"

"You'll sit her down and tell her your truth, then offer for her to be with her real family. You and Trenton. And me," Kyllian added.

Quinn frowned. "You?"

"If you'll have me. I know we just met, and we have a lot to work out, but we're mates, Quinn. You know that. Our animals know it too. We're meant to be together."

Quinn's Wolf yipped in her head. It wanted nothing more than to bare its neck for Kyllian's Gryphon. Quinn still wasn't convinced it was the right thing to do no matter how much she longed to have what her parents had before her mom was killed. "What about being a Master? I'm not sure I can handle you going off to the club and being intimate with others."

"I said I wouldn't be intimate with anyone if I found my mate." Kyllian pressed his fingers into Quinn's back. "If that's not enough, I'll give up being a Master completely."

Quinn's eyes widened, and she tried to pull away, but Kyllian kept her within the circle of his arms. "Just like that? You said earlier you would compromise, but giving up something you enjoy isn't compromise, and that's not fair to you."

Kyllian pulled Quinn closer until they were chest to chest. Dipping his head, he pressed his mouth to her ear. "What's not fair is finding my mate, then not doing everything possible to keep her. And Quinn? I want to keep you. We have a lot to learn about one another, but something you can learn right here, right now? When I want something, I go after it. I'm a Lazlo, and you should know we're a tenacious bunch."

Quinn pressed her cheek to his chest. Instead of agreeing or arguing further, she asked, "Why a kitten?"

Kyllian smoothed his hand down her back. "Say what?"

"The tattoo on your back." Quinn noticed the cartoon figure when he was naked outside her home.

Kyllian huffed out a laugh. "Fucking Havyk. My brothers and I like to bet each other, and I lost one to Hayden. He likes to call my subs 'kittens', so he drew the cartoon. He also got to choose where it would be inked on my body, the bastard."

Quinn smiled at the fond tone Kyllian had for his youngest brother. She had always wondered what it would be like to have a sibling. Someone to share secrets with. Get in trouble with. "So he knows about your lifestyle?"

"He does. Besides Maveryck, Hay is the most outgoing, fun-loving one of us. He joined me at the club one night just to see what it was like. None of what went on appealed to him, and that's okay. But he watched me doing a demo, and it allowed him to understand better what it is I do. Now he knows, and unlike Ryker, Hay doesn't judge me for it."

"Ryker's not good with you being a Master?" Quinn had met Ryker briefly, and the male had been all business.

"He doesn't understand it. Ryot says he'll try to do better with the judgmental bullshit, but that's to be seen. He probably searched the term Master and saw only the ones who had slaves and assumed that was the type I am. It's not, and I told him that. Having a slave holds no appeal to me, but I don't judge those who are into that dynamic. There are so many different kinds even I don't understand, like puppies and littles, but it's not for me to understand, just as it isn't for them to get why I inflict pain. When I'm not in a scene, one of my jobs is to provide security and make sure the club is a safe place for everyone who enters the doors."

Quinn leaned back, but not before she rubbed her face against Kyllian's neck and cheek. "Puppies and littles?"

"Yes. Puppies are…" Kyllian looked around. Quinn also felt a shift in the air and turned to find the wolves strolling their way. "Did you find anything?" Kyllian asked Jeremy. Quinn didn't step away. Instead, she turned sideways, snaking her arm around Kyllian's waist. He already admitted he wanted her as his mate, so she took advantage of that knowledge. Seeking comfort was something mates did, right?

"We tracked her scent about half a mile past the bus station down the sidewalk. She entered a diner, and when we showed her photo, the waitress behind the counter remembered Nikita. Said she ordered a soda and kept her nose glued to her phone while she sipped it. After about thirty minutes, she went toward the bathroom, but the waitress didn't remember seeing her come out. She thought she just missed her when a large group came in. We circled the building, and Nikita had exited through a back door. Her scent led us about six blocks before it disappeared."

Mercy bounced on the balls of her feet. "We figure she got into a car because we scoured the area and nothing."

"Shit," Quinn muttered. "She's just a kid."

Kyllian released Quinn's waist and turned, tipping her chin up with a knuckle. "Yeah, but she's strong. Unless she got into a car with another shifter, she can take care of herself." Kyllian pulled out his phone and showed Quinn as he texted Bishop with the information, asking the male to tap into any CCTV cameras in the area. It was a long shot but worth it to try. When he put his phone away, Kyllian told the group what he'd requested. "It's late. Unless you want to keep going, I suggest we all get some shuteye."

"No." Quinn gripped his arms. "We need to keep going."

Kyllian searched her eyes, so she made sure he could read the determination there. He dipped his chin, then turned to Mercy and the other wolves. "If you guys need to rest, go ahead. You can catch up with us afterward."

Mercy shook her head. "No way. We're going with you."

"Okay. Then let's head toward the RC pack. If Bishop happens to catch sight of Nikita, we can always double back if we're going the wrong way."

Kayos

WHEN THEY PILED into their vehicles, Mercy rejoined Kyllian and Quinn. "I hope you don't mind, but there's more room in here." The female stretched her legs across the seat with her back to the door and closed her eyes. So much for not needing rest, and there wasn't any less room in the other two cars. Something felt off about the she-wolf, but until she gave him a reason to distrust her, Kyllian would keep an open mind. Quinn leaned her head back but turned it so she was facing Kyllian. She, too, closed her eyes after giving Kyllian a smile, and he was left alone with his thoughts. He put his phone on vibrate in case Bishop called. The females obviously needed downtime but were too stubborn to say so. It was a good thing he was a Gryphon and didn't require as much sleep as humans. Or wolves.

Kyllian had been driving a couple hours when his phone vibrated, only it wasn't Bishop. Instead of using the Bluetooth, he put the phone to his ear. "Devil, talk to me." Kyllian kept his voice low, knowing his nephew would hear him.

"No sign of Nikita, but we're definitely in wolf country. If we weren't Gryphons, we would have never seen them prowling the area. There's fur everywhere."

"Any trouble?"

"None so far, but I have a feeling that won't last long. Not only are there wolves patrolling, but there are bikers out even this late. They fell in behind us, keeping their distance. Since we don't know exactly where the pack lives, we continued on about forty miles. That must have satisfied the other bikers, because once we passed the county line, they turned back."

"Shit. I should have had Quinn tell you exactly where the pack is located. Once she wakes up, I'll have her call you. We talked to the ticketing agent at the bus terminal. Nikita did come through the building, but she didn't get on another bus. The wolves lost her scent a few blocks from a diner. We assume she got into a vehicle, so I called Bishop and asked him to check CCTV cameras."

"It would be helpful if he can see what kind of car she got into, because there are no cameras out this way. The area we passed through where we encountered those bikers is nothing but nature. At least not that we saw."

"I was afraid of that. Hang tight where you are, and if I hear from Bishop, I'll let you know."

"You got it."

As Kyllian disconnected, Quinn raised her head and leaned forward, stretching. "What's the plan?"

"If we don't hear from Bishop, I think we need to split up and cover all the roads heading toward the pack. Not that we'll know what kind of car Nikita is in, but maybe we'll get lucky and recognize her."

Quinn reached over and placed her hand on Kyllian's nape, playing with his hair. "And do what? We can't sabotage the driver."

Mercy roused in the back seat. "No, but if we do

see her, Jeremy or I can flag her down."

Quinn turned in her seat, keeping her hand on his neck. "Nikita's on the run for a reason. Do you think she'll stop for you? Or will she panic?"

"Only one way to find out," Mercy said tartly. Kyllian narrowed his eyes at her image in the rearview mirror. Ignoring his anger, she asked, "Where are we anyway?"

Kyllian shot a glance at the GPS. "About thirty miles from San Rito."

Quinn removed her hand from his hair, then leaned closer and glanced at the dash. "You might want to stop for gas soon. We don't want to run out once we get onto the back roads." Instead of moving back to her side of the car, she remained stretched across the console. Kyllian didn't know if she was changing her tune about them being mates or if she just needed to be near. Whatever the reason, he liked having her close to him.

Kyllian took the next exit that had a sign for a gas station. The wolves pulled up to the pumps as well, and everyone spilled out of the vehicles. Everyone except Quinn. She was staring out the windshield, and Kyllian followed her gaze. About a hundred yards down the road, several bikes were parked on the shoulder with their riders leaning against the machines. Kyllian's Gryphon took notice as well.

Looks like trouble.

Sure does.

Wanna cause a little chaos?

No, but it might not hurt to get some answers.

You're no fun.

110

I'm all kinds of fun, and you know it.

When the pump clicked off, Kyllian replaced the nozzle and finalized the transaction. He stepped between the pumps where Jeremy was finishing up. "I'm going to pull around to the side of the store and park. See those bikers down there?" Jeremy looked to where Kyllian indicated and nodded. "I'm going to go have a little chat with them."

"Do you want me to go with you?"

"No. Stay here and watch over Quinn for me."

"Do you think you should go alone? What if they're armed?"

"I'll— shit, it's too late." The rumble of motors rent the air as the bikers loaded up and took off in the opposite direction. Using his Eagle's keen vision, Kyllian studied the last male's kutte. The one percent patch beside the howling wolf didn't surprise him. It was the name of the club that did. *Wolves of Chaos.* Kyllian would have to show them his own brand of Kayos.

"Think they're from the River Canyon pack?" Jeremy asked.

"Yep," Kyllian responded.

"Kyllian?" Quinn called out, holding his phone. "It's Bishop." Kyllian strode to where she was standing in the open door. "Normally, I wouldn't answer your phone, but I saw his name on the caller ID."

Kyllian smiled. "I'm glad you did." He let his fingers brush hers as he took the phone. "Bishop?"

"Hey, Kayos. I think I have something. It might not be Nikita, but there was a teenager riding in the passenger seat of a blue sedan..." Quinn ran her

111

fingers down his arm and pointed inside while mouthing "bathroom." Her touch distracted him momentarily.

"I'm sorry, Bishop. Can you repeat that?" Kyllian kept an eye on Quinn until she was safely inside the small store. As the Hound repeated what he'd seen on the CCTV camera, Kyllian kept waiting. When she didn't come back soon enough to appease his gut, he told Bishop to hang on. "Jeremy." When the male walked over, Kyllian handed him the phone. "This is Bishop. He has some information on Nikita, but I need to go check on Quinn." Kyllian took off across the parking lot and pushed open the door to the store. He checked the overhead signs and rushed toward the bathrooms. "Quinn?" he called out when he reached the door to the women's. When she didn't respond, he knocked. "Quinn?" he asked loudly. Being a wolf, she would be able to hear him whisper, but he was frantic. With no answer, Kyllian opened the door and peeked in, not caring if anyone else was in there. The restroom was empty, so he retraced his steps to the door and looked out at the vehicles, making sure she hadn't exited while he was in the back hallway. Not seeing her, Kyllian ran outside.

"Mercy, with me." When the wolf reached his side, he said, "Quinn's gone."

"What?"

"While I was on the phone, she said she was going to the restroom. She's not in there."

Kyllian continued jogging around back of the building with the wolf at his side. Several barks sounded in the woods off to the east followed by a howl. Kyllian's Gryphon tried to break free, but there were too many humans around. He took off running in the direction of the noise with Mercy at his side. Several sets of feet beating pavement sounded behind them, but Kyllian didn't slow to wait on them. He was already breaking the rules by running faster than humanly possible, but he didn't care. There was no path through the trees, so Kyllian made one.

Snarls and growls were getting louder as tree branches struck Kyllian as he shoved through the dense foliage. "Quinn? Quinn!"

Someone yelped, and Kyllian prayed it wasn't his mate. He pushed on as his beast yelled in his head to turn him loose. Kyllian didn't have time to strip and shift. Why couldn't Gryphons have the same kind of magic dire wolves did? And why was Quinn in the woods fighting?

When another howl rose, Mercy cursed, then shifted, her clothes shredding. The smaller grey wolf took off, and Kyllian's Gryphon took control. His clothes fell away as his body morphed into his Eagle. Its sleek body flew through the trees with ease, darting over and around the branches he'd seconds before been fighting in his human body. Scanning the area, Kyllian caught sight of Mercy running toward a larger wolf. No, no, no. She was no match for a dire wolf, but she didn't slow down. The larger animal turned its head at her approach and bared its teeth. Kyllian dove toward them, screeching. The dire wolf froze at the sound, giving Mercy a temporary reprieve. When he broke through the trees, Kyllian increased his Eagle's size. That was one bit of magic he did have.

With talons stretched out in front of him, Kyllian aimed for the wolf's head. Before he could latch on, Mercy lunged, the force of her speed knocking the larger animal to the ground. It was back on its feet quickly, though. Kyllian flapped his wings, changing course in midair, putting his body between the dire wolf and Mercy. Several motorcycles revved their engines, and a vehicle roared to life. Shit, Quinn! Mercy was no match for the other beast, but Quinn was his mate.

When two more wolves broke through the trees, Kyllian prayed to Zeus they, along with Mercy, could handle one dire wolf. He sped toward the sound of the bikes, catching up with them soon after. Stretching out his talons once more, Kyllian grabbed the first rider's shoulders and flung him sideways. The bike careened, then slid, catching the attention of the next male. With his attention on the wreckage, Kyllian latched onto him, tossing him aside as well. With no rider to control it, that bike teetered back and forth before falling on its side and sliding off the road. By the time Kyllian dispatched all the riders, the SUV had disappeared around a curve.

Kyllian flew hard and fast. He was nearly upon the vehicle when the passenger side window was rolled down and a pistol appeared. A shot rang out, and Kyllian swooped hard to the right. Fuck. He was no match for a bullet. Choosing to live to fight another day, he circled back to where the bikers were stumbling to their feet. Shifting, he landed on two legs, and used his Gryphon voice before any of them could pull a weapon.

CHAPTER EIGHT

Quinn

QUINN FELT UNEASY walking down the semi-dark hallway, but she really had to pee. When she reached for the doorknob to the women's restroom, a hand covered her mouth. Quinn struggled, but whoever was at her back was stronger than her. The back door opened, and she was shoved through. Quinn struggled with all her shifter strength.

"Grab her feet," the man behind her demanded, and the other did as he was told. Quinn squirmed in their grip, moving her legs back and forth until she was able to break one foot free. She kicked out, hitting the one holding her legs in the nose. He dropped her other leg to cover his bleeding face. With her lower body now free, Quinn used the momentum of her legs falling to carry her forward, flipping the man behind her over her back. As soon as she was out of his clutches, Quinn called forth her Wolf, and then she ran.

The convenience store backed up to dense woods, and Quinn headed that direction instead of circling the building where humans wouldn't react well to seeing wolves. The vegetation was thick, but Quinn bullied her way through the branches and undergrowth. Snarls and snapping of jaws sounded close behind, so Quinn urged her Wolf faster. The trees opened up slightly, and Quinn had a moment of hope until she caught sight of more wolves. These weren't your garden variety timber wolves either. Like her, they had silver fur covering their backs, with black on their bellies and legs. She was no match for six dire wolves, but that didn't mean she wouldn't hurt as many as possible before they finally took her down.

Quinn shifted, biting and clawing until they turned loose. She took off running, but they were hot on her trail through the woods. Then there were more of them. Quinn fought as hard as she could, but she was outnumbered. If the males were regular wolves, she might have stood a chance. But they weren't. She let out a howl, knowing Mercy and the other Ozark wolves would hear. Kyllian would as well, but since he wasn't lupine, he wouldn't know what her call meant.

Once they subdued Quinn, they shifted back to their skin and bragged about how their father would reward them for finally bringing Quinn to him, which meant they were both her uncles. But how the hell had they known she was there at the store? Or in New Mexico for that matter? Fuck. Someone had betrayed her, and when Quinn found out who? She was going to tear them apart, adding another shifter to the long list of those she wanted to see dead. Her grandfather for having her mother killed. Blake for taking Nikita from her. And now, whoever told the River Canyon pack she was headed their direction.

Her uncles dragged her to an SUV and tossed her

in the back seat. Her beast wanted her to fight, but Quinn needed to be smart. Kyllian would come for her.

"What the fuck is that?" Henry, the driver of the SUV, was intent on something in the rearview mirror. Quinn turned to look out the back window. A large eagle grabbed one of the bikers following them and tossed him off his motorcycle.

Kyllian.

"Shoot that fucking bird," Henry instructed his brother.

Quinn lunged for the male sitting in the passenger seat when he aimed a pistol out the window. Henry swerved before regaining control of the SUV. Bradley cursed as he turned the gun on her. "That was a mistake." She didn't respond. Instead, she glared at her uncle who was snarling at her.

No, the mistake had been leaving the safety of Kyllian and the wolves to go into the store alone. There were only a handful of pack members who knew she was there. Mercy claimed she and Jeremy were on Quinn's side, but were they? And Scott... Quinn remembered him from her time with the pack. If Blake hadn't gotten to Quinn and declared them mates, she would have fallen for Scott's easy smile and boyish good looks. He had been one of the first to befriend her, but as soon as Blake claimed Quinn, Scott's presence had been scarce. Had he seen her being with Blake as betrayal? Enough to hate her and try to ruin her life? If so, she would be the one to ruin him. First, she had to get away from her mother's people.

The drive would have been gorgeous if Quinn wasn't being taken against her will. The road leading away from civilization wound through lush trees, and the farther away she got from Kyllian, the more dread filled her heart. Kyllian, her tatted guardian. Her fierce Gryphon. Her mate. Quinn regretted not claiming him the moment he strode through her front door. True mates were scarce, and she'd denied hers.

He'll come for us.

Her Wolf was right. Kyllian wouldn't stop until he found her. With him taking down the bikers, she had no doubt he was using his Gryphon voice to find out exactly where they were taking her. It was a matter of him and his Hound family getting to her without getting shot. Quinn needed to be smart. To bide her time in captivity until Kyllian came up with a plan. She would do whatever it took to stay alive, and that meant she couldn't attack her uncles. Not when one of them kept his weapon trained on her.

Quinn was expecting living arrangements like the Ozark pack had with a subdivision of similar houses. Instead, small cabins dotted the tree line, and those didn't appear to be in top condition. When Henry pulled to a stop in front of a massive structure reminiscent of a lodge, she guessed that's where all the pack's money went.

With the pistol aimed at her chest, Bradley opened the back door. "Get out. And if you try anything stupid, I *will* shoot you, niece or not."

Quinn could tell her Wolf was trying to communicate with Kyllian's Gryphon. She didn't know if it succeeded, and she didn't have time to ask. An older man strode out of the lodge, his alpha pheromones licking the air. Quinn had no doubt this was her grandfather. Several more wolves followed. Only a couple were female. Every single one of them had the same coloring as Dennis. Were they all Quinn's aunts and uncles? Cousins? Her mom made it clear the RC pack didn't accept outsiders, so did that mean... No, that was too disgusting.

Her uncle nudged her back with the barrel of the pistol. "Bow to your Alpha."

"He's not my Alpha."

Dennis glared but didn't argue the point. "You look just like your mother."

"Are you going to kill me for that?" Okay, so maybe Quinn only thought she would be able to remain calm until Kyllian got to her.

"I didn't kill the bitch. She did that to herself when she betrayed the pack." Dennis spit tobacco juice onto the ground, then wiped his mouth with the back of his hand. She wasn't impressed. Looking down the driveway he asked, "Where are the others?"

Her uncles glanced at one another, and the one with the gun shrugged. "They were right behind us, but a big ass bird attacked them, and they wrecked."

"A big— Bradley, you're shitting me right now, right?"

"No, Alpha." Bradley bared his neck to his father. "I swear that's what happened."

Dennis narrowed his eyes, looking from one son to the other. "Henry?" When Henry nodded, Dennis spit again. "Well, if five fucking wolves can't handle one fucking bird, it serves 'em right." Turning his attention back to Quinn, he asked, "Did she give you any trouble?"

"Nothing we couldn't handle, sir." Bradley waved the gun in Quinn's direction.

"Good. Take her inside. You know where to put her." With that, Dennis strode down the steps and continued walking toward a group of males gathered around an old truck. A couple of spotlights shone down on the vehicle. Quinn wondered if that's what they considered entertainment for a Friday night.

Henry grabbed Quinn's arm and pulled her toward the lodge. She didn't fight him. She had counted no less than thirty wolves in the area, and she didn't have a death wish. The room her uncle led her to was toward the back of the first floor. He shoved her inside before pulling the door closed and locking it from the outside. Quinn looked around, finding nothing in the room except a bucket. Considering she'd needed to pee for a couple hours, Quinn swallowed her pride and used it, praying no one walked in on her. The relief was instant.

Once her pants were pulled up and fastened, she walked over to the window and looked out, surprised there weren't bars covering the outside. Pushing back the thin, sheer curtain, Quinn found two wolves sitting on the ground underneath, both facing her. She let the material fall back in place before sliding down the wall.

Having read her mother's journals cover to cover numerous times, Quinn felt as though she knew this pack. Finola not only recorded everyday life, but she documented traits of every person within the pack. Who was alpha, beta, and omega. Which females tended the gardens. Which ones did the cooking and cleaning. Those who held outside jobs. They were few, but Dennis allowed it because the pack needed money. Quinn knew from the journals that Bradley and Henry weren't her only uncles. She had four more as well as three aunts, possibly more. Dennis took as many mates as he saw fit to keep the family line going. Those aunts and uncles had numerous offspring, and Quinn figured there were many more considering it had been over thirty years since her mother's passing.

No, her mother's murder. Quinn wasn't foolish enough to believe she could challenge Dennis. The longer a wolf lived, the stronger they became, and Dennis was over a hundred by a few years. Quinn leaned her head against the rough paneling and thought about the nearby pack. Were they still around, or had Dennis run them off? They had to have been close for Finola to know of their existence but not close enough she knew the Alpha had a fated mate. Thinking of mates, Quinn turned to her Wolf.

Can you reach our Gryphon?

It is distracted. Trying to keep Kyllian calm.

Quinn could only imagine. Kyllian had been sent to protect Quinn, and she had walked away from his safety into the arms of her enemies. Speaking of enemies…

Tell our Gryphon not to trust anyone. Someone gave away our location to Dennis.

Quinn felt the magic of her Wolf reaching out to Kyllian's beast. Was this what it had been like for her parents? Finola didn't mention being able to mind-speak with Trenton, but they had been fated mates, so it made sense they would have the ability. Goddess, her father was going to have a stroke when he found

121

out Quinn had been taken. Her cell phone was back in the rental, but even if she'd had it on her, Quinn had no doubt her uncles would have taken it from her.

Voices echoed through the hallway, and Quinn focused on the muted conversation. A female argued with someone.

"Francine, you're not getting in there."

"I am still the Alpha Mate, and that is my granddaughter you have locked up. If you don't get out of my way—"

"You'll what, old woman? I do not take orders from you, Alpha Mate or not."

"Bradley, please. I just want to see her."

Quinn wasn't sure if she wanted to meet her grandmother. She didn't know how to feel about someone remaining with their mate, Alpha or not, after said mate ordered their child killed. But Quinn remembered everything her mother journaled, and Francine wasn't allowed to leave pack lands. None of Dennis's mates were. With no outside job, she had no money. No way to survive if she were able to escape. Finola had help in getting away from the pack, and they still found her. Fear was a heady deterrent, and Dennis ruled with an iron claw.

When the lock turned, Quinn pushed off the floor. She wouldn't allow anyone to see her as anything but strong. Crossing her arms over her chest, she held her breath. Instead of her uncle, an older female entered the room. Quinn's breath left her chest in a whoosh. If she didn't know better, she would think the female in front of her was Finola. Trenton had photos of her mother safely tucked away, but he shared them with

122

her whenever she wanted to see them. And since Quinn was the spitting image of her mother, she could see what she would look like later in life.

Bradley stuck his head in the room. "You have five minutes." He closed the door and turned the lock once again.

Francine's eyes filled with tears. She reached out a trembling hand, but pulled it back when Quinn didn't move. "Oh, goddess," she whispered. "You look just like her."

"And she looked just like you, and for that, I'm grateful." Dennis was handsome in a rugged way, but his demeanor detracted from his looks, making him the ugliest being Quinn had ever encountered. Considering what she did for a living, that was saying something.

Francine wrapped her arms around her own waist. "I'm so sorry, Quinn. You have no idea how much. Your mother was such a strong-willed child, but nothing I said got through to her. I always figured she would try to leave. As soon as she started working outside the pack, a change came over her, and..." Francine shook her head and sucked in a breath. Tears streamed down her cheeks, but Quinn remained glued to the floor. "Please tell me she was happy."

"She was. My father was her fated mate, and even though they had to move often and hide from Dennis, they had each other. At least for a short while." Quinn didn't feel the least bit guilty for getting that dig in.

"And then they had you."

Quinn shifted on her feet but didn't move closer. "For three years, she had us both. Then your mate had her killed. Nothing, not even pack, excuses the murder of your own child." Quinn's claws elongated, and Francine gasped, taking a step back. Quinn willed her Wolf to stand down. As angry as she was, Quinn tried to remember this female was without any choices in life.

Your mother made a choice.

And look where it got her.

With her mate and child. Happy for a while.

That was true. Finola found joy in Trenton and Quinn, if only for a short time. Trenton always reminded her they would have made the same choice again even knowing the outcome. Their happiness was tragically cut short, but he had the memories of their time together to sustain him.

"What happens now? Am I going to be killed the same as my mother? Or will I continue to remain locked in this cell the rest of my life?" Quinn gestured to the empty room.

"I-I don't know. I had no idea you had been found."

"I wasn't lost. I have a life. At least I did."

"And your pack, are you happy with them?" Francine asked wistfully.

"I have the best pack in the world." Quinn didn't tell her grandmother it was a pack of two. She didn't need to know that. "What I don't understand is why I'm here. According to my mother, Dennis only wants pure bloods in his pack. It's why he had her killed, because she chose to follow her heart and mate with my father. Since my father is half human, that makes me part human as well."

Francine sighed. "Our numbers are dwindling. The bloodline is dying out."

"So he's, what? Letting the riffraff in to keep the pack going?"

Francine winced at Quinn's harsh tone, but Quinn didn't care. The bastard hadn't cared enough for his own daughter to allow her happiness, but now he was willing to... "He plans to pimp me out?"

Francine lowered her eyes, and Quinn turned, punching the wall. Francine yelped, and the door flew open.

"Time's up." Bradley leered at Quinn. "A good Alpha does whatever's necessary for the well-being of the pack." As suspected, her uncle had been outside the door listening. "And it's not pimping if he isn't getting paid."

"You can tell your Alpha I'll kill myself before I allow a single one of you to touch me. I have a mate, and he doesn't share."

Bradley pointed to Quinn's neck. "Yeah? Where's your mate mark?"

Well, hell. She forgot about that. If she hadn't been so stubborn upon meeting Kyllian, she might have the bite mark proving she was taken. Then again, she doubted Dennis would care if what Francine said was true. Still, she needed to say something, so pulled up a smirk, placed a hand on her hip, and cocked her head to the side.

"His kind doesn't leave a mark. But don't worry. You can ask him all about it when he comes for me, because he is coming. And I cannot wait to see your face when he rains fire down on this pack."

"What the fuck kind of noise are you making right now? His kind? There is nothing stronger than a dire wolf."

"You keep telling yourself that. Just make sure you have plenty of clean underwear, because when you do see there's something stronger? You're going to shit yourself."

Francine covered her mouth, eyes wide. Whether it was from Quinn's crude words or the fact that she was talking back to Bradley, Quinn didn't know. Didn't care. She prayed to the goddess she wasn't lying, and Kyllian did rain hell down on the lot of them. Okay, maybe not all of them, but Dennis and all those who followed his path. What was it Kyllian had asked? If this pack was like a cult? Yes. This situation was similar, and Quinn would take a page out of the Lazlo book, helping Francine and anyone else who wished for a better life.

Bradley's claws came out, and Quinn was ready to turn her Wolf loose, but Dennis appeared in the doorway. "What the fuck are you doing in here, Francine? Get your ass back to your room."

Francine bared her neck. "Yes, Alpha." Quinn's grandmother rushed out the door, turning sideways as if she didn't want to touch Dennis. Quinn didn't blame her.

"Change of plans. Corbin returned. You and Henry failed to mention there's a group of wolves with Quinn."

"And he didn't take care of them?"

Dennis punched Bradley in the stomach. "Watch your tone, pup. While six of you were fighting one bitch, he took on four wolves by himself. I think a change in rank is due, wouldn't you say?"

Bradley hung his head. "Whatever you think best, Alpha."

Dennis spit his nasty juice at his son's feet. "I'll give you one chance to redeem yourself. Take Quinn to the cliffs. If you think you need backup, grab one of your brothers. Stay there until I send word it's safe to return."

"I won't let you down." Bradley turned away from his father. "Let's go."

Quinn didn't let her excitement show. Getting away from the pack was better for her. If Kyllian's Gryphon could locate her, he would only have one wolf to tangle with. Two at most. When she moved to walk past Dennis, he gripped her arm hard enough to bruise.

"Don't do anything stupid."

"Wouldn't dream of it," she snarled, glaring at him. His eyes flashed the bright amber of his Wolf, but Quinn wouldn't cow down to this male. He wasn't her Alpha. Her Alpha was out there looking for her.

CHAPTER NINE

Kayos

KYLLIAN WAS LIVID. Quinn had been lied to by someone in their group. There was no other explanation for how the RC pack found her. After grilling the bikers, he wiped their minds of his Eagle taking them out. He then sent them on their merry way, far away from their home. That might have been a mistake, sending rogue wolves out to live among the humans, but at the moment, he wasn't thinking straight. Between fighting with his Gryphon for control and reining in the desire to kill the four wolves, he had his hands full. Yes, he killed people for a living, but those who met his fangs and claws deserved it. He couldn't justify taking four lives for following the orders of their Alpha to kidnap Quinn, even if she was his mate. They hadn't marked one another, but they would. He knew it in his heart.

Instead of shifting back to his Eagle, Kyllian walked back to where he'd left the others fighting the dire wolf. When he arrived, only three wolves were waiting.

"What happened to the dire wolf?"

"It took off when it couldn't handle all of us,"

Mercy answered.

Kyllian strode to where his clothes had fallen when he shifted. He lifted the shirt, but it was in tatters. He had no shame in being naked, but somehow, he needed to get back to the rental still parked at the gas pump.

"Where's Scott?" he asked when he realized which one of the wolves was missing.

"He went to move the cars so the clerk didn't call the cops," Jeremy said.

"Naked?"

Mercy bit her lip, looking at the ground. "No. He never shifted."

Kyllian pulled on his Gryphon, letting his Lion's mane and fangs come forth. "Which one of you betrayed Quinn?"

With wide eyes, all three wolves shivered at the sight of his Lion and the power in his voice, but it was Jeremy who answered. "It had to be Scott since the three of us were here fighting to help save Quinn."

Kyllian reined the beast in, taking deep breaths. "I'd lay odds he isn't waiting back at the store. Stay here. I'm going to have a look." Kyllian shifted into his Eagle and took off. As he expected, one of the SUVs was gone. Luckily, the one he rented was still sitting where he left it. Thanking Zeus the lot was empty of other customers, Kyllian shifted back, keeping the car between him and the store. Opening the door, Kyllian leaned in and grabbed his phone. There were several missed calls, one of them Trenton. Kyllian closed his eyes and blew out a breath. He didn't want to tell the male his daughter was missing. Instead of calling Quinn's father, Kyllian dialed Devon.

"Hey, Uncle. Everything okay?" Devon answered.

"No. No, it's not." Kyllian relayed the events of the last half hour. "I'm going to kill that fucker Scott, but first, I'm going after my mate."

"Tell me what to do," Devon said.

"Call Bishop. He had news about Nikita, but I took off after Quinn before he could tell me what he found. You, Joker, and Storm follow up on whatever he tells you, and I'll ask the wolves if they want to come with me or help you. Quinn's my priority right now. I know where the pack is located, and I'm going to do a flyover, get the lay of the land. If I find she's in mortal danger, I won't wait for backup. If she isn't, I'll regroup."

"Keep us posted, and we'll do the same if we can get a bead on the girl."

After disconnecting, Kyllian moved both cars to the side of the building. Kyllian dug in his duffel for clothes and pulled them on. He then went inside and wiped the clerk's memory of anything he might have seen, including Kyllian's shifting from Eagle to two legs. Before returning to the woods, Kyllian pulled clothes out of the other car and headed back toward the wolves. They were sitting where he left them. Kyllian tossed the clothes at their feet. "Get dressed." He crossed over to where his boots were. Whenever he shifted, his boots were left intact since his shifter feet were smaller. Wings, however, were hell on shirts.

"I was right about Scott. He took off, so it's safe to assume he was the one who told the dire wolves where she was. What I want to know is why."

Brett bent over to tie his boots. Without looking at

Kyllian, he said, "When Quinn first arrived at our pack, she and Scott became friends. Good friends. He wanted more and felt like she did as well, so when Quinn hooked up with Blake, Scott took it hard."

"Hard enough he'd try to ruin her life? I mean, I get teenage angst, but that's a little harsh." Kyllian thought back to his one and only brokenhearted experience. He was sixteen at the time, and the girl he thought was his forever broke up with him to date an older guy. Kyllian had been crushed, but two weeks later, he found someone else who made his heart sing. His high school days were rife with young lust, but his first crush was just that, and he got over it. He couldn't imagine holding onto a grudge for eighteen years.

"Scott had to watch Blake raise Nikita, the child Scott wanted for himself."

"Then why did you let him come with you if there was a possibility he'd turn on Quinn?"

Mercy stomped her feet into her shoes. "He was the first to volunteer. We" — she gestured to Jeremy, then herself — "had no idea he had ulterior motives."

"I hope you aren't good friends with the male, because the next time I see him, I'm going to gut him."

Brett lifted his chin. "I'll hold him down for you."

"What did Bishop have to say when you spoke to him?" Kyllian asked Jeremy.

"Said he saw Nikita not too far from here, but that's as much as I got before I heard the commotion and came running to help."

"I know you're here for Nikita, but Quinn is my first priority. I asked Devon to call Bishop, and they're going to follow up on whatever else he had to say. I

131

understand if you want to help them find the girl. It's probably better that you do. It's going to be hard enough getting Quinn away from Dennis. I really don't want to have to rescue Nikita as well."

"From listening to Quinn talk about the RC pack, I don't want Nikita anywhere near them." Mercy gazed over Kyllian's shoulder, and he let her have time to decide. When she looked back at him, she said, "I'm going to work with the Hounds to try and intercept her. If we do manage to get her before she reaches the pack, I'm not sure what'll happen. She ran away for a reason."

"I would suggest you take her to one of my sisters. Between the six of them, they have plenty of experience with angsty teens."

"Won't that be awkward? They don't know Nikita, or me for that matter."

"No. Our family specializes in helping those who need a safe place to land. Then again, if they get their hands on Nikita, I might never get her back. The girls – that's what my mom calls my sisters – they love hard."

Mercy puffed up. "*You* might never get her back? You've never met her."

"No, but she's Quinn's daughter. Quinn is my mate; therefore, Nikita is mine as well. Yes, I'm getting ahead of myself, but when I said my sisters love hard? It isn't only them. Once you have a Lazlo in your corner, that's all there is to it."

Mercy stared at Kyllian a beat, studying him. He let her take his measure. Not that her opinion mattered. Yes, she had some sway over Nikita, but in the long run, it would be Quinn and Kyllian who took care of the girl. It might take a while for Nikita to believe her mother had her best interest at heart, but he would make sure it happened. If he needed to enlist the girls help, he would.

"Look. Devon and his mate recently helped one of my brothers with a situation involving a child. They took the child and her mother in. Poppy is Devon's mother. Please think about going to her for help. There's nowhere you'll be more protected than with my family."

"If you think they won't mind, I'll take her there."

"They won't mind at all. Like I said, it's what our family does." Kyllian gestured to Jeremy and Brett. "Are you two going with Mercy?"

"Yes. Quinn is your priority, but Nikita is ours. She might be Quinn's daughter, but she's still part of our pack."

She wouldn't be for long if Kyllian had anything to say about it, but he kept that thought to himself. "Okay, let me call Devon and tell him the three of you are going to meet up with the Hounds. Jeremy, I'll give him your number, and I'll be on my way to find Quinn."

After calling his nephew and getting everyone on the same page, Kyllian got into the rental and headed west. The RC pack's land wasn't too much farther, but Kyllian needed to find somewhere to park away from the watchful eyes of the wolves. He had no doubt the wolf Mercy and the others fought would have arrived home and alerted Dennis to what went down. The wolves already had an advantage with their numbers. Kyllian needed his Hounds at his back when he went

133

in to get Quinn, but he could scout the area while Devon and the others searched for Nikita.

Devon had mapped out the route the Hounds took earlier, so Kyllian made sure to stay away from that area. He drove until he found a secluded road leading away from the river and parked. He put his cell phone and keys in a small pouch before stripping. He deposited his clothes on the front seat and locked the car. Kyllian then shifted to his Eagle, grabbing the pouch handle in his beak before taking flight. The land below was gorgeous, but it was the river that called to him. Each Hound had their own element, and his was water. Unable to resist, Kyllian flew lower until his talons dragged the surface. If he weren't in a hurry to get to Quinn, he would let his Eagle snag a fish or two. After getting his fill of communing with his element, he angled back to the sky.

Staying well above the tree line, Kyllian continued on to where the bikers had said the pack land was hidden away, well off the main road. When he noticed small cabins nestled back in the woods, he knew he was in the right place. Kyllian continued until he caught sight of the Alpha's residence. The cabins were nothing more than two room shacks while the main house was a sprawling, three-story lodge. Kyllian expected Dennis to have better accommodations, but this was ridiculous. It was apparent the Alpha cared more about himself than his pack.

Circling the area, Kyllian kept his Eagle eyes open for any sign of Quinn. He doubted Dennis would allow her to remain out in the open, but he searched anyway. Motorcycles were parked all around the property. Most of the cabins had at least one bike parked next to it. He cringed thinking of the wear and tear on the machines from sitting in the elements. Several men stood around an older model truck, the hood up with one male leaning over working on the engine. Quinn said all money earned from outside jobs went back into the pack, but it was clear where the money was focused, and it wasn't on the individual members if that junker was any indication.

Kyllian hovered as the front door opened and Quinn walked out followed by a man with a gun. Fuck. If these dire wolves were such badasses, why did they need weapons?

You carry a gun.

Yes, he did, but only at Ryker's insistence for their merc jobs. Kyllian kept his eyes trained on his mate as she was escorted to the same SUV she'd been in before. The wolf gestured to the back, and Quinn complied. The gunman slid into the backseat with her while another got in to drive. Where were they taking her? Kyllian followed from above as the vehicle left the compound. Instead of turning right out of the driveway, the driver went left. Kyllian could handle two wolves, but at least one of them was armed, and he couldn't risk Quinn getting shot. Shifter or not, if a bullet hit a vital organ, it could be lights out.

A few miles farther down the road, they turned left once again. From the looks of the area, it appeared as though they were headed up. *Where are you taking her?* From somewhere below, a scream filled the air followed by growls and a single howl. Scanning the area below, Kyllian found the source of the disturbance. Without flying lower, he felt in his soul he'd found Nikita.

Kyllian was torn. Did he abandon his mate to whatever fate awaited her at the end of her drive and go after her daughter? Would she hate him if he continued following the car, then something happened to Nikita because he left her to fight on her own? He cursed, and it came out as a loud screech.

Go after the girl.

Nikita

NIKITA CROUCHED BEHIND a tree, begging her Wolf to calm down. She needed to shift to heal the wounds from jumping out of a moving vehicle, but if she did, she was afraid the beast would take over completely. Nikita had always prided herself on being a good judge of character, so when the old man who offered her a ride turned out to be a creep, well, it wasn't her finest moment. Neither had been running from home, but something weird was going on back in her pack.

She was different from everyone else in her pack. When Nikita took to her fur, she was larger than the other wolves her age. She also had different coloring. The best thing about her Wolf was she didn't have to strip. Her clothes magically reappeared when she took to her skin again. She'd asked her dad about it, and he said it was because she was special. Blake sat Nikita down and told her the truth of her birth. How her birth mother had walked away from the pack two days after Nikita was born. In essence, had walked away from Nikita.

She didn't believe him for one second, but Nikita was an excellent actress. She had witnessed pups being born. She had seen the joy in each mother's eyes when they first held their baby. And she had felt the fierce protectiveness they displayed if anyone tried to get near the baby. Anyone other than the sire or the Alpha would be eviscerated, at least verbally.

It wasn't until she was older and her best friend Tarryn told her the truth. Nikita's biological mother had been distraught upon finding Nikita gone. So much so she killed the Alpha, Blake's father. Learning the truth was the moment everything changed inside her mind. Tarryn swore Nikita to secrecy, but her whole life had been a lie. She went to the one person she thought would be on her side, realizing too late it was her own mother who killed her grandfather, and the pain in her Gran's eyes was proof she blamed Quinn Shepherd for everything wrong in the world.

Then why did she tell you where your mother lived?

That was an excellent question. Nikita explained to Gran that she wanted to find out where she came from. To learn the truth of the dire wolves. Gran had willingly offered up the location of her mother's old pack. She even went as far as giving Nikita money for bus fare and food, but she also made Nikita swear she wouldn't divulge where the money came from. When Nikita thought about traveling to New Mexico, she had been excited. She'd never traveled farther than the Texas border with her parents and siblings. Now, here she was, stuck in a strange place with nothing but twelve dollars and some change to her name.

Her plan to find Quinn hadn't included hiding in the dark while other wolves roamed the area. Nikita thought she'd be able to waltz right up to the door and ask for her mother. If this was her mother's pack, they wouldn't hurt her, right?

Someone's coming! The Wolf took over just as a man approached.

"Well, well, well. What do we have here?" The man in front of her felt familiar somehow, but she didn't know this pack. Heck, she didn't know her mother.

Nikita growled, baring her teeth. Returned snarls encircled her, and the male standing a few feet away just grinned. Well, hell. Nikita shifted back to her skin and put her acting skills to the test. "Oh, thank goodness. I was so scared. I thought for sure you guys were the enemy. You're with the River Canyon pack, right? Because if you're not, I apologize for intruding in your territory."

"Who are you, little girl, and what are you doing out here alone?"

"I'm Nikita, and Quinn is my mom. That's who I've come to see."

The man's eyes flashed amber, and the other wolves growled, baring their own sharp teeth. "Quinn, huh? You're in luck," he said, a feral grin on his face. It was then Nikita realized something was bad wrong. The male who'd done the talking grabbed her arm, and

Nikita squirmed.

"Get off me!" Nikita jerked her arm out of his grasp and turned in a circle, trying to keep an eye on all of them at one time. The man took to his fur once again, and Nikita's Wolf pushed to be turned loose. A loud squawking came from overhead, capturing not only Nikita's attention, but the wolves as well. "What the...?" Even in the darkness, Nikita could see a fantastical beast bearing down on them. With the head and wings of an eagle and the body of a lion, the creature tucked in its wings in and flew faster. As it neared, Nikita feared being eaten by the large beak or torn apart by the sharp talons. Still, she couldn't move. Within the blink of an eye, the creature shifted into a man and yelled, "Nikita, run!" before turning back into the winged beast just as quickly.

Gryphons weren't real, yet here was one, getting closer. It spread out its magical wings and took out two of the men. Nikita took advantage of the distraction and ran. Snarls sounded behind her, and she pushed her body faster, but it wasn't enough. Hands grabbed both her arms, and Nikita was dragged back toward the fighting. She kicked and screamed, but it was no use. She wasn't strong enough to fight two grown dire wolves.

CHAPTER TEN

Kayos

KYLLIAN'S BEAST WAS right. Quinn was smart. She could hold her own until he could find her. Nikita didn't stand a chance against a larger wolf, even if there had been only one. Changing trajectory, he flew fast to where the girl was surrounded by four dire wolves.

"Get away from me!" The girl's claws were out, and she was moving in a circle, doing her best to keep an eye on each wolf. His Eagle was no match for the beasts below, but his Gryphon could handle them with ease. Shifting mid-flight, Kyllian called on his own beast. His Lion's roar would be more impressive, but his Eagle when in Gryphon form was loud enough to get the wolves' attention. He squawked, causing the animals to avert their attention from Nikita momentarily. Kyllian shifted to his human form long enough to yell, "Nikita, run!" then he shifted back to his Gryphon just in time to take out the two closest with his powerful wings. The wolves flew through the air, landing twenty feet away. Kyllian landed and turned back to find one of the wolves had shifted and was aiming a gun his way.

Well, fuck. He shifted so he could pull up his Gryphon's voice, but the male pulled the trigger. Kyllian dove, but he wasn't quick enough. The bullet tore through his shoulder. Kyllian transformed into his Eagle, but the bullet was still lodged inside his body, making it impossible to fly. Nikita was being dragged back to the fray, kicking and screaming. Releasing her sharp canines, she clamped down on her captor's arm, and he shoved her to the ground. She took advantage of being free and ran toward the male holding the pistol. Kyllian returned to his human form to tell her to stay back, but the girl charged forward, shifting in mid-air, tackling the male. The gun disappeared into the high grass, and Kyllian found his voice, yelling, "Freeze." All the wolves, including Nikita, stopped in their tracks. The two Kyllian had dispatched with his wings had found their feet, but didn't come any closer.

"Nikita, find the gun," he instructed the girl. "The rest of you do not move." When he was sure they would obey, Kyllian shifted into his Lion, doing his best to expel the bullet. Getting shot hurt like a motherfucker, but he had bigger issues than a non-life-threatening wound. Snarls and shouting sounded from close by, and Kyllian was out of time. Returning to his skin, he said, "Nikita, I hope you aren't scared of heights."

The girl stood empty-handed, her eyes wide. "Who are you? Better yet, *what* are you?"

Nudging with his shifter voice, he said, "I'll explain later because right now, we have company. Just know I'm a friend. I'm going to shift into my Gryphon, and I want you to climb on."

141

Nikita nodded, still wide-eyed. Kyllian shifted, then lowered his body so she could get on his back. When he felt her grab hold of his feathers, he lifted off as gently as possible. He had only ever carried the twins like this, and the two of them together didn't weigh what the girl did. As he took to his wings, males shouted from below, and a bullet whizzed close enough to his chest it ruffled his feathers. He couldn't talk to Nikita in this form, so he prayed to Zeus to keep her safe as he banked hard right, pushing his wings harder, which was easier said than done with his wounded shoulder. More gunfire erupted, but his god must have been listening, for they made it away unharmed.

Nikita kept a tight grip on his feathers and clenched his sides with her knees. Kyllian headed to where he had parked, needing to get the girl on the ground as quickly as possible. Before they were halfway there, she let out an exuberant "yeehaw." Kyllian's Gryphon huffed, as close to laughing as possible. His girl was made of stern stuff.

It wasn't until the car was in his sights that Kyllian realized he had dropped the pouch containing his keys and phone. His clothes were locked in the car, and he seriously didn't want to stand around naked with a teenager he didn't know. He'd have to figure something out though, because he needed to make sure Nikita was okay. He landed as gently as possible, and she slid from his back, her knees wobbling. Needing his voice, Kyllian walked around the car and shifted to his human form.

"Man, that was insane." Nikita pushed her windblown hair off her face.

"I'm glad it didn't freak you out too much. My name is Kyllian Lazlo, and I'm a friend of your mother's. Your real mother," he added, hoping she didn't take offense. "We have a small problem, though. I dropped my keys, and my clothes are in the car. I'm going to bust out the window so I don't have to stand here in all my glory."

Nikita wiggled her eyebrows. "Don't mind me."

Kyllian huffed out a laugh and shook his head. "You're gonna be trouble, aren't you?"

"Who me?" She clutched the collar of her shirt and batted her lashes.

"Yes, you. Now please turn around so I can get in the car. Unlike dire wolves, I don't have the same magic that allows my clothes not to shred when I shift. It's really unfair."

"I don't know. I think I might be willing to give up that boon if I could change between three different creatures. That's so cool." She cocked her head to the side and pointed to his shoulder. "You're hurt."

"Yeah, bullets'll do that." When she stood there eyeing his bare chest, Kyllian made the twirling motion with his finger.

"If you insist." Nikita did as he asked and turned her back. Kyllian waited to make sure she wasn't going to peek, then walked to the back window and broke it with his elbow. He reached in and pulled on the lever to lower the hatch and grabbed his duffel. Shoving his legs in his pants first, he told her she could turn around. While pulling on a shirt, he got a good look at Quinn's daughter. There was no doubt they were related.

"What about you? You have some scratches." Kyllian pointed to his own cheek.

Nikita waved her hand in the air. "Eh, just a flesh wound. They'll heal pretty quickly. You said you're a Gryphon, right?" she asked as Kyllian slipped on a pair of socks.

"Yes. Why aren't you more freaked out about that?"

"Well, I did hit my head when I dove from a car, so maybe I'm dreaming. But if not, is it really so unlikely there are other supernatural beings in the world?"

Kyllian thought about the Gargoyles. Nikita was right. It wasn't unlikely at all. "Wait, back up. You dove from a car?"

"Yes. That old man seemed harmless when he offered me a ride. Turns out the geriatric can still be creepers." Nikita rolled her eyes, and Kyllian grinned at her sass. He wondered where she got it from. "Thanks for that back there. I thought I was a goner for sure." And just like that, she was serious again.

"You're welcome. The RC pack isn't very nice."

"RC? Oh, River Canyon. Then why does Quinn live with them?" Nikita pulled the band holding her ruined braid out of her hair and shook out her long locks before combing through them with her fingers. She re-tied her hair off her face, looking so much like Quinn. Kyllian's heart thumped wildly, both from the remaining adrenaline of the fight and the fact that Quinn was still in trouble.

"She doesn't. Your mom lives in Upstate New York and has for many years. It's a long story that I promise

144

I'll tell you, but first, we need to get out of here. I have no doubt there are more wolves coming our way. You don't happen to have your phone on you, do you?"

Nikita reached in the back pocket of her jeans and pulled out a burner. "Sure do." She handed it over. "You and my mom are friends?"

"I'll explain later. I need you to open your phone, ping this location, and send Tarryn a text that reads 'Kyllian lost his phone and needs a ride.'"

Nikita narrowed her eyes. "How do you know Tarryn?"

"Again, I'll explain everything once we're secure. Please, Nikita."

"Fine. I don't know why you think Tarryn can help though. She's hundreds of miles away," she said as she tapped the buttons on the phone. "Done. Now, explain."

Kyllian did. He told her from start to finish about Mercy showing up, about Blake and his father lying to Quinn when she was a teenager, and finishing with how Quinn had been taken.

"She hasn't left her house in eighteen years? Man, I'd go crazy."

Kyllian gaped at the girl. "That's your first question?"

"What else would I ask? I already figured out Quinn didn't abandon me the way Blake claimed."

"You call your dad Blake?" It wasn't that odd considering he and his brothers often called their dad by his name.

"I do now. He lied to me my whole life. Made me think she didn't want me when he stole me from her.

145

And don't get me started on Bethany. How could a female do that to another female? All I see on the internet is how women are supposed to stick together, but taking part in kidnapping a pup? Then raising it as your own? No wonder Quinn killed my grandfather. That makes more sense than she was feral."

"She may have been feral in that moment. But to answer your question, yes. Quinn has remained a recluse all these years, hiding from your pack as well as her mother's. She only left to come help rescue you before she was caught by Dennis's wolves."

"They almost got me too. What I don't get is why my grandmother told me where the pack was if she knew Quinn wasn't with them."

"I can't answer that, but it seems that family is a bunch of liars." Kyllian scrubbed a hand down his face. "I need to stay here and find Quinn. My nephews are here with Mercy, Jeremy, and Brett. I need you to go to my sister's house while the Hounds and I go after Quinn. Mercy said she'd take you there."

Nikita shook her head. "No, I want to help you."

"I appreciate that, but you saw what they're like. These wolves don't care about you. They killed Quinn's mom for mating outside the pack. They kidnapped Quinn, and who knows what they have planned for her? Please, do this for me. I need to focus on getting your mom back without worrying about you getting hurt. As soon as I rescue her, we'll come to you at my sister's, and we can figure things out from there."

"Do you think Quinn still wants me?" Nikita's bottom lip quivered, and Kyllian closed the distance and wrapped his arms around the teen.

"I do. We both do." Kyllian pressed a kiss to her hair. "You don't know either of us, and Quinn and I still have some things to discuss, but you're her daughter, and she's my mate, which means you're mine now too. If that's not too weird." Nikita gripped his shirt tight in her fists and nodded against his chest.

"It is too weird?"

"No. Sorry, I'm a little overwhelmed. I can't believe you'd want me."

Kyllian leaned back and used his thumbs to wipe away the tears leaking from the corners of her eyes. He was proud of Nikita. She'd been through some shit that night and was only then letting her emotions free. "Why wouldn't I? From what Mercy told us, you're smart. You're tough, and you have an excellent bullshit meter. You set out to find your mom and kept yourself safe. Plus, you rode on my Gryphon like a champ."

"I did, didn't I?" Nikita grinned through the tears.

Kyllian grinned back. "And you're sassy. You'll fit in with the Lazlos well."

"Are all your family Gryphons?"

"For the most part. My brothers' mates aren't. One of them is a witch. Another was an assassin. Quinn is the first wolf in our family." Kyllian thought about Wynter, but technically, she wasn't family. He didn't know if she and Hawk were even mates. "Gryphons aren't pack the way wolves are, but family is everything to us, and let me tell you. When you meet my mom? Rory is going to go all Lioness on you. Then she'll probably go after Blake and your grandmother herself. No one touches Rory's cubs and gets away

147

with it."

Nikita got a dreamy look in her eyes. "She sounds wonderful."

"She's the best." As they waited on the Hounds to arrive, Kyllian kept Nikita entertained with stories about the twins and their antics while keeping his senses open to trouble. It took another twenty minutes before Devon and the others found them.

Mercy was the first to exit the vehicle, and she took a tentative step toward Nikita. "Goddess, am I glad to see you safe."

Nikita grabbed Kyllian's hand. He looked down at the teen, and she smiled up at him. "It's all thanks to this guy. If he hadn't found me when he did…" Nikita shivered. "Are they like you?" She tilted her head toward Devon, Joker, and Storm.

"Yes." Kyllian introduced her to the Hounds before explaining what happened to Quinn. "Two of the RC pack led her away from the compound. I was following when I heard Nikita squaring off against four wolves. There were more on their way when we took off, so I doubt we have much time before they find us. I'm surprised they haven't already. Now that Nikita's safe, we need to move." Turning to the teen, he said, "My sister, Poppy, is going to put you and the other wolves up while the rest of us go after Quinn."

Mercy closed the distance between them. "Come on, kiddo. We'll get you out of here while the Hounds go find Quinn."

Nikita squeezed Kyllian's hand, and he smiled at her again. "Go ahead. I'll catch up to you as soon as I can." Nikita released her grip and flung her arms around his waist. Kyllian hugged her tight, pressing another kiss to her hair. He breathed in her scent, letting it settle his beast somewhat. When she finally turned loose, she walked away with her pack. Kyllian's heart was torn watching the girl get into the car with the other wolves. He wanted to keep her close, but he needed to find Quinn so the three of them could start their lives together. Kyllian might be getting ahead of himself, but there was no way he would allow Blake or his mother to have any more influence on Nikita.

Devon waited until the wolves were gone to speak. "You've got it bad, Uncle."

Kyllian rolled his shoulder. "Right? A week ago, I didn't know she existed, and now I want to build a life with her and her mother."

"Are you injured?" Jericho asked.

"Yeah. One of those fuckers shot me in the shoulder. These bastards don't play fair."

"Let me look," Storm said. "I was a medic in the army." Kyllian tugged off his tee and let the Hound assess the wound. "Devil, you need to call Theo."

Kyllian pulled his shirt back on. "It'll take too long for him to get here. Can't you dig the bullet out?"

"I could if I had the necessary equipment. I don't even have a first aid kit on my bike."

Kyllian rolled his shoulder. He really wanted the slug out. "As much as I want to storm the castle, we're going to need guns of our own. What we need is a sniper."

"Do you know one?" Joker asked.

"Quinn's father was a sniper in the army. Quinn didn't want him involved, but if that were my child, I wouldn't have stayed behind in the first place."

When a phone rang from inside the vehicle, Devon asked, "Why is the window busted on the car?"

"I dropped my pouch. My keys and phone were in it. When Nikita and I got back here, I needed to get inside for my clothes," Kyllian replied as he crawled through the back, climbing over the seats until he found the culprit. Locating it on the passenger side floorboard, he figured it was Quinn's. When he saw Trenton's name on the screen, he sighed. He had to talk to the male sooner or later. Kyllian unlocked the door and climbed out before answering.

"Trenton, I've got good news and bad news. The good news is we found Nikita, and she's safely on her way to my sister's house. The bad news is Quinn is with the RC pack."

"Dammit, Kyllian. You promised to keep her safe."

"Yessir, I did, but she went inside a convenience store to use the restroom while I was on the phone. Long story short, one of the Ozark pack had history with Quinn from when she was a teen, and he betrayed her. The RC wolves took Quinn from the back of the store. I was able to trail them to the compound, and then two of their males put Quinn in a car, and I was following when I heard Nikita being targeted by four of their wolves. Trenton, I was torn between following Quinn and helping the girl."

Trenton sighed on the other end of the line. "No, you did the right thing. She's just a kid. So what are you going to do to get Quinn back?"

"The wolves are armed. I've already taken a bullet to the shoulder, so we're going to have to get our

150

hands on weapons of our own."

"Send me your location. I'll charter a plane and bring my rifle. I owe those fuckers for killing Finola."

Kyllian hesitated in agreeing. Quinn hadn't wanted her father anywhere near the dire wolves, but he did have a point. Who was Kyllian to deny the male his revenge? Besides, they needed a sniper. "I will text you our location as soon as we disconnect, but bring Ace and Ripper with you. I'm going to text a few things I need them to bring as well."

"Done. We'll see you as soon as we can get there."

Kyllian disconnected. Turning to Storm, he said, "Guns are on the way. Now tell me what you need for this," he said, pointing at his shoulder. He texted the list to Ripper, then sent up another prayer up to Zeus, asking for Trenton and the Hounds to get there safely but quickly, and for him to watch over Quinn until they could get to her.

Chapter Eleven

Quinn

WHEN DENNIS TOLD Bradley to take her to the cliffs, Quinn was expecting to be dragged to the edge and dangled over the side by her ankles. Instead, she found herself in a rudimentary dwelling carved out of the side of the mountain. What probably started off as a cave, the room was large and filled with the comforts of home, if the dweller were a hunter seeking shelter for the night. Or a wolf looking to hide his niece from her mate. Bradley shoved Quinn down on a worn sofa and took an old armchair across from her.

"Grab me a beer, would ya?" he said to Henry who was digging around in a cooler. Henry tossed a can to his brother, not bothering to offer Quinn one. Not that she'd have taken it, but still. Quinn took in the cavern while both males popped the tops on their cans. Henry returned to the opening and sat with his back to them. Bradley glared at Quinn, but she refused to look at him. She was used to a solitary existence. She and Trenton coexisted well with her father giving her space more often than not. That didn't mean they never spoke, but they could go hours without seeing one another in their large home.

Quinn really needed to pee, but she refused to drop her pants in front of these males, uncles or not. She had no idea if they held any amount of honor. She would fight claw and fang if they ever moved to touch her inappropriately.

Bradley drained his can, then let out a belch. He tossed the empty aside but didn't move to get a refill. He waited until Henry got up from his spot to grab another. As the minutes turned into hours, her uncles switched places several times. Whoever sat in the chair held the gun. The beer cans piled up; their shifter metabolism burned through the alcohol as quickly as they drained it. Eventually, Henry dug through a bag Quinn hadn't noticed and pulled out what looked like beef jerky. Again, they didn't offer her any.

Nikita is safe, and the Hounds are coming for us.

Quinn thanked the goddess for that blessing. She didn't know her daughter, but she wanted to. She needed to find out if she'd had a good life. If she was happy. She wanted the chance to explain her side of the story, even though Mercy said Tarryn had told Nikita the truth about what happened all those years ago. Would Nikita want to move to New York? Leave her friends and siblings behind? Quinn had no idea what it was like to have others her age to hang out with. Confide in. No, that wasn't true. She'd had that for a short while when she first met the Ozark pack. Scott befriended her, and Quinn had felt normal for the first time in her life.

Then Blake happened. Claimed she was his mate. Quinn had felt honored. After he and his real mate took off with Nikita, Quinn wondered how Bethany felt about her mate having sex with another female. Did she feel less than because she wasn't a dire wolf like Quinn? It was the reason Blake had seduced Quinn. To have a pup with dire DNA. But to what end? Quinn was only half dire herself, which meant Nikita was a quarter. And if she had her own pup, it would be even less of one unless she were to find a full-blood. And if Quinn hadn't killed Stewart, if she had stayed with the pack, would someone else have taken her as a mate?

"This is bullshit. I'm going to hunt," Henry grumbled. He shifted to his animal before leaving the cavern.

Bradley set the gun on the arm of the chair and pulled a pack of tobacco out of the bag on the floor, sticking a wad in his jaw. He held the pack out to her. "Want some?" he asked with a smirk.

"I'll pass." Quinn seriously needed to pee. She would have to suck it up and go in front of her uncle. "Is there a bathroom in this place?"

"You're a fucking wolf. Go piss outside."

She hadn't thought of that. Quinn could shift, and it wouldn't be as horrific. When she rose from the couch, Bradley grabbed the gun. "You try to run, and I'll put a bullet in your hide."

"I'm not going to run." Quinn stretched her neck from side to side, then twisted at the waist. She had no idea how long she'd been sitting in one position. "Do you have underwear in that Mary Poppins bag of yours?"

"Mary Pop— What the fuck are you going on

154

about?"

"Just curious if you have a change of briefs. Like I said before, you're going to need them." Quinn took to her fur and padded to the entrance. Bradley cursed her insolence, following a few steps behind. Instead of trotting like she wanted, Quinn kept her steps slow.

"That's far enough," Bradley barked.

If she could, Quinn would have rolled her eyes. Instead, she turned so she was facing her uncle and squatted. The relief was instant. Quinn took a few steps to the side of the puddle and stared off into the distance. The valley below was quiet, and the crescent moon glowed above. She usually loved this time of morning with its peacefulness. Except for those nocturnal creatures who roamed after twilight, most everything else was asleep. She often sat outside early enough to observe as dawn broke. It was such a gradual occurrence. Magical in its happening. She stretched out on her belly, ignoring her uncle.

A few minutes later, flashes of red caught her attention followed by the sounds of guns going off. Howls rent the air, and Quinn got to her paws. Bradley took a step closer, the gun hanging down beside his thigh, his attention on the chaos below. Quinn had no idea where Henry was or when he would return. She eyed the pistol. If she were going to take a chance, now would be the time with her uncle distracted by whatever was happening below. The phone in Bradley's pocket rang, and Quinn lunged, clamping her jaws around his wrist. Bradley howled as the gun dropped to the ground. Quinn shifted and dove for the weapon, landing on her back with the pistol gripped in both hands.

"You fucking bitch! I'm gonna gut you." Bradley shoved to his feet, his eyes flashing amber.

Quinn didn't hesitate. She fired off a shot that echoed through the cliffs like a cannon, thankful for her father's training in weapons. She took out Bradley's knee, and her uncle writhed on the dirt, cursing her, her dead mother, and everyone else he could think of. Bradley howled, his Wolf trying to push to the front. His face elongated into a snout. Claws protruded from his fingertips, and fur covered most of his body. Quinn scrambled to her feet, keeping the gun pointed at the male. If wolves could grin, his did as he looked at something over her shoulder. Quinn had been so focused on Bradley that she hadn't heard Henry coming up behind her. Quinn turned, ready to shoot, but Henry was already in the air.

"Quinn, get down!" someone who sounded strangely like her father yelled. She didn't hesitate. Quinn flattened herself to the ground, waiting on Henry to pounce. A shot rang out, and Henry fell in a heap. His body shifted back to his human form, and the blood pooling beneath his chest was all the proof she needed her uncle wouldn't be rising ever again.

"No!" Bradley screamed before trying to shift again.

"Quinn!" another voice yelled, this one closer. She turned the pistol back on Bradley, keeping him in her peripheral as she scanned the area. Dawn had crept in without her noticing, and she was able to make out a large bird flying her direction. No, not a bird. She hadn't seen Kyllian in his Gryphon form, but her beast recognized him.

"Wh-what the f-fuck?" Bradley's voice tremored as Kyllian landed between Quinn and her uncle. The Gryphon shifted into his Lion, and the scent of urine filled the air.

"I told you you'd need clean underwear," Quinn muttered as she admired her mate's feline form. Kyllian roared as he stalked closer to Bradley. And there it was – the stench of Bradley soiling himself. Kyllian wasted no time in clamping his sharp fangs over Bradley's throat, shaking his mighty head back and forth, ripping through skin and tendons until they reached his spine. With one final, fierce shake, Kyllian ended Bradley's life. Kyllian dropped the body and turned to face her, shifting to his skin.

Quinn eyed his naked body from top to bottom. Instead of being scared, she was turned on. Who knew murder was an aphrodisiac?

"Quinn." Kyllian's voice was low. Deep. Thrilling. She took her time meeting his eyes, because naked Kyllian was a sight to behold. "Quinn," he repeated, this time with his alpha voice. Or maybe it was his Gryphon voice because she had to obey. By the time she looked at his face, he was inches away.

"Hi." She couldn't help but grin at him.

Kyllian shook his head, letting out a huff. He grabbed her around the waist, pulling her flush to all that glorious, inked skin. He took her lips in a kiss that would have sent her to her knees had he not been holding her tightly. Kyllian's tongue plunged into her mouth, and Quinn returned the kiss with equal fervor. She dropped the gun so she could grab his hair with

157

both hands. Kyllian fisted her ponytail with one hand and her ass with the other. His fingers splayed over her jeans, toying with the seam between her legs. Too soon, he broke the kiss and took a step back. His erection strained toward her, and she wanted nothing more than to drop to her knees and taste him.

"Later, Pretty Lady. Right now, we need to get out of here." Kyllian's chest rose and fell with each breath as he cupped her cheek. If she wasn't sure about claiming him before, the warmth in his eyes sealed the deal. She had never felt as wanted. Or as precious.

"Is that my father down there?" she asked, looking back at Henry.

"Yes. He's the only reason I'm not stripping you bare and claiming you right now."

"Why is he here? Not that I'm complaining." She gestured to Henry's human form. Wolves shifted back to their skin upon death.

"We needed a sniper." Kyllian held out his hand, and she grabbed it. "We really need to go. The other Hounds have done well holding off the RC pack, but they're running out of ammunition."

"Nikita—"

"Is safe." Kyllian squeezed her hand. "How do you feel about riding a Gryphon?"

Quinn arched a brow, and her Wolf growled.

Kyllian gave her a sexy smirk. "That kind of ride is definitely happening, but it'll have to wait. I meant how do you feel about flying?"

"Are you sure it's safe? Not that I don't trust you, but if the pack has guns, won't we be targets?"

"Do you have another option?"

158

"The car my uncles brought me here in is just down that path."

"You just want to keep me naked," Kyllian husked, his eyes gleaming.

"There's that. Plus, you can tell me everything that's happened since I so stupidly went into the store by myself."

Kyllian growled again, and this time, it wasn't sexy. Quinn had screwed up, and she would apologize later. "What's it going to be? Drive or fly?"

"I really don't want to sit my bare ass where one of them sat, but it does make the most sense. Any idea where the keys are?"

"I'm assuming in Henry's pocket since he drove." Quinn gestured to her uncle.

Kyllian walked the few steps to where Henry's body lay and dug in his pockets. Quinn kept her eyes averted. She hired killers for a living, but that didn't mean she was immune to the stench of death. The coppery tang of blood was only lessened by being outside where the cool, early morning breeze floated on the air.

"Got 'em." Kyllian stood and strode to Bradley and removed his shirt, wrapping it around his waist. Quinn may have pouted because Kyllian's ass and other assets were worthy of sonnets. He held his hand out to Quinn. She picked up the pistol, then placed her free hand in his, and they made their way to the car. A phone rang behind them.

"That's probably Dennis checking in. When they don't answer, he'll have someone headed this way."

"Then we need to be gone before they get here."

159

Kyllian opened the passenger door and guided Quinn in before going around to the driver's side. Once seated, he adjusted the shirt so it covered his lap. "Did they hurt you?" he asked once the car was in motion.

"No. According to my grandmother, the pack is dwindling in numbers, so I think they wanted to use me as a brood mare."

Kyllian growled low in his chest, and Quinn reached over and laced their fingers. "I'm safe now, thanks to you. I'm sorry for going into the store alone. I know it was stupid, but… How did they find us?"

"Scott. We don't know how he got in touch with the RC pack, but after you were taken, he fled in one of the SUVs."

"I thought he was my friend. I mean, it's been years since I was around him, but when I first met the Ozark pack, he and I were close."

"Mercy said he felt more than friendship, and when you and Blake hooked up, Scott took it hard."

"Goddess, I was so foolish. Still am. Kyllian, I'm sorry "

Kyllian squeezed her hand before bringing it to his lips and kissing it. "Stop apologizing. I've got you back now, and I'm not letting you go."

"You're my mate," she blurted.

"I figured as much. Well, your Wolf told my Gryphon. They're rather chatty." Kyllian's voice was warm, and in that moment, Quinn knew they'd be okay. She would be an idiot to let her past get in the way of her future. She didn't know how they'd make it work, only that they would.

"Tell me about my daughter."

160

Kyllian laughed. "She's a trip. Zeus, she's like Mercy said. Smart. Tough. A lot like her mother. Not afraid of Gryphon rides. I have something to confess." Kyllian took a deep breath and blew it out before continuing. "I knew you were at the compound. I saw them put you in the car, and I was following, but then I heard Nikita yell out, and I had to make a choice. Continue following you or go help her." Kyllian kept his eyes on the road. "I chose her, Quinn."

"As you should have. She's still a kid."

Kyllian rolled his shoulder, and Quinn focused on her mate. "You're hurt."

"One of the wolves got a shot off. Hit me here." He released her hand long enough to point to his opposite side. "Ripper brought supplies, and Storm was able to get the bullet out."

"How did my dad end up here? I didn't want him involved."

Kyllian threaded their fingers again. "He called while Nikita and I were waiting on the other wolves and the Hounds to find us. I knew he would be more upset not knowing what was going on than hearing the truth, so I told him what we were up against. That we needed a sniper. He didn't hesitate, Quinn, and I'm glad. That shot he took was perfect. Since you were being held by two of the RC pack, I wasn't sure whether or not we could get close, so..." Kyllian shrugged. "It was the right call. The two Hounds who were watching over him gathered up some guns, and the three of them chartered a private flight. Mercy, Jeremy, and Brett took Nikita to my sister's house in Texas to get her away from the fighting. Storm was shot, but he's going to live. The RC pack is used to the area. They know the landscape and where to hide, but we got in some shots of our own."

A car headed their direction on the narrow road. Quinn ducked down in the seat until they had passed. "Are they turning around?"

Kyllian glanced in the rearview mirror. "Doesn't look like it. I'm surprised they didn't recognize the car."

Quinn rose and turned to look out the back window. "If it was pack."

"With the number of wolves in the area, I'd bet on it." Kyllian sped up a little, and Quinn was glad for it. She wanted to put as much distance between them and the cliffs as possible.

"What happens next?"

"Now that Trenton is here, he plans on going after Dennis."

Quinn gasped and clutched his forearm with her free hand. "Kyllian, no. He's no match for a dire wolf. You can't let him do this."

"Sweetheart, Dennis killed your mother. Trenton needs to do this for his own peace of mind."

"Dammit, Kyllian. He's all I have in this world. I can't lose him."

Kyllian stiffened, and Quinn realized what she said. "No, that's not true. I have you now. It's going to take a while for it to sink in that it's not just me and Dad anymore. It's been just the two of us for so long." Kyllian relaxed, so Quinn did too. This mate stuff was going to take some getting used to.

"You aren't a pack of two now. You have me,

Nikita, and a whole lotta Hounds."

"I have Nikita? She doesn't hate me?" During the hours of sitting in the cavern, she'd thought about what it would be like to have her daughter in her life. Both Nikita and Kyllian. It had been too much to hope for, but she still prayed to the goddess for it anyway.

"No, she doesn't. Like I said, the girl is smart. She figured out Blake was lying about you abandoning her all those years ago. I told her the truth, and she was furious. She can't wait to meet you. But before we go to her, we need to help Trenton see his vengeance through."

"He's not strong enough to fight a dire wolf and win."

"That's the thing about vengeance, Pretty Lady. It can come in many different forms. You saw what he did to the male on the cliff."

"Henry. He and Bradley were both my uncles. Wait, are you saying Dad is going to snipe Dennis?"

"That'd be my guess. Trenton is smart enough to realize he can't take him down with claws, and dead is dead."

"Okay, that makes me feel better. When they took me to the lodge, I spoke to my grandmother, and I realized she's stuck there. I have a feeling all the females are. If Dad takes out Dennis, that's going to leave the pack without an Alpha. One of my other uncles might step into the role, but I don't feel right about leaving her there with no way out."

"That's the good thing about having the Lazlos on your side. Remember when I told you my parents track down The Ministry?" Quinn nodded. "There are often people being held within the cult who don't want to be there. My family gets them out, sets them up in therapy, offers training or school if needed. Things like that. With someone like your grandmother who's always lived off-grid, they would find her a place within a household as a caretaker or cook. Something along those lines. *If* it's what she wants. But Quinn, you have to be prepared for the possibility that she doesn't want to leave. This is the only home she's known for a lot of years. This is her family. Her kids and grandkids are here. And who knows? Without Dennis leading the pack, someone better might step into the role as Alpha."

Quinn hadn't thought of it that way. "You're right. We'll wait and see what happens. Give her the choice, and let her decide."

"That's my girl."

Quinn's heart swelled at Kyllian's words. She was his. As frightened as she was about giving her heart away, it also excited her. After reading her mother's journals, Quinn had prayed to the goddess for a love like her parents had. She never thought it would happen. Never thought she'd get over Blake's betrayal, but her prayers had been answered, and her destined mate was there in the flesh. Quinn glanced over at her mate and took in all the flesh on display.

"Quinn," Kyllian warned.

She didn't have time to apologize for admiring everything his god had given him. Kyllian pulled up alongside an SUV, and her father emerged from the passenger door, his smile as big as she'd ever seen.

CHAPTER TWELVE

Kayos

WHILE QUINN WENT to greet her father, Kyllian waited on Jericho to bring his clothes. He pulled his jeans on while sitting in the car, then got out to finish dressing. "Where is everyone?" he asked as he tied his boots.

"Spread out. A few of the wolves ran when the shooting started, and Dad figured they went back to the Alpha to report."

"Excellent." Kyllian clapped his nephew on the shoulder as he passed by to join Trenton and Quinn, who were in a heated discussion.

"Quinn, please. I want you out of here."

"Dad, if you're staying, then so am I."

"Kyllian, would you talk some sense into her?" Trenton begged.

Kyllian knew from watching his parents that this was where he had his mate's back. "Quinn has her own mission, same as you. There are females at the compound who might want to leave after you take out Dennis. We're going to give them every opportunity to start over somewhere else."

"Without an Alpha?" Trenton turned to Quinn.

165

"Are you going to step into that role for them? Honey, I understand wanting to help, but if these females have never lived outside this pack, they won't be able to function."

"You'll be their Alpha if you take out Dennis. As far as the females are concerned, that's where the Lazlos come in. It's what they do for those they rescue from The Ministry."

Trenton closed his eyes and let his chin fall to his chest, releasing Quinn's arms. She moved closer to Kyllian, and he wrapped an arm around her shoulder, pressing a kiss to her temple. He wanted her to know he had her back in every situation. He might not like or understand her decisions, but until they were mated, until they had time under their belt where they learned to compromise, he would defer to her wishes. She was a grown woman who ran a mercenary business. Not single-handedly because Trenton helped, but for the most part, she was in charge. She had been making her way for many years with little input. Kyllian wouldn't take that away from her now. Or ever. He would offer guidance and backup, but he would never try to tamp down the strong female she was. It would be like Sutton trying to bench Rory.

Jericho stepped up beside Kyllian. "I don't mean to interrupt, but we need to move. I just got a call from Dad that more wolves are headed this way."

"What's the plan?" Kyllian asked Trenton once he opened his eyes.

"I'm going to kill Dennis Hightower."

"Then you need a distraction to bring him out of the house."

"Do you have something in mind?"

Kyllian squeezed Quinn's shoulder. "I do, but you aren't going to like it."

Before Kyllian told him the plan, they left to meet the other Hounds. Instead of hanging around where the RC pack could possibly spot them, they headed back to New Santa Rosa, and Kyllian secured a hotel suite where they could grab some breakfast from room service while making plans. While waiting on food to arrive, Kyllian reached out to Mercy to check on Nikita and discuss the broken window of the rental car since it was in her name. After they squared away the details for the car, Mercy handed the phone over to Nikita.

"Hey, Trouble," Kyllian greeted Nikita when she answered.

"Hi, Ky," the teen responded.

"Nope. Try again."

Nikita laughed. "What? You can give me a nickname, but I can't return the favor?"

"Sure you can, just not that one." Kyllian winked at Quinn who was sitting next to him, biting her lip. He reached over and thumbed the flesh.

"Ian?" Nikita asked.

"My niece called me that a few times, but it didn't stick. Besides, I already have a nickname. It's Kayos."

"That sounds like a biker name."

"Smart girl. I am a biker."

"Kayos, I like it. Will you take me for a ride?"

"Anytime you want. And if you stick around, I might get you your own sidecar."

"Really? Wait. Why would I need a sidecar?"

"Because your mom will be riding behind me. And

167

if you don't cause too much trouble, I'll even have Hayden customize it for you."

"That's your youngest brother, right? The one mated to the woman with the car name."

"Correct. Her name's Mercedes. We're going to be finishing up here today, and then we'll come meet you at Poppy's."

"At this rate, you might beat us there. Mercy insisted we stop for the night."

"Everyone had a rough day, so that's understandable." Kyllian pointed to the phone and raised his eyebrows. Quinn bit her lip again and shook her head. "Look, kiddo. I need to go and make a few arrangements. You stay out of trouble, and we'll see you soon, yeah?"

"She doesn't want to talk to me, does she?" Nikita asked, her voice wobbly.

"She absolutely does, but your mom wants to do it in person. There are a lot of people in the room with us, and what the two of you need is a little privacy, okay? I promise she's looking forward to meeting you."

"Gryphon's honor?"

"Gryphon's honor. I'll never lie to you, Nikita. No matter what." And he wouldn't. He might have to skirt the truth sometimes considering her age, but Kyllian found honesty worked best, even if it hurt or was hard to hear.

"Thanks, Kayos. For everything. Do you need to talk to Mercy again?"

"No, I'm good. I'll see you soon."

"See you soon."

Kyllian disconnected, and Quinn buried her face in

her hands. Kyllian pulled her to him and onto his lap sideways. "I wasn't lying, Pretty Lady. The two of you need privacy when you talk for the first time."

Quinn rested her head on his shoulder. "You're right, but I don't know what to say to her."

"Just tell her the truth." A knock sounded, and Jericho opened the door to their breakfast after looking through the peephole. "Let's get some food in us, then we'll figure out how your dad's going to take Dennis out with the fewest casualties."

Kyllian had been right. Trenton didn't like his plan. At all.

"They still have plenty of ammunition, Kyllian. I won't let you sacrifice yourself."

"I'm not that altruistic. I'll issue the challenge, and they won't shoot me."

Trenton ran both hands through his hair, pulling the short strands. "If you get close enough. No. There has to be another way."

Quinn had been quiet up until then, and when she finally spoke, Kyllian's beast preened inside. "Dad, Kyllian can do this. Unless you want to ride in on Gryphon back and shoot from above."

Trenton pointed at no one in particular. "See, that's a better plan. Take him out from farther away."

Trenton was letting his human half lead. "Don't you want to look him in the eye and let him know who it is who's ending his life and why?"

When Trenton's eyes clouded over, Kyllian knew he had the male.

"Dammit. Okay, we'll do it your way, but if something happens to you, I won't be the one facing

169

Sutton."

"If my pop were here, he'd be the one leading the way."

Quinn clapped her hands once. "Let's do this. I have a daughter I want to meet."

Kyllian counted on his Gryphon voice to keep any of the wolves from shooting. At least that was the plan. The Hounds left their bikes parked in the underground garage of the hotel. Devon had rented a car while Kyllian argued with Trenton. Storm patched himself up, and the Gryphon was almost back to fighting form. When it was time to go, he insisted on being with them. Kyllian didn't argue.

As they neared RC territory, Kyllian kept his window down and voiced every wolf he came across as did Devon from the car behind. When they reached the turnoff, one of the pack stood with a rifle trained on them. Kyllian quickly said, "I'm here to challenge the Alpha. Tell everyone to stand down and let us pass." The wolf's eyes grew wide, but he couldn't disobey neither Kyllian's voice nor the challenge. The male inclined his head and let out a howl. Several howls answered. Kyllian found that ability fascinating. The Gryphons couldn't communicate in such a way.

When they rolled to a stop in front of the lodge, Dennis stood outside waiting. As planned, Kyllian stepped out of the vehicle first and voiced everyone. "Dennis Hightower, I challenge you. The rest of you will put your weapons down. You will not interfere in any way."

Everyone who held a weapon laid them on the ground. The smirk Dennis wore faded quickly.

"You can't challenge me. You aren't wolfkind."

Kyllian grinned. "No, I'm not." With that, he removed his jeans. He hadn't bothered dressing all the way knowing he would need to shift. As soon as his pants were kicked off to the side, he called forth his Gryphon. He'd not been able to wipe the minds of the wolves they fought the day before, but he would need to do so with everyone at the compound. The other Hounds walked around and picked up the dropped guns since they were out of ammo. They kept their backs to Kyllian, watching for any sign of wolves who might not have been voiced.

Dennis stood there glaring at Kyllian. "You killed my sons."

"He only killed Bradley. I killed Henry," Trenton said, his rifle aimed at the Alpha's chest.

"Who the fuck are you?" Dennis asked, spitting tobacco juice toward Kyllian's talons. Kyllian's Gryphon squawked in disgust.

"I'm Trenton Shepherd, mate to Finola. Father to Quinn."

Realization hit Dennis, and he took a step back. Kyllian pushed off with his Lion's paws and captured Dennis mid-shift. Pack members gasped, but Kyllian ignored them. He tossed Dennis to the ground where he completed the transition to wolf. Snarling, Dennis rose to his feet, but Kyllian didn't wait for the animal to attack. He wanted this done. Kyllian made quick work of tearing through fur with his Eagle's razor-sharp talons. He used his powerful beak to snap limbs. With Dennis unable to walk, Kyllian stepped back and shifted to his human form. Gesturing toward the nearly

171

dead wolf, he told Trenton, "He's all yours."

Trenton wasn't strong enough to take down an alpha dire wolf, so Kyllian did the majority of the damage. The killing blow would be Trenton's to take. Quinn handed Kyllian his jeans as Trenton stepped closer, stripping as he went.

"You don't deserve a quick death, but the sight of you makes me sick. This is for Finola." With that, Trenton shifted to his smaller wolf and lunged. He opened his jaw and clamped his sharp teeth into the fur at Dennis's neck, and with one shake of his head, it was over. When he turned with blood dripping off his snout, the rest of the RC wolves shifted and bared their necks.

Trenton returned to his skin and stood before the pack. Technically, his pack. "Which one of you killed Finola?" Kyllian handed over his clothes so he wasn't addressing the group naked.

An older male shifted so he could speak. "That was Henry, Alpha."

Trenton let out a deep breath. He had already ended the life of his mate's murderer. "Rise and return to your skin," he commanded. Once everyone complied, he stared them all down. "My mate was one of you. As much as she loved her mother, she loathed how her father led. She wanted out, and by the grace of the goddess, we met. Fate had something different in store for her. For us. Fated mates are a gift of the goddess; one you should never turn you back on. Finola didn't. She chose a life with me and Quinn. But Dennis was speciesist. He felt I wasn't good enough because I wasn't a dire wolf. For whatever reason, the

172

goddess chose me for Finola. To the goddess, I was good enough. My life is not in New Mexico. I didn't come here because I wanted to lead this pack. However, I will remain long enough to make sure you have the means necessary to turn things around."

Kyllian stepped up beside Trenton. "With Trenton guiding you, you will change your ways. You will no longer guard this land with weapons. You will welcome wolves of any kind into your territory. You will not treat your females as property and use them as nothing more than omegas to bear children or slaves to cook and clean for you. Francine, step forward." Quinn's grandmother had watched from the doorway. She walked down the steps and stopped a few feet away, tilting her head in obedience to Trenton before turning her attention to Kyllian.

"Quinn has advised me on the situation here with you and the other females. If you wish, we can help get you set up with new lives. You'll be given a place to live, money to spend, and any training you wish to receive to help in your new lives. I understand this has been your home for many years, and if you want to stay and help see it flourish, that is also your choice. It is the choice for all your females. If you remain, you will be treated with the respect you deserve." Kyllian eyed every male as he spoke next. "Females should be cherished. They are the bringers of life. The mothers to our offspring. They are not your property to be kept underfoot or paw. Every male here will go out and get a job. You will provide for the pack. You will ensure everyone has suitable housing, not just whoever is in charge."

Kyllian took a breath and continued. "Your offspring should be cherished and raised to be honorable. It is up to you to give them every opportunity to succeed in life. Give them the tools they need to succeed as adults, not as one-percenters of a motorcycle club. I'm not saying clubs are a bad thing because I'm a member of one. But instead of causing chaos, we do good in the community. We raise our children to do the same."

One of the males stepped forward. "Excuse me, Alpha. May I speak with Francine?" He bared his neck to Trenton. When Trenton nodded, the wolf closed the distance between himself and Quinn's grandmother, taking her hands in his. "Franny, this is our chance."

Francine's eyes filled with tears. "What are you saying, Eddie?"

"I'm saying I have loved you for all these years. You are my mate, but Dennis wouldn't allow us to be together. Our time has passed to have young ones of our own, but we could do good here. Together. If..." Eddie cleared his throat. "If you wish to go, I won't stop you, but please consider staying here with me. They need our guidance. Our love and support."

Another female stepped off the porch and stood beside Francine. She placed her hand on the other woman's shoulder. "They all need our guidance, and with the Alpha's influence, I think our pack could be a good one once more."

Quinn gripped Kyllian's hand before stepping closer to her grandmother. "Who is the strongest wolf in the pack?"

"Eddie is," Francine answered, and the male

blushed.

Quinn turned to her father, her eyes speaking to him without words. He nodded, then addressed the crowd. "As I said, my life isn't here. Once I assess the financial situation and am assured things will go forward as planned, Eddie will be your new Alpha."

Eddie released Francine's hands and bowed his head. "You honor me, Alpha."

Kyllian eyed everyone, searching for signs of discord. To be sure, he said, "If there is anyone who wishes to leave the pack, now is the time. If you leave, you will never return. If you remain, you will do everything within your power to make this pack thrive with love, not hatred and violence." Kyllian waited for them to make their decisions. When no one made a move to leave, he spoke to Eddie. "Take a look around. How many wolves are out there?" Kyllian gestured past the trees.

Eddie silently counted as he searched the compound. "Seventeen." He rattled off the names including Henry and Bradley. That number was more than the wolves they had taken down in the firefight, then Kyllian remembered the ones who'd shown up at Quinn's.

"Good. Then there shouldn't be any surprises." With one more thing left to do, Kyllian wove a different tale of Trenton taking down Dennis and leaving Eddie as Alpha and wiped all their memories of fighting Gryphons.

Quinn

AFTER SAYING THEIR goodbyes to Trenton, the Hounds returned to the hotel to retrieve their bikes. Ace and Ripper remained with Trenton as he spent the rest of the day with the pack before taking the chartered plane back to New York. Kyllian and Quinn made a detour to locate the pouch he dropped with his phone. With the wolves now under Trenton's command, Kyllian assured Quinn they were safe to search the area. Quinn shifted into her Wolf while Kyllian took to the sky as his Eagle. It took almost an hour, but Kyllian flew to where Quinn was sniffing around and squawked at her, the pouch clutched in his talon. She barked in return, and the two met back at the SUV. Once that was handled, they headed to the rental car company and returned the extra vehicle, allowing Devon and company to get on the road to Texas, expecting Kyllian to be not too far behind. Too far was too soon because Quinn wanted alone time with Kyllian before setting off. They still had the hotel room, and she wanted to make good use of it. Quinn was ready to claim her mate.

"Are you hungry?" Kyllian asked as they entered the suite.

"Ravenous." Quinn pushed Kyllian against the door, her fingers scratching a line down his chest. When she got to the button of his jeans, Kyllian stilled her hands. Had she read him wrong?

"Are you sure about this?" His eyes searched hers, and she liked what she saw. This male wasn't demanding. He was offering, and Quinn knew in her heart he would never make her regret this decision.

"About claiming my mate? I've never been more sure about anything in my life. Sitting at the cliffs, wondering if it was my last minutes on earth, I realized how stupid I was to deny you the moment you stepped through the front door. My Wolf knew. She wanted to drop down and show you her belly. Bare her neck, and bend to your will. I was too stubborn to let her lead after what happened with Blake. There are so many things we'll need to figure out, but I don't want to go one more minute without you as my mate. If that's what you want."

"Oh, I want." Kyllian lifted her hands to his mouth and kissed her knuckles. "I want you naked on the bed. I want to sink my teeth into your neck as you do the same to me. I want the world to know you are claimed, just as I want everyone to know I am owned completely." Kyllian dropped her hands and scooped her up bridal-style, returning to the bedroom. Instead of putting her on the bed, he placed her on her feet and knelt in front of her. "Lift your foot." Quinn did as instructed, and Kyllian removed one shoe, then the other. He unfastened her jeans and lowered them oh so slowly down her legs, his knuckles grazing bare skin.

Quinn shivered as goose bumps rose along the same path his fingers took. She carded her fingers through Kyllian's thick hair as he placed kisses on her thighs. She was nervous. She'd had sex with Blake, but it hadn't been slow and seductive. It had been a means to an end. He took care with her the first time since it was her very first time, but after that, it was nothing more than him wanting an heir. He said the right words to make her feel worshiped, but his touch hadn't been this gentle. This attentive. He—

Stop thinking of that bastard.

Her Wolf was right. Quinn could compare notes later. She needed to give Kyllian her undivided attention. There would never be another claiming. Never be another first for them, and she wanted it to be memorable. Kyllian nuzzled her mound over her panties, inhaling deeply. He pressed kisses against the silky material as his hands splayed across her stomach and grazed her skin as he pushed them higher underneath her shirt. When he reached her bra, he pushed it up over her breasts and cupped both in his calloused hands. Quinn arched into his touch, wanting more. She pulled her tee over her head and unclasped the bra, the straps slipping down her arms and falling to the floor.

"I need to see you," she husked. "Please."

Kyllian stood and pulled his own shirt off, then bent to unlace his boots. While he was bent over, Quinn stroked her fingers down the broad plane of his back, nails scratching outlines of his ink. There was so much ink, and she couldn't wait to explore every inch of it. Kyllian stood and toed his boots off as he pushed his jeans down his muscled thighs, taking his briefs with them. Quinn was no stranger to a man's penis, but it had been a while since she'd been up close and personal with one. When she and Blake had sex, it was just that. No blow jobs. No stroking him for pleasure. Quinn wanted to pleasure Kyllian, but she wanted him inside her more.

Still, she reached out and wrapped her hand

around his erection, feeling a man's flesh for the first time. Velvety skin covered a hard shaft. She paid special attention to the vein beneath the skin. Quinn ran a fingertip from base to tip, finding a pearl of liquid glistening at the slit. She touched the bead and drew it onto her finger, sucking it into her mouth. It was a little salty and not at all sweet, but she didn't hate it. She wondered what it would be like to take all of his ejaculate in her mouth if she ever got the nerve up to give him head.

Kyllian grabbed her wrist and sucked the same fingertip into his own mouth. His brown eyes had darkened further, and Quinn was lost in their depths. He removed her finger and grabbed her ponytail in a fist, angling her head so he could kiss her. She opened for him, tongues meeting again for a slow, seductive dance. His free hand slid down the back of her panties, and Kyllian dipped his fingers down her crack. Lower until he found the wet juncture. Quinn spread her legs for him, and Kyllian toyed with her opening.

Breaking the kiss, Quinn tightened the hold she had on his shoulders, her fangs itching to come out and claim him. "Please, don't make me wait."

Kyllian removed his fingers, released her hair, and in one swift move, ripped her panties down the back. Goddess that was hot. Kyllian leaned over and pulled the covers down before picking Quinn up and placing her in the center of the bed. When Kyllian didn't immediately cover her body with his own, she propped up on her elbows. He started at her ankles nipping and sucking at both her legs. He licked the back of her knees before continuing his torturous path toward her core. When he reached the top of her thigh, Kyllian nuzzled her pubic hair, inhaling once again. Then the true torture began. Kyllian fingered her open and used his tongue to tease her clit and taste her wetness. He nipped and sucked on her clit, flicking his tongue on the bud. He brought her to the edge of orgasm before backing off. After several times of the teasing release, Quinn couldn't take any more.

"Kyllian, please. I need you inside me."

"You beg so prettily. How could I say no?" His voice was deep. Husky. "I'll only ask once more; are you sure? Because when I get my cock in your pretty pussy, I'm going to bite you. Claim you as my mate."

"I'm sure." Quinn's fangs elongated, and when she felt the tug of her Wolf coming out, she shouted to her animal in her mind. *No!* The animal retreated, but it wasn't happy about it.

Kyllian crawled up her body, sucking on a nipple before he finished the climb. He lifted her legs, propping them open over his forearms and lined his cock at her entrance. Kyllian eased in, her slick flesh allowing him to glide smoothly. She expected him to fuck her hard and fast, but that wasn't what she got. Not at first. Her badass biker made love to her. Tenderly. He kept his gaze on hers, and for a second, she got a flash of his Gryphon. His eyes changed from dark to golden, then back. She flashed her own amber eyes, answering the call.

"Fuck, you're so wet. I could drown in your pussy and die a happy male." The cords in Kyllian's neck strained, and his breaths came in heavy pants. "Gotta fuck you hard now. Tell me you want that."

"I want it. Give it to me hard, Kyll." Quinn didn't know if he was okay with a shortened version of his name, but it felt right.

"Kyll. I like it. Now hang on." Kyllian pushed her legs higher and set a fast pace, pumping harder with each thrust. Quinn's claws came out, and she gripped the bedding, shredding it as he grunted. Quinn whimpered as her orgasm crept closer. She'd never gotten off having sex like this. But this was her mate. The one intended to be hers forever. It made sense Kyllian would be able to satisfy her. "I'm close, Quinn." He dropped her legs and lowered his chest, propping on his forearms. His fangs dropped, and Quinn braced herself for the sting of the bite.

"Do it. Bite me."

CHAPTER THIRTEEN

Quinn

QUINN ANGLED HER head, baring her neck to him. Kyllian thrust harder, faster, and then he struck. His sharp teeth found flesh, and the intense pain morphed into something else. Something euphoric. Quinn gasped as her orgasm spread through her core, muscles clenching his cock. Kyllian stilled his lower body, retracting his fangs and licking the wound closed. She couldn't hold her Wolf at bay any longer. She answered his bite with one of her own, and Kyllian shouted as his cock hammered home again. The tang of blood flooded her mouth, and she drank from her mate, the bond flowing through them. Making them one. She urged her Wolf back, and it obeyed. Kyllian came again, their releases mixing together. When he pulled out, Quinn felt empty. Except she wasn't. Her heart and mind were full of promise. A future with her fated mate. Her forever.

Kyllian rolled to the side and continued until he was on his back with Quinn lying on his chest. She reached up and brushed his hair off his forehead, relishing the lushness. Neither spoke for a few moments. Words weren't needed. Kyllian tipped his head up, taking her mouth in a tender kiss. She never would have expected a Master of pain to be gentle, and maybe he wasn't with others. She didn't want to think about all the women he'd been with. It wasn't like she was a virgin. Hell, she had a kid. He promised to leave being a Master behind if it was what she wished, but Quinn wouldn't be that selfish. As long as he kept sex out of the equation, she would compromise.

"You're absolutely perfect. You know that?" Kyllian asked as he ghosted his fingers down her spine.

"No, I'm not, but I'm glad you think so." Quinn ran a fingertip along the ink over his eyebrow. "One day, I want you to tell me about all your ink."

"I can do that." Kyllian tugged at the band holding her ponytail, and her hair fell down over her shoulders, brushing against his chest. He ran his fingers through the strands, careful of the tangles. "I like it down," he muttered, more to himself than her. Using her toes, she pushed her body farther up his until she could easily reach his mouth. Kissing Kyllian was her new favorite thing in the world, right after sex. His dick lengthened against her stomach, and Quinn pushed up until she was straddling his waist. With his hands in her hair, Kyllian wiggled until his erection was at her still slick passage and pushed inside. Quinn took over, placing her hands on his chest, and rode her Gryphon. She wasn't a skilled lover, but she didn't need to be. Kyllian placed his feet on the bed and moved in time with her. She'd read somewhere that sex was like dancing, and in Kyllian, she had the perfect partner.

After another orgasm and lots more kissing,

Kyllian ordered room service when he heard Quinn's stomach rumbling. He took Quinn to the shower and got on his knees, pleasuring her with his wicked tongue once more. The waiter bringing their food knocked on the door while they were drying off, and Kyllian walked naked back to the bedroom to dress with Quinn admiring his ass.

Quinn towel-dried her hair, then got the tangles out before pulling on jeans and a sweater. She joined Kyllian in the living area where he'd placed their food on the small dining table. They were both quiet while they devoured their meals. Quinn had been starving when they arrived at the hotel, but mating with Kyllian took precedence over food. Kyllian tossed his napkin on the empty plate and leaned back, patting his stomach. Quinn was ready for round two – or was it three? – in bed, but Kyllian's phone rang.

"Hey, Poppy. How's Nikita doing? Say what?" Quinn felt Kyllian's anger like a sentient beast from a room away. Quinn set her fork down and pushed her chair back, not wanting to get within striking distance of the claws on his hands. Not that she thought he would ever hurt her. "Okay, yeah. Let me call Mercy." Kyllian disconnected and turned to Quinn. "They never made it to my sister's," he said as he tapped away at the phone. Quinn stood and went to her mate. They both waited as it rang, but it went to voicemail. "Mercy, it's Kyllian. Call me back."

"You don't think—"

Kyllian kissed her hard before pressing his forehead to hers. "Let's not borrow trouble yet." He took a deep breath and tapped the screen again. A robotic voice answered, and Kyllian stabbed at the screen, silencing the noise. "Let's get dressed. I want to hit the road." Kyllian's phone rang, and he punched the screen so hard Quinn thought he'd crack it. "Bishop?"

"I thought Nikita was going to your sister's."

"She was supposed to be, but Poppy said they never made it. Why? Do you have something?"

"Tarryn just got another text from Nikita. It said Mercy was taking her back to the pack."

"I'll kill her. I'll fucking gut that wolf."

"Brother, I don't think she had a choice. Nikita said something about the Alpha's call."

Kyllian took a deep breath. "We're headed to the Ozarks now. Keep me posted if you see any more texts."

"Will do."

As soon as Kyllian disconnected, Quinn returned to the bathroom and grabbed her hairband, twisting her hair in a messy knot on top of her head. She was livid. And scared. But mostly livid at the thought of Blake getting his hands on Nikita.

"Hey." Kyllian wrapped his arms around her from behind and set his chin on her shoulder. "I promise you we'll get her back."

"How? Blake's her father. He has custody, and I'm noth—"

"Don't you fucking dare finish that sentence." Kyllian turned her around and gripped her upper arms. "You are my mate. Nikita's mother. Trenton's daughter. Handler of mercenaries. You, my Pretty Lady, are not nobody. Yes, Blake is her father, but she's eighteen. Her birthday was two weeks ago, which means she's now able to make her own decisions, Blake be damned."

Quinn clutched Kyllian's shirt, tugging him closer. He kissed her temple before pushing her back. "Come on. The sooner we're on the road, the sooner we get there."

Quinn gathered her things as Kyllian loaded his own duffel. Not bothering to stop off at the front desk, he directed her to the rental and took her bag, tossing it along with his in the back. Handing his phone over, he said, "Please look up the quickest route for me."

According to the app, it was just over twelve hours from their location to the Ozarks. There was no assurance they could get a flight to Arkansas faster than they could drive. And being alone in the car would give them time to talk.

"You told me about your family, but I want to know more about you. When you're not at the club or out killing bad guys for me, what do you do?"

Kyllian settled lower in the seat, one hand on the steering wheel, the other holding Quinn's. "I hang out with Hayden mostly. Or at least I did before he found Sadie. I still go by the clubhouse when he's working on bikes. I spend as much time with the twins as possible. Man, I cannot wait for you to meet those two. They're something else. Major is outgoing, outspoken, and he's going to be hell on wheels. Marshall is his brother's shadow. Just as cute but much quieter. They have this thing where they run into the room where Natalia is and call out 'Lolly, Tolly, Lollipop.' You'd think for an assassin who was raised by the Russian mafia she wouldn't be good with kids, but she's the best. When Lucy's in town, Hay and I go over there and shoot pool or swim. We used to guard the estate, but now that she's mated to Tamian, she doesn't need us."

"Yeah? Why's that?"

Kyllian hesitated before answering. "Remember the call about Rafael Stone and his brothers?"

"Yes. You said they're good men."

"Well, they are good, but they're Gargoyles, and Tamian is one of them. Since we're mated now, you'll meet Lucy and Tamian eventually. The Goyles are this huge Clan of shifters. They aren't the stone creatures you see attached to buildings, although I heard that those were a calling card of sorts. To let others of their kind know they were in Goyle territory. That Clan has been through some shit, let me tell you. Crazy uncles. Kidnappings. Bombs. For centuries, they went without mates because they didn't know they could bond with humans. The females of their kind were almost extinct, and they'd given up hope. Anyway, that's a story for another day. What about you? I know you've not left your house for a long time, so what did you do to occupy your time?"

"I read. A lot. I stream movies, and spend time with Dad." Quinn turned in her seat so she was facing Kyllian. "How's this going to work? Am I moving in with you? I love my dad with everything I am, but I can't see us living with him and having all the sex we're going to have."

"All the sex, huh?" Kyllian grinned, and Quinn smiled back.

"Yes. All the sex. I mean, look at you. Do you

honestly think I'll be able to keep my hands to myself? That's a big fat nope in case you were wondering."

"I would love for you to move in with me. My house is nice, but it's nothing like yours. If you like, we can find a new place that's just ours. But I have to ask, will Trenton be okay on his own? Not that he isn't capable, but he's had you there twenty-four seven for a lot of years."

"He'll be fine. Maybe now that I have you, he will start living for himself again. Get out and see his friends. Your dad and he are still close, so maybe Sutton can coax Dad out of the house now that he doesn't have to worry about me." Quinn ran her finger over the ink on Kyllian's hand. "And what about Nikita? Do you think she'll want to live with us?"

"I don't see why not. She's going to want to get to know you, plus she'll have all the Lazlos wanting time with her as well. But then so will your dad. Maybe Nikita will be the impetus in getting Trenton out of the house more. She has two more months until she graduates. We should figure out what that's going to look like. I want to be there when she walks across the stage. Our girl is something else. I cannot wait for you to meet her. You're gonna love her."

"Our girl? You're claiming her just like that?"

"Yes, I am. Just like Hayden claimed Mateo when he mated with Sadie. Just like Natalia claimed the twins, and Rhiannon claimed Mac even though she isn't that much older. Nikita's part of you. You're a package deal. And did I mention how awesome she is?"

Quinn laughed. "Once or twice. But her living with

188

us puts a damper on all the sex."

"Nah. I'll get her some noise-cancelling headphones. Then again, maybe I should take a page out of Ryker's book and build a house with two wings so she'll be on the opposite side of the house. Headphones may not be enough to shield her from all the dirty things I plan on doing to you."

"Do you have a sex dungeon in your house?"

Kyllian snapped his head around, his eyes wide. He growled low in his chest. "Why? Are you interested?"

"No. Maybe." Quinn rolled her eyes when he wiggled his eyebrows. "I told you I read a lot, and some of the books have BDSM in them. So yes, I've thought about what it would be like, but I can't say much of it appealed to me except maybe the Shibari. I think that might be something I'd like."

"You'll want to talk to Charlie. She's Spyder's female, and he's a Shibari Master. They recently mated. Oh, Charlie's friend Wynter is a wolf shifter too. Until her, we didn't realize there were more than two kinds of shifters in the world. Gargoyles have always been on our radar. A long time ago, one of our Gryphons met a Goyle and that knowledge has been passed from generation to generation, although the Gryphon voiced the Goyle, and they didn't know about us until Lucy met Tamian. Now we're aware of wolves, and it makes me wonder how many other types of shifters there are out there we haven't met."

"If there are others, they're probably like the rest of us and keep the knowledge quiet. Can you imagine if humans found out there were shifters in the world? It

189

would be chaos."

"Yes, and not the good kind."

"There's a good kind of… Oh, I see what you did there." Quinn loved Kyllian's wit. She sent a quick prayer of thanks to the goddess for her mate. "Do your parents call you Kyllian or Kayos?'

"Mom calls me Kyllian if I'm not in trouble, then it's Kyllian Donovan Lazlo. You know you're in deep shit when she brings out the middle name."

"Donovan, I like it."

"It's her maiden name, so she talked Pop into using it as all the boys' middle name. As for Pop, most of the time I'm Kayos to him. He was the Pres of our MC for many years until he handed the gavel over to Ryker. What's your middle name?"

"Trinity after the triple moon goddess."

"Rhiannon has a triple moon tattoo. She's a witch, like her mother before her. Now that's a story you need to hear. All the mates have their own stories to tell, but hers is a doozie. As a matter of fact, Ryker was on his way home from the meeting with you when he found her. He had stopped to get gas when this little slip of a thing ran past him and hid in a dumpster. She was running from The Ministry."

"That's the cult responsible for the near apocalypse, right?"

"Yes. Talk about a small world, but Rafael Stone's uncle, the one who caused so much trouble in their family, funded The Ministry. He had a hard-on for Jonas Montague, who happens to be another Gargoyle, so when Alistair heard the cult was planning world domination, he made a bargain with them. He would

190

back their play if they would make sure to take out Jonas."

"Wait, isn't Jonas Montague the scientist who cloned the first baby?"

"One and the same. And that baby? He's Lucy's mate, Tamian. Like I said, small world."

"Holy crap. I feel like I've stepped into one of my fantasy novels."

"Right? And now we have our own chapter to add to this sordid tale. You'd think the gods and goddesses would go easy on us, but I guess they want us to appreciate what it means to finally find our mates. My parents had an easy time of it, as did all my sisters, but here lately, it's been one crazy ride after another. Maybe I should have mentioned all this before I bit you."

"No way. My life has been a little boring up until now. I think I'm due a little excitement. And chaos."

Kyllian growled again. "Keep talking like that, and we'll never make it to Arkansas."

Kayos

KYLLIAN COULDN'T BELIEVE how happy he was. It was only a couple weeks ago that he felt like the loner in his family. He'd been mostly content with his life until Bonnie ended things with him. He hadn't loved her, but she'd been a bright spot in his nights. Now Kyllian couldn't imagine even looking at another female. He thanked Zeus again for Quinn. He would also thank his pop for insisting Kyllian be the one to watch over her. Had Sutton somehow known Quinn was the one for him? Stranger things had happened over the years. Not only did he have an amazing female, but they had a daughter too. Nikita might be almost grown, but he believed they would be the perfect family of three until he and Quinn had a child together.

"Do you want more kids?" he asked.

"I wouldn't be opposed to it, but not anytime soon. You and I just met, and I'd like to spend some time getting to know one another. Plus we'll have Nikita to think about."

"Where'd you come up with her name? It fits her."

"Don't laugh, but I watched a movie about this badass female assassin, and her name was Nikita. I always dreamed that's what I'd name my daughter if I ever had one."

"Not to bring up a sore subject, but Blake didn't have an opinion on her name?"

"Oh, he did, but I told him when he carried a pup for three months and pushed it out, he could choose the name."

There was so much Kyllian didn't know about wolf shifters. Quinn had given him the Cliff's Notes version when they first met. "This is going to sound stupid, but uh, do wolves give birth to babies or pups?"

"Babies, and that's not stupid. Most kids don't shift for the first time until they're around five or six. Sometimes later, and sometime sooner. Depends on the pup." Quinn sighed. "I missed that with Nikita. I missed her first words. Her first steps. Her first shift. I fucking hate Blake for it. I hate the whole pack. Maybe not Mercy since she kept up with where I was and came for me when Nikita needed me."

"How do you want to play this? I can voice every single one of them, or I challenge Blake the way I did Dennis. Let you get your revenge."

Quinn sighed again, her distress palpable. "I... I don't want to kill him. I know I said I would rip his throat out, but as much as I hate him, I don't think he deserves that. I already have one death on my hands, and it still haunts me. And Nikita might say she hates him, but he's still her father. I won't be the one to take him away from her."

Kyllian lifted Quinn's hand to his mouth and kissed it. He'd rather kiss her lips, but he couldn't afford to get distracted any more than he was while driving. Because his mate was definitely distracting just sitting beside him. "I love your heart. You've been through some shit, yet you still take the high road." Kyllian was falling hard and fast. Gryphons didn't have fated mates, yet that's what he was to Quinn. So why couldn't she be that for him? He had never felt as complete as he did in her presence. Had never had the urge to tell someone he loved them outside his family. Until her, he was content – mostly – being a bachelor who had sex with whomever he pleased. Now the thought of being with anyone else made him nauseated. If that wasn't love, he didn't know what was.

"My heart was shattered all those years ago with Blake's lies and betrayal. I never thought it would mend, but you did that. You made it whole again. I'm not perfect like you think. Unless I'm working, I get lost in my head. Being around others is going to take some getting used to."

"I'll be beside you every step of the way. I'm so fucking proud of you, Quinn. You stepped out of your sanctuary to go after Nikita. That took guts. My niece, Mac, she rarely leaves the house. Not because she's a recluse, but she got an awful scar when one of the Ministry leaders sicced his dog on her. The mates are helping her come out of her shell more by taking her places. And her boyfriend, Elijah, he makes her feel beautiful regardless of the blemish on her face."

"Wow, your family has been through a lot."

"They have. But we Lazlos are fierce when it comes to loving. The mates are all special in their own ways, but I really think you and Natalia will hit it off being in the same field. She worked as an assassin for Nexus. Plus there's Wynter. You're both wolves, so there's that. What I'm trying to say is you might be nervous at first, but our family will welcome you with open arms and do whatever it takes to help you. I have a feeling we won't see Nikita much in the beginning. Rory is going to kidnap her newest granddaughter."

"Do you think Rory will like me? She knows what it is I do for a living."

"She'll love you. And if she held your job against you, that would be hypocritical considering all her sons work for you."

"That's right! I'm your boss," Quinn said with a whimsical giggle that hit Kyllian right in the solar plexus. He doubted she had much reason to laugh over the years, and he vowed to hear more of it.

"You can boss me all you want, Pretty Lady. In the bedroom and out."

"Kyll," she groaned.

"I know. I know. If we weren't in a hurry to get to Arkansas, I'd find a spot to pull over and... Okay, change of subject. Quick." Kyllian released her hand so he could adjust his dick. Quinn laughed again, and Kyllian scowled. His female laughed harder.

Kyllian turned on the satellite music app and told Quinn to find them a song. She switched stations until she found a rock channel. Yep, his mate was perfect. His singing voice was decent, but Quinn couldn't carry a tune in a bucket.

When he encouraged her to sing louder, she complained, "No. Nope. Then you really will know I'm not perfect."

"Do you like to sing?" he asked.

"Yes, but it doesn't mean I do it well."

Kyllian flipped on the turn signal and hit the next exit. "That doesn't matter. If you enjoy something, you should do it."

"I enjoy you," she deadpanned.

"Woman, I swear you're trying to kill me," he muttered, but Quinn sat back in her seat with a satisfied grin. Kyllian loved that she was letting more of her true self shine through. "Are you hungry? We need fuel, so we can grab some snacks."

Quinn shook her head. "No, I'm not sure I could eat, knowing where we're going and who I'll be facing."

Kyllian wanted to go into whatever afterlife wolves

believed in, find Stewart Aberdine, and kill him all over again. If he thought it wouldn't upset Quinn, he would rip Blake apart as well. He kept those thoughts to himself as he found a gas station.

After filling the tank, Kyllian got them back on the interstate. The next hour was made with idle talk and lots of singing. Quinn finally found her voice, and even though her tone was nowhere close to the artist, it was a thing of beauty. Yes, Kyllian had it bad. When he noticed she'd stopped singing, Kyllian checked on his mate. She was slumped against the door, her eyes closed. He spent the rest of the drive with the radio off and the sounds of Quinn's breathing as company.

CHAPTER FOURTEEN

Quinn

IF QUINN DIDN'T believe Kyllian was her fated mate before, she certainly did after spending hours in the car with him, talking and singing. She knew she sounded horrible, but Kyllian encouraged her to enjoy herself, so she did. She'd always loved music. It and books were the two bright spots in her self-imposed reclusiveness. She always wanted to go to concerts, but she had to make do with watching highlights of them on the internet. She would have loved to attend book signings and meet her favorite authors. Instead, she interacted with them via social media. She didn't think she was ready to put herself out there with thousands or even hundreds of people just yet, but she would get there.

With Kyllian by her side, Quinn saw a bright future where she no longer hid from the world. First, she had to get through the next few hours of confronting her past. The one that caused her so many years of missing out on everything the world around her had to offer. If what he said was true, she had a large family waiting on her back in New York. Other mates who had trauma of their own to overcome. A ready-made clan who would welcome her with open arms. The one she was most excited about was Rory. Quinn didn't remember her mother or the feel of an older woman's open arms.

Not even when she ran off and became part of the Ozark pack for a few months had any of the females offered a mother's love and affection. When Stewart welcomed her into the pack, Karen had been standoffish. She hadn't been cruel, but it was apparent by the way she often scowled at Quinn she wasn't happy with the situation. Had it been because she knew Blake already had a mate? Had she loved Bethany like a daughter and found what her mate and son plotted to be reprehensible? Quinn never met Bethany. She often wondered how the female handled her mate seducing someone solely for a dire offspring. How had she treated Nikita? Raising someone else's child couldn't be easy, especially under the circumstances.

The important thing was making sure Nikita was safe. Someone told her where the RC pack was, and Quinn didn't believe whoever it was that sent the teen there had her best intentions at heart. Who would send a child off on their own into unknown shifter territory? Maybe Quinn would get answers to all her questions. Maybe she wouldn't. If it weren't for Kyllian, she would be worried about stepping foot onto Ozark pack land. Blake had threatened her life after all.

The GPS voice instructed Kyllian to take the next exit. That was Quinn's cue to pay attention. She'd only woken a few minutes earlier when Kyllian shook her gently. As she'd done with the RC pack, Quinn had used satellite maps to locate the Ozark community. She never intended to return, but she still wanted to know exactly where her daughter was being raised. Quinn had been tempted many times over the years to fly south and try to get a glimpse of her child, but she'd been too scared. During their drive, Kyllian asked that Quinn let Kyllian go after Nikita alone, but she nixed that idea. Nikita was her daughter. Her responsibility now. She appreciated him wanting to protect her, but this was something she needed to do. To face her past. And her fears.

The area looked the same as it had eighteen years ago, and Quinn took a deep breath, attempting to quell her nerves. She doubted if Blake still lived in the smaller house where she stayed with him. It wasn't large enough for a family of five, so she directed Kyllian to the house Stewart and Karen had called home. If Blake wasn't there, Karen might be, and she could tell them where her son was. Kyllian pulled into the driveway. When he shut the engine off, he held out his hand and Quinn took it. "You ready for this?"

"If you weren't with me, I'd say no, but I know you won't let anything happen to me."

Kyllian raised her hand and kissed it. "No, I won't." He removed the keys from the ignition and got out of the car. Quinn opened her door and pushed to her feet. The front door opened, and Blake stepped outside.

"Can I help— Quinn," he seethed. "You shouldn't have come back." Blake partially shifted, and Kyllian stepped in front of her. Blake tilted his head back and howled.

"Shit." Kyllian pushed Quinn behind him. "Where's Nikita?" he asked. Quinn recognized the power in his voice.

Blake stomped down the steps. "She's not here. You'll never get your hands on my daughter."

"You will tell me where she is," Kyllian said with more force.

Shaking his head as though he could resist, Blake repeated, "She's not here."

"Blake, what's going on? Who are these people?" a woman asked from the porch.

"Get back in the house, Bethany."

"I'm Quinn Shepherd, Nikita's mother." Quinn stepped up beside Kyllian and crossed her arms over her chest, scowling at the female. Bethany's eyes widened.

"You!" Karen walked out of the house and stopped beside Bethany. Before Quinn could blink, Karen shifted into her Wolf, her clothes ripping, and sprang from the porch. Quinn's Wolf took over and met the smaller animal in the air. It was no contest. Quinn took Karen to the ground hard.

Blake howled again, and Kyllian yelled Quinn's name. Quinn had no desire to hurt the female, so she used her larger frame to keep Karen where she was. Karen thrashed and growled, but she was no match for Quinn's size or strength. Quinn growled, and Karen whined, baring her neck in submission. Quinn took a step back and returned to her skin. "I'm not here to hurt anyone. I just want Nikita."

Shouts and growls came from several pack

members as they raced to answer their Alpha's call, some on two feet, most in their fur.

"Stop," Kyllian commanded. "Don't come any closer."

The pack froze where they were, and Blake's eyes narrowed. "Who are you?"

"Quinn's mate. Like she said, we don't want to hurt anyone. We came for Nikita."

Blake gritted his teeth. "She ran away. I sent my betas to find her."

Quinn's claws came out, digging into her palms. "Who told Nikita about the River Canyon Pack?"

"That little bitch, Tarryn."

"No," Kyllian argued. "She only told her they were in New Mexico. Who told her exactly where they were and that Quinn was there?"

Blake's face turned red. Looking around, his eyes fell on his mate. "Bethany, did you betray me?"

Bethany gasped. "What? No. I love Nikita like she's my own."

"Yeah, Dad. She loves Nikita more than her real kids." A teen standing off to the side of the porch had her arms crossed, her face as dark as Blake's.

Bethany took a step toward the girl but stopped when her daughter lifted her chin. "No, I don't. Why would you say that?"

"Because she's a dire wolf. You all think she's so much better than the rest of us, even Nathan, your own heir. She's not even an alpha, and yet she's the golden child."

"That's enough," Blake hissed. "Who told Nikita where to find the River Canyon pack?" he asked, his

201

prime Alpha voice in full effect.

Karen rolled to her knees, her head bowed. "I did."

"Mom? Why would you do that?" Blake stared at his mother like she was a stranger. Maybe in that moment she was.

Karen lifted her face to her son. "It's like Carrie said; you dote on Nikita like she's the goddess incarnate. And that one"— Karen pointed at Quinn — "killed my mate."

"I'll deal with you later," Blake seethed.

They were getting nowhere with the family bickering, so Quinn asked, "When's the last time you spoke with Mercy?"

Before Blake could answer, Kyllian's phone rang, and he held up his hand. "Nobody move." He tapped the screen and put it to his ear.

"Kayos," Bishop responded. "I'm afraid I don't have good news. I didn't call until now because I've been working nonstop, but here's the thing. Jeremy texted someone with a cryptic message. All it said was 'it's time.' It took forever, but I finally tapped into the receiver's phone and figured out it was someone named Kinsley."

Kyllian tilted his head. "Kinsley, Kinsley…"

"That's Jeremy's mate," Quinn reminded him.

"The last location for all their phones was just outside New Tulsa. That was an hour ago. Either they're waiting for something or someone, or they left the phones and are traveling without them. Nikita hasn't sent any new texts to Tarryn either."

Kyllian growled low, and Quinn understood. It was a frustrating situation. "Why would Nikita tell

Tarryn that Blake commanded Mercy to return to the pack?"

Quinn brushed a stray strand of hair behind her ear. "Either to throw someone off, or Mercy gave Nikita that excuse as to why they didn't take her to Poppy's."

Kyllian took Quinn by the arm and led her away from the pack. Whispering, he asked, "If the Alpha gives a command, does a wolf have to obey?"

"If he uses the Prime Alpha voice, then yes. It's much like your compulsion."

"What's a Prime Alpha?" Bishop asked.

"In wolf hierarchy, there are alphas, betas, and omegas. The alphas are the more dominant of the species. The Prime Alpha is the leader of the pack. His word is law, and that's usually enough to have the pack obey. When he wants to make sure of it, he uses the power of the prime position to ensure it."

"So it's possible he didn't use the prime voice and Mercy disobeyed?" Bishop asked.

"It is. But I don't understand why she wouldn't answer our calls if that's the case. Why not take Nikita to Poppy's like planned? Kyllian..." Quinn didn't know what to ask for. Her mind was going several directions, each scenario worse than the last.

Kyllian took her hand with his free one as he returned to where Blake was struggling not to shift. "Did you speak to Mercy yesterday and tell her to return Nikita here?"

"No. She won't answer her fucking phone."

"Where's Kinsley?" Quinn asked. If she was texting with Jeremy, she had to know their plan.

203

Kyllian's phone buzzed, and he looked at the screen. "Bishop, I've got a call coming through from an unknown number. I want you to trace it if you can."

"I'm on it."

Kyllian tapped the screen, then put the phone to his ear. "Hello?"

"Kyllian, help." Quinn's knees about buckled at the panicked voice.

"Trouble, is that you?"

"Yes. I don't know what's going on, but Mercy has lost her fricking mind. They all have."

"Where are you?" Kyllian wrapped his arm around Quinn's waist, and she gripped his tee over his heart.

"The mall in Tulsa. I'm borrowing someone's phone. Mercy took mine."

"How did you get away?"

"You don't want to know," she whispered.

"You need to find a security guard. Tell them—"

"Crap! They're coming." Pounding feet sounded in the background as did voices yelling.

"Nikita," Kyllian called out, but she didn't respond. "Damnit."

"H-hello?" a scared voice asked.

"Yeah, this is Nikita's stepdad. Can you tell me what's happening?"

"The girl – Nikita – tossed my phone at me and took off running. There's two men and a woman chasing her through the mall. Man, they're really fast."

"What's your name?"

"Bailey."

"Bailey, thank you for letting Nikita use your phone. If you happen to see a security guard, can you let them know what's going on? The ones chasing my girl kidnapped her. Her mom and I are on our way, but we're a couple hours out."

"Yes, I can do that."

"Thank you, Bailey." Kyllian disconnected and closed his eyes.

Quinn looked around. "Where is Kinsley?"

When no one immediately spoke up, Kyllian growled, "Answer her."

A female cleared her throat. She was standing toward the back of the pack, and she raised her hand like she was in school. "She left earlier. Said something about an appointment in town."

Quinn dug her fingers into Kyllian's bicep. "Shit, she's going to meet them."

"I'll have Bishop track her phone in case she doesn't meet them at the mall." Kyllian pried her fingers from his arm, turned so he was facing her, and kissed her forehead. His gentle demeanor changed to something she never wanted to see aimed in her direction as he strode toward Blake. "We're going after our girl, and she will not be coming back here. Ever. You stole Nikita from her mother, your mother plotted to send a teen out by herself into unknown territory where those wolves were the worst of the worst. You're lucky I found her when I did, or we'd be planning a funeral and so would you. You don't deserve the title of father, and you sure as fuck don't deserve to be Alpha. Once I get *my* girl back, I'll deal with Mercy and Jeremy myself." Kyllian let his Lion's head come forth. He shook his mane and roared so loud it came close to shattering the windows. When he returned to his human form, he pointed to Bethany. "You. Go inside and get a pen and paper."

While the female did as he commanded, Kyllian took a menacing step toward Blake, his Eagle's talons elongating. Blake's eyes widened, and Quinn expected him to piss his pants. Bethany returned, and Kyllian continued. "Write this down." He slowly gave her a New Troy address, and Quinn assumed it was his own. "You will pack up Nikita's things and ship them to that address at once. When that is taken care of, you will lose the address and you all will forget about Nikita and Quinn. None of you will remember either one of them or me."

Kyllian turned and stalked to the car, leaving the pack staring after them. Quinn had to wonder how Nikita would feel about Kyllian making such concessions with her life, but she trusted her mate. He'd met the teen, and considering he was the one she turned to when in trouble, Quinn knew in her heart Nikita trusted him too. She jogged to catch with his long strides. Once they were both seated and secure, he blew out a breath and looked over at her. She couldn't help but smile.

"What?"

"That was so sexy. And scary. But mostly sexy."

"You're ridiculous." Kyllian turned his head to start the engine, but Quinn caught the smirk.

Nikita

NIKITA WAS STILL coming down off the high of fighting other dire wolves and being saved by Kyllian. Riding on his animal had been better than anything she'd encountered in her eighteen years. The tatted biker was fierce yet kind. Charming with his bad boy vibe. When she talked to him on the phone after he rescued her mom, Nikita's heart sunk when Quinn wouldn't speak to Nikita, but she trusted when Kyllian told her the reason. She trusted him more than anyone in her life. Her life that had been full of lies. She spent much of the car ride dreaming of a life with him and Quinn. He promised her a sidecar of her own if she enjoyed riding motorcycles. Nikita would so rock a pair of biker goggles. And a leather jacket. And boots.

Her whole life, she had been the perfect daughter. Wearing clothes Bethany chose for her. She made good grades. She didn't pick fights with her siblings even though she wanted to throttle Carrie more often than not. Her little sister was a pain in the ass. Always whining about something. Nathan got away with everything being the heir. Jake was the only one she didn't mind spending time with. He didn't consider her the enemy, but it was only a matter of time until that changed. Nikita had towed the line so Blake and Bethany would keep her around and not ditch her like they said her mother did. But that wasn't what happened.

Getting ready to graduate, she was supposed to be figuring out her life. Things like what to study at college, not that Blake would let her go. However, with

207

these new revelations, all Nikita wanted was to get to know both Kyllian and her mom. Find out all about her family on her mom's side and meet all Kyllian's many siblings and mates. And his parents. Kyllian painted this wonderful picture of life with the Lazlos. So many Lazlos.

Nikita Lazlo. Yep, it had a good ring to it. Was eighteen too old to be adopted? She hoped not. She wanted to belong to a family who had her back. Who didn't demand a mated wolf seduce a young woman just to have a dire offspring. Now that Nikita was aware of how she came to be, she wanted nothing to do with Blake. If she never saw her sire again, it would be too soon.

Getting out of this vehicle would also be too soon. Nikita didn't do well being still for long periods of time. She sat up in the seat and took in their surroundings. She'd never been to Texas other than the stop on the bus. Something was wrong. Nikita knew it down to her soul when the signs on the interstate pointed north instead of east. Nikita sat back and observed the adults in the vehicle. Brett, who was sitting next to Nikita, had his arms crossed over his chest. Jeremy was driving, but his hands were gripping the steering wheel tight enough to turn his knuckles white. And Mercy? Mercy had never been the most stable female, and now she was giving off some eerie vibes. Nikita long ago learned to trust her Wolf, and it was telling her to get as far away from Mercy as possible.

"I thought we were going to Texas to stay with Kyllian's sister?" If Nikita hadn't been watching

Jeremy's face in the rearview mirror, she would have missed the way his eyes shifted sideways to his sister. Brett stiffened beside Nikita but didn't comment.

Mercy shrugged without looking back. "I don't know those people, and I'm not trusting your safety to strangers."

"I trust them. Kyllian and his family put their lives on the line for me. He saved me." It was Mercy's turn to stiffen, but Nikita kept talking. "If we aren't going to Texas, where are we going? Because I don't want to go back to the pack."

"I'm sorry, but the Alpha gave me an order. You know I can't ignore it."

Nikita sent Tarryn a quick text, praying Kyllian's fellow Gryphon was monitoring the messages. It's how they found Nikita in the first place.

Nikita: *Mercy is taking me back to the pack. Said Blake demanded it.*

Tarryn: *I'm sorry. I know things are shitty right now, but hey. You only have a couple more months until graduation, then you can get out of there. My parents already said you could come here.*

Nikita: *Tell them thanks. I guess I'll figure something out then.*

Tarryn: *Keep me posted.*

Nikita needed a plan. If Bishop was keeping tabs on her whereabouts, he could get word to Kyllian. She needed to stall to give him time to catch up. "I'm hungry, and I gotta pee."

Mercy turned and glared at her. "We just ate. And you're not a child; you can hold it."

Nikita crossed her arms over her chest, mirroring

Brett. She chewed her lip as she wondered what awaited her back home. Blake would be furious and probably ground her. Bethany would use her disappointed look, the one she reserved for Carrie. Her grandmother would… Her grandmother was the one who gave her the money to go looking for Quinn, so hopefully she wouldn't be upset with Nikita. Unless Blake used his Prime Alpha voice, Nikita wouldn't admit his mom gave her the money.

About an hour later, Mercy told Jeremy, "Take the next exit. According to the internet, there's a mall there, and we can get what we need."

Nikita didn't know what they needed other than food, but a mall was good. Lots of places to hide if she could get away from them. Jeremy followed Mercy's directions and parked in the lot outside the food court entrance. Once inside, the four of them ordered burgers and sat amid the myriad of shoppers and families. As she ate her food, Nikita searched the area. It was set up much the same as the mall close to home with smaller stores just past the food court and the larger stores on each corner of the building. This one was two levels as well. It was now or never.

"I still need to pee. I'll be right back," she said, standing.

Mercy held out her hand. "Leave your phone here. Brett, go with her."

Shit. She didn't need to give Mercy any reason to doubt she was going anywhere other than the restroom. "Sure. Here you go." She slid the phone across the table. Mercy couldn't get in it without Nikita to unlock it. Putting on her best fake smile, she said,

"We'll be right back."

Nikita set up a quick pace. When she continued past the entrance to the restroom, Brett grabbed her hand. "The restroom is right there."

Nikita gave him a sheepish grin, leaning in whispering. "I know, but I'm on my period. I don't have any tampons, so I need to see if there's a small market of some sort." As she suspected, Brett flinched. Why men were so grossed out by a natural bodily function, she didn't know, but she used it to her advantage. She took him on a circuit of the ground floor, crossing through the middle of the concourse, and hopping on the escalator. When they were almost at the top, Nikita kicked Brett in the chest, sending him crashing into shoppers behind him. She took off running and darted into one of the larger stores. She continued to the opposite side where she exited into the mall and entered the first clothing store for teens.

Seeing someone close to her age texting, she ducked behind the clothes rack. "Hey, can I borrow your phone? There's some creep following me, and I need to call my dad."

"Yeah, sure." The girl handed her phone over, and Nikita prayed Kyllian had found his phone. She had memorized the number even though it was stored in her phone.

After several rings, the best voice in the world answered, "Hello?"

"Kyllian, help." Nikita peered around the clothes, keeping an eye on the door.

"Trouble, is that you?"

"Yes. I don't know what's going on, but Mercy has

lost her fricking mind. They all have."

"Where are you?"

"The mall in Tulsa. I'm borrowing someone's phone. Mercy took mine."

"How did you get away?"

"You don't want to know," she whispered. Ah, shit. Brett was looking in the store, and Jeremy and Mercy were with him.

"You need to find a security guard. Tell them—" Nikita didn't hear the rest of what Kyllian was saying. She tossed the phone back to its owner. When Brett and the others turned right, Nikita took off running to the left. Kyllian had the right idea. If she could find a security guard, that would get Mercy off her back for a bit. At least long enough for security to question who they were and why they were chasing her.

"Help! Security!" Nikita yelled as she ran, shoving people out of the way as she made her way back to the escalator. She needed to get to an exit before the others caught her. She ran down the escalator, apologizing as she pushed a couple to the side on her way down. She continued yelling for help as she headed away from where they parked. As she reached the entrance to one of the larger stores, a uniformed guard came into view. "Oh, thank the goddess. You have to help me." Nikita hid behind him and pointed over his shoulder. "Those people were chasing me." Mercy, Jeremy, and Brett slowed to a stop. Mercy glared at her, Jeremy blew out a breath and looked toward the ceiling. And Brett? He turned and walked away. Smart man.

"Let's go, Mercy. Your revenge isn't worth going to jail for," Jeremy said. It wasn't loud enough for the guard to catch, but Nikita's Wolf heard him just fine.

Nikita glared back, daring them to come closer. The guard was no match for wolves, but she didn't think Mercy was crazy enough to cause more of a scene where the police would be called in.

The man lifted a microphone off his shoulder and spoke to whoever was on the other end, telling them of the situation and to call the police. When he received an affirmative, he put his arm around Nikita's shoulder. "Come on. I'll take you to the office while we wait."

Nikita glanced over her shoulder. Jeremy was walking away as he typed on his phone, but Mercy had already disappeared into the crowd. Nikita didn't understand. Revenge? Against who? She'd never done anything to the female, so Mercy must be using Nikita as a pawn. Once inside the office, she said, "May I please use the phone to call my parents?"

CHAPTER FIFTEEN

Kayos

KYLLIAN'S ADRENALINE WAS still pumping by the time they hit the interstate. Knowing Quinn was a badass was one thing, but to see her in action? His Gryphon wanted to rip Karen apart for challenging Quinn, but he got it. Sort of. If someone killed his mate, he'd be hellbent on revenge too. Still, he'd pulled his beast back knowing Quinn could handle herself. She was the sexy one with all that gorgeous silver and black fur. If it weren't for the fact that their girl needed them, he'd have pulled over and found somewhere to claim her all over again. Instead, he got his thoughts off his dick and where they needed to be.

He pressed the button on the steering wheel and said, "Call Bishop."

"Kayos? Everything okay there?"

"No, it's not. Somehow Nikita got away from Mercy and Jeremy, and they were chasing her through the mall. She'd borrowed someone's phone to call me. According to one of the pack members, Kinsley had an appointment in town, but we all know that was a lie."

"I've got a bead on her phone, and I'd say you're

right. She's headed west toward New Tulsa. I'll keep an eye on her. If her path changes, I'll let you know."

"Thanks, Bishop. We're on the road west as well." Kyllian's phone buzzed, and he glanced long enough to see who was calling. "Pop's calling. I'll check back in soon." He switched over and said, "Hey, Pop."

"Kyllian Donovan Lazlo." Rory using his pop's phone plus Kyllian's full name didn't bode well. Kyllian cringed, and Quinn slapped her hand over her mouth, trying to suppress a laugh.

"Hey, Mom. I take it you've heard about Nikita?"

"Rory, give me the phone, Love. Let me handle this," Sutton said.

"Why did I have to hear from your sister that you're in New Mexico battling wolves? Wolves, Kyllian."

Kyllian opened his mouth, not sure what to say, but Sutton came on the line. "Kayos, I'm putting you on speaker even though I don't need to. Your mother is sitting on my lap so she can hear you too." Kyllian grinned. He couldn't help it. His parents were just as in love now as they were when they mated a hundred years ago. "Son, not only did Poppy call your mom, but Trenton called me to give me a heads-up on the River Canyon Pack and Nikita being Quinn's daughter."

"Shit, Pop. So much has happened, and we haven't had time to get in touch with Trenton since we left. Long story short, some wolves from the Ozark pack were supposed to take Nikita to Poppy's where we were going to pick her up after dealing with the RC pack. Instead, they kidnapped her. Currently, they're in Tulsa. Nikita managed to get away and call me, but the ones who took her found her again, and she's on the run. Quinn and I are headed there now."

"That poor girl," Rory said. "You better find her, Kyllian. Find her and bring her here. She needs the Lazlos to watch her back."

"That's the plan, Mom. I've already instructed her sire to pack her things and send them to my house."

"Sire? Is that like her father?" Rory asked.

"The bastard doesn't get that title. You're gonna love her mom. Her and Quinn both."

"Am I the only one?"

Kyllian rolled his eyes at his mother's lack of subtlety. "Nope. Quinn and I are mates. I have the bite mark to prove it."

"And you didn't lead with that?" Rory's indignant tone had Quinn laughing out loud. "Oh, hello Quinn. I'm Rory, and I can't wait to meet you." Indignant to sugary sweet in point-five seconds. That was Rory.

"Hello, Mrs. Lazlo. I can't wait to meet you all as well."

"None of this Mrs. Lazlo business. You call me Rory, or Mom, whichever you prefer."

Quinn gasped, and her fingers in Kyllian's hair froze. Yep, Aurora Rose Lazlo was the best mom ever. He had no doubt his pop had already given Rory the scoop on Trenton's past. She would be aware Quinn didn't have a mom of her own and hadn't since she was a toddler. Rory would step into the role if Quinn would let her.

"Hey, Pop, can you do me a favor? Like I said, Nikita's things are being delivered to my house. I have no idea how much stuff she has, but if you could keep an eye out for it, I'd appreciate it."

"You got it, Son. Anything else you need?"

"Not right now, but thanks."

"Kyllian, you said all her stuff is being sent, but does that include her birth certificate?" Rory asked.

"Shit, Mom. I don't know. Even if they send it, it's going to list Blake as her sperm donor, and I doubt the dickhead put Quinn down as the mother. I'll need to check on that."

"Why don't you call Lucy? If anyone can get it settled, it's her. Or Julian if she can't."

If his mom was suggesting calling Julian Stone for help, they hadn't heard of the latest trouble with the Gargoyles. With Lucy and Tamian in the mix, he didn't want to worry his mother. "I'll ask Bishop if he can handle it. If not, I'll call her."

"Sounds good. You stay safe. Both of you." The line went dead, and Kyllian glanced over to check on his mate. She'd gone still when Rory told her she could call her "mom."

"You okay, Pretty Lady?"

"Y-yeah." Quinn cleared her throat. "They both sound really nice. I can see why my dad thinks so highly of yours."

"They're the best. I was thinking once we rescue Nikita and you and she have a chance to talk, we should bring her back here to finish out the school year. If she wasn't getting ready to graduate, it would be different, but I want her life to be as easy as possible going forward. We can stay in one of those hotels for people who need long-term options. It'll only be for a couple months, then we can head home."

Quinn moved her fingers again, her nails scratching softly. "Do you think she'll really be okay moving so far away from Tarryn and her other friends? And what if she misses her siblings?"

"We don't know where Tarryn is. I could get Bishop to figure it out, but I think she'll be okay. We'll promise to let them visit one another if it seems upsetting to her. As for her siblings, you heard how there was no love lost from her little sister. I wanted to shift into my Gryphon and scare the shit out of her. I get being jealous, but that was over the top."

"I love your fierce heart. I've only met Ryker, but I bet all your brothers are built the same. How can you not be with the parents you have?"

"I've met some shitty people who have great parents. I've also met some great folks whose parents aren't worth spitting on. We were all raised that being kind and caring is more important than the size of the house we live in or how much money we did or didn't have. It's why Pop's so adamant about bringing down The Ministry. Those fuckers tout Godliness, but they wouldn't know a god if one punched them in the face. I don't know how Nikita was raised, but somehow, she turned out good." He'd only spent about an hour with Nikita, but the girl had claimed his heart with her easy smile, her sass, and her strength. "Our girl is smart. We exchanged numbers, but considering Mercy took Nikita's phone, she had to have memorized my number since she called from a stranger's phone. She's got a good head on her shoulders considering what she's going through. I want to give her the best life

218

going forward."

"It's going to be a big change for all of us." Quinn propped her elbow on the door and cradled her head in her hand. "I won't lie to you; I'm nervous. I get being mates. I understand the goddess or fates chose you for me, but I'm worried about moving in together. I'm worried about Nikita accepting not only me as her mother but the new living arrangements. I'm worried you'll resent me when I might not be able to handle you being a Master. It's a lot of change in a short time."

"I get it, Pretty Lady. I do. I'm nervous too. I'm pretty sure Nikita's going to surprise you. We had a good, if short, conversation after I rescued her. We'll ask her what she wants. Listen to her concerns, and we'll do what's best for her. She might not want to live with us, and if that's the case, we'll have to accept it for now, but I honestly don't see that happening. She ran away to find you. She wants you in her life. As for you and me? We'll be fine. Will there be learning curves? Of course. Will it take time to figure out what the other wants and needs? Yes. I wouldn't have mated with you if I wasn't willing to put in the work. I've never been in a relationship, and I've never been a father figure, but I've observed my parents over the years. I can't say I'd be okay with us living apart. I want you with me. I want to get to know you and vice versa. I've already told you I'll give up being a Master if that's what you need because your happiness comes first."

Quinn sighed. "But you shouldn't have to. I should be willing to make compromises too. If you promise me nothing sexual will happen, I trust you mean it."

"You could always come to the club with me.

Watch what it is I do so you can see for yourself what it's about. If you still aren't comfortable, I'll hand off my female subs to someone else. My friend Gunnar is handling things while I'm away. Hell, I might get back and have no subs left. They might decide he's a better fit. Everyone except Brandon. I'm not ready to hand him off. He's going through some shit right now, and I'd feel better keeping him with me. I can make sure Charlie and Wynter are going to be there on those nights so you'll have other females to talk to."

"Wynter's the wolf, right?"

"Yes. It might be cool for the two of you to compare notes. Find out what her pack is like. Your dad might like to meet up with others of your kind too. Speaking of, if he's half wolf, does his family not have a pack?"

"Not really. They decided to live as humans. Like Dad, they only shift and let the beast out whenever their animal gets too restless. I've only seen Dad in his fur a handful of times. As far as I know, it's been years since he shifted. Then again, he might shift and sleep in his fur. We don't talk about it."

Kyllian couldn't imagine suppressing his Gryphon. "Maybe once we find our balance, he will too. I have a feeling he's going to want to be in Nikita's life. You know how much money I make because you pay me for the mercenary jobs. I haven't been doing that as long as Ryker and Mav, but another thing Pop taught us all was about investing. I worked construction during high school. I love being outside, so it was the ideal job for me. Pop helped me open a checking and savings account. I had to put at least half my paycheck in savings. When I had several thousand dollars, he showed me how to invest in both stocks and crypto. By the time I was old enough, I knew I didn't want to go to college. Since I planned on joining my older brothers in the merc business, I didn't see the need in wasting the money. Mercy said Nikita's top in her class, so if she wants to go on to college, there's plenty of money to ensure she doesn't need student loans if she doesn't get enough in scholarships or grants."

Quinn gripped the strands of Kyllian's hair and tugged. "I appreciate that, but you have to know that I'm not without money. I've lived with my father, and we split the income from the company. The house is paid for. He refuses to let me pay for groceries, and I don't have a car. What little I do spend is on books, music, and clothes. Considering I never go anywhere, my wardrobe isn't much."

"So, what you're saying is you're loaded? That I got me a sugar momma?" Kyllian winked.

Quinn laughed and shook his head side to side using the grip on his hair. "I'm saying we'll never have to worry about money. Like if we want to build that house you mentioned with two wings? We could pay cash."

"In that case, I think we should look for some land as soon as we get our girl graduated. You'll both need somewhere to run."

"What about you? Don't you need to let the Lion out every once in a while?"

"Being able to take to my Eagle and fly is usually enough to appease the beast. I do like to let the Lion out and lie in the sun though. And if we buy some property, I'll be able to let him run more than in the past." Kyllian thought back to when they chased each other outside her home. He wanted more of that. He'd never considered frolicking to be something he'd find fun because come on; he was a badass Gryphon. But another thing he'd learned from his pop was that when you found your mate, you'd find the badassery took a back seat to the gentleness. "I can't wait to run with you every chance I get. Let me call Bishop and see about Nikita's birth certificate."

Bishop was good at hacking into phones and security cameras, but his skillset did not include getting his hands on a birth certificate, so Kyllian called Lucy. She was distracted but wouldn't tell him with what. She assured him she was fine and would take the time to get Nikita's birth certificate. After speaking with Quinn to get the correct time and date of birth, Lucy told them to be safe and hung up. Kyllian trusted the Gargoyle to keep his niece safe, but he still worried about her. She was important to their family in more ways than one.

By the time they arrived in New Tulsa, Kyllian was pretty sure Quinn was ready for their future. He assured her more than once he would do whatever it took to make theirs the best relationship ever. She agreed to come with him to the club before she asked him to give up being a Master. She was looking forward to seeing Spyder do a Shibari scene with Charlie and to meet a fellow she-wolf in Wynter. But first, they had to find Nikita.

Bishop forwarded all the messages that Kinsley received. He also sent them her location, which was a downtown hotel. Instead of driving around looking for Nikita, Kyllian came up with a plan. According to the texts, Mercy and Jeremy were still chasing Nikita, but they didn't say where they were. New Tulsa was a large city, so they could be anywhere. Kyllian parked down the street from the hotel, and he and Quinn entered the hotel and bypassed the front desk and headed to the elevator, going up to the sixth floor where Kinsley's room was.

Quinn knocked on the door and called out, "Room service," standing off to the side in case Kinsley looked through the peephole.

Kinsley opened the door. "I didn't—" Kyllian pushed past the female with Quinn on his heels. "What are you doing? Get out of my room!"

"Quiet," Kyllian commanded, and Kinsley clamped her mouth shut. "Why did your mate and Mercy kidnap Nikita?"

"How do you know..." Kinsley peered over his shoulder, and her eyes widened. "Goddess, you look just like her."

"Answer the question, Kinsley. Why did you all plot to take my daughter?"

Kinsley wrapped her arms around her waist and paced the living area of the suite. She muttered to herself about stupid betas and bad ideas. She stopped in front of the sofa and plopped down, rubbing her temple. When Kinsley raised her head, there was resignation in her eyes. "Mercy hates you. And Blake. Before you came along, Stewart promised Mercy's parents she and Blake would be mates. We all grew up together in the pack. Hung out and went to school together. Everyone knew Blake would become Alpha one day, and Mercy had her sights on being the Alpha mate. For Mercy, the sun rose and set with Blake. Her parents assured her it would happen, but then Bethany and her family moved to the area, and Blake fell in love. Said Bethany was his fated mate."

Kinsley rose and went to the table where bottled water sat alongside an ice bucket. She unscrewed the lid and swallowed half the bottle down. Instead of returning to the sofa, she sat at the dining table and set the bottle down, picking at the label. "It caused dissension in the pack. Mercy went from riding the high of thinking she'd be Blake's mate to disrupting everyone's lives. Mercy's family was well loved, but Stewart gave Blake anything he wanted. When Blake told Stewart Bethany was it for him, Stewart went to Mercy's parents and basically paid them off if they promised to keep Mercy in line. Blake and Bethany completed the bond after high school with plans to take over the pack one day, but you came along."

Quinn walked over and sat down across from the other female. "That's something I never understood. If Bethany was his fated mate, why did Blake seduce me? Now having a destined mate myself, I could never be with anyone else."

"Stewart demanded it. When he found out you were a dire wolf, he ordered Bethany to stay away while Blake convinced you the two of you were mates so there would be a dire wolf in their family. Up until you arrived, dire wolves were a thing of the past. We didn't know they still existed. I honestly don't know what Stewart thought having one in the family would do. Anyway, he told Blake if he didn't follow orders, he would never become Alpha. I don't know all the details, and I don't know how Mercy found out either. But not only had Bethany come along and taken Blake from her, she saw you as the enemy as well. She followed you when you went after Nikita. She followed you back to your apartment, then she kept tabs on your every move."

"But why? With me in New York, I was no threat to her."

"No, but you had something she didn't – Blake's child. She became obsessed."

"I take it the two of you are close if you know all this."

Kinsley smiled, but it was sad. "No. To Mercy, I was another female she felt she was in competition with. She and Jeremy were always close, and when we mated, I took up most of his time, and she resented me for it. Anyway, none of us respected Stewart when he demanded Blake seduce you, and when you took Stewart down, we were hopeful you'd stay and become Alpha. When it was apparent you weren't coming back, Blake took on the role."

"And no one challenged him? If they didn't like what he and his father did, why would everyone sit back and let things remain as they were?"

Kinsley tapped her nails on the glass-top. "Nobody wanted the responsibility. Quite a few families left to start their own pack somewhere else while ours was in flux. Blake waited almost three months to ensure you weren't coming back. He was an alpha, but you? You're an alpha dire wolf. He wouldn't stand a chance against you."

Kyllian crossed the room and stood behind Quinn, placing his hands on her shoulders. "So what was the plan? Why does Mercy want Nikita so badly?" Kinsley downed the rest of the water. As a stall tactic, it was effective. "Kinsley," Kyllian put a little force behind the name.

She blew a strand of hair off her face and clasped her hands together. "Revenge."

When Quinn's body tightened, Kyllian rubbed his thumbs across her nape.

Kinsley explained, "Mercy thought by sending Nikita to the River Canyon pack, Quinn would storm the pack and be taken out, then Mercy could swoop in and play both hero and mother to the girl. Their parents were among those who left the Ozark pack and started somewhere new. She was planning on taking Nikita there after this was all over."

"But how did Mercy know where the RC pack was located? I only ever told Stewart and Karen," Quinn said.

"Mercy befriended Karen when her parents left. When I say she's been plotting this a while, I mean years. She sympathized with Karen over you killing Stewart. Convinced her Nikita was going to turn on the pack. Turn on her father. Karen had lost a mate, and she wasn't willing to lose her son as well, so she went along with Mercy's plan."

"How do you know all this, and why did you go along with it?" Kyllian asked.

"Mercy might not like me, but she trusts Jeremy. He loves his sister, but he didn't agree with her, so he and I decided we would do whatever it took to keep Nikita from harm. She's really a great kid. Super smart."

"Was it really Scott who told the River Canyon pack where I was, or was that all Mercy lying again?"

"That was Scott doing Mercy's bidding. He's tried for years to get her attention. When you turned to Blake, Scott was upset, same as Mercy. They bonded over their mutual heartbreak. But where Scott got over it and moved on, she didn't. She used Scott's affection against him. Strung him along all these years. The idiot couldn't see she was playing him." Kinsley's phone beeped, and she looked at it, then at Kyllian.

"Read the message aloud."

Kinsley fumbled with the device. Her eyes widened, and she cleared her throat. Turning the phone around, she showed them the screen.

Jer: *It's over. I won't go to jail for Mercy. I'll meet you there in twenty minutes.*

"What does that mean? Where's Nikita?" Quinn slammed her palm down on the table.

Kyllian's phone rang, and he pulled it out of his back pocket. Another unknown number. *Please, Zeus, let her be okay.* "Hello?"

"Hey, Dad. I'm at the New Tulsa mall in the security office. I ran into a little trouble. I'm okay, but can you come get me?"

Kyllian squeezed Quinn's shoulder. "Hey, Trouble. Your mom and I will be there soon. You sit tight."

"I will," she choked out. "Thanks." The line went dead, and Quinn shoved out of her seat.

"Let's go." She headed for the door, but Kyllian

227

told her to hang on a second.

He focused on Kinsley and said, "You will not remember Quinn and I being here or the conversation we had." Kinsley nodded like a bobblehead, and Kyllian left her sitting at the table.

Quinn was quiet during the drive, holding Kyllian's hand so tight he thought she might break a few bones, but he didn't complain. She was meeting her daughter, and the circumstances weren't optimal. They would have to figure out a story to tell the security guard.

Once inside the mall, they asked for directions to the office, and standing outside the door, Quinn was shaking. "Hey. Look at me." When Quinn gave him her eyes, he kissed her hard. "I promise it will be fine." Quinn squared her shoulders, turned, and knocked on the door.

Instead of a mall guard, a deputy stood in the doorway. "Mr. and Mrs. Lazlo?"

"Yes. Where's our daughter?" Kyllian was taller than the cop, and he could see Nikita over his shoulder. "Nikita!" Kyllian pushed past the cop.

"Dad!" Nikita rushed across the room and threw herself against his chest. He held her tight, and opened an arm for Quinn to join them. Nikita, feeling her presence, looked up. "Mom," she whispered before leaning over and shoving her face against Quinn's neck. Quinn took her daughter from Kyllian and held on while the two of them silently became acquainted.

The police officer inclined his head, so Kyllian stepped away with him. "Your daughter won't talk about what happened. The security guard said she was running through the mall screaming for help. There were two men and one woman chasing her. That much we've ascertained from video footage. But Mr. Lazlo, your daughter was with these people at first. They walked in together. Sat in the food court and ate together. Then your daughter got up and walked away with one of the men. When they get on the escalator, she kicked the man, causing him to fall into a couple, then took off running."

Kyllian's pride kicked up a notch. "Yeah, she's badass that way."

"Excuse me?" The cop seemed perplexed that Kyllian would think that of his kid.

"Look, Officer." Kyllian smiled while bringing forth his Gryphon. He hadn't used his voice as much in his whole life as he had these past few days. "My daughter is fine. Those three are her aunt and uncles, and this was a training simulation. Nikita wants to go off to college, but her mother fears for her safety. They're royalty, and her mom thinks she needs a bodyguard twenty-four seven. We've been putting Nikita through the paces to see how well she handles herself."

"Training? Royalty?"

"Yes, but you'll keep all this information to yourself. I appreciate the fine job you and the security guard did today in keeping my girl safe. Now, we'll be going. You have a nice day."

Kyllian left the cop standing staring over at Quinn and Nikita, probably trying to figure out who they were. Quinn was Kyllian's queen and Nikita his princess. So yes, royalty.

229

"Let's go." Kyllian opened the office door, ushering his girls out of the room. "Keep your eyes peeled for Mercy," he whispered as they put Nikita in the middle and escorted her out of the mall. He opened the back door, and Quinn slid in beside her daughter. When Kyllian was seated, he turned and grinned at Nikita. "Definitely trouble."

CHAPTER SIXTEEN

Quinn

QUINN COULDN'T STOP touching Nikita. Staring at her to make sure she was really there. Her beautiful baby girl. In all her years, Quinn never imagined meeting her again, much less where Nikita wanted to know her. As Kyllian drove away from the mall, Quinn held Nikita's hand. She stared at her daughter who looked almost identical to Quinn at her age. Nikita's hair was a shade lighter, but she had the same blue eyes. The same nose. Even her ears were shaped like Quinn's, a little on the large side and slightly pointed.

"A training simulation? Really?" Nikita was grinning at Kyllian, and it was clear she was enamored with him.

"Hey, I had to tell him something that didn't require someone trying to erase all the footage of you tearing through the mall. Who did you kick down the escalator?" Kyllian asked, pride in his voice

"Brett. Mercy sent him with me to the restroom. Can one of you tell me what the hell is going on?" Nikita gripped Quinn's hand tighter.

"It's a long story," Quinn responded. "Before I get

into it, because I promise I'll tell you everything, we need to decide where we're going."

Nikita's eyes widened. "I'm not going back to the pack. You can forget it."

Quinn cupped Nikita's cheek. "Never, my darling girl. But you still have two months left until you graduate. Kyllian thought we might get an extended stay hotel suite close to the school so you can finish out the year. Graduating is a big deal."

"But what about Blake? Won't he be looking for me?"

"No," Kyllian said. "I need to tell you what I did and get it out of the way first. It's one of those beg for forgiveness instead of asking permission situations. As a Gryphon, I have the ability to influence minds. Make people do things or forget things. I made your whole pack forget about you and Quinn."

"Seriously? That's... that's a little scary."

"It can be, but I promise you now I will never use it on you. Gryphons were given the gift in case our human mates couldn't handle the knowledge of our existence. We don't have fated mates or destined mates. There aren't that many Gryphons, so not all of our kind get to mate with other Gryphons. Most have human partners. To keep our existence a secret, we can voice them if needed. I might have overstepped in making your whole pack forget about the two of you, but it seemed like the easiest solution. I'm sorry if it's not something you wanted. If you want to keep in touch with anyone from your pack, I can undo the command." Nikita chewed on her lip, and Quinn held her breath. Nikita said she would never go back, but that didn't mean there weren't those who she loved. Who were important to her.

"It's sad to say, but Tarryn is the only one I care anything about. Well, I'll miss Jake, my little brother, but I figure it's only a matter of time before he falls prey to Blake's influence the way Nathan has. Without me there, Carrie won't feel neglected, and Nathan won't feel threatened. As far as school, I'm pretty much done. I asked Tarryn to get my assignments while I went off searching for Quinn, but even if I never turned in another assignment, I'll still have a 4.0 average. I'm taking mostly AP classes this year. Can we, I don't know, call the school and tell them I'm sick or something? See if I can do the work remotely? They can mail my diploma to me, right?"

Quinn's heart swelled with pride, but at the same time, it broke hearing Nikita wouldn't miss anyone from her life. "You don't want to walk across the stage with your classmates? And Mercy said something about you being top in your class. Won't you need to make a speech?"

"Tommy Connors and I have the same GPA and are co-valedictorians. If I don't show back up, he'll still do his speech, but I won't have to. And before you ask, yes, I'm cool with that. Finding out about my past put me in a tailspin, and I couldn't focus on what I wanted to say to my class anyway."

"I'm so sorry," Quinn whispered. "I should have never given up trying to find you."

"Why did you?" Nikita didn't sound accusing only curious.

"I was your age. Lost and alone." Quinn took a

deep breath, turned so she was facing her child, and told her everything from the beginning. Starting with her own parents, she laid it all out for Nikita.

Nikita remained silent, taking it all in. When Quinn finished, Nikita smiled. "Thank you for coming for me now." She leaned over and hugged Quinn the best she could with her seatbelt on. Quinn held her daughter, breathing in her scent, and thanking the goddess for her beautiful child and her fierce mate. When Nikita released her, she turned to Kyllian. "So, about that sidecar."

Kyllian laughed, shaking his head. "Nothing but trouble."

Nikita grabbed Quinn's hand and put hers next to it. "It's incredible how much we're alike. When I saw you back at the mall for the first time, it was surreal."

"Wait 'til you see a picture of my mom. The genes are strong in our female line. I met her mother back at the RC pack, and I had the same reaction. If I hadn't known better, I'd have thought it was Finola standing there."

"I'm glad I look like you because you're gorgeous. I can't wait to see your Wolf. I wonder if they're similar too."

"They are," Kyllian said. "Quinn's Wolf is slightly larger than your own, but your markings are the same. Speaking of, Quinn and I were talking."

"Seems like you've been doing a lot of that," Nikita teased.

"Yes, smartass, we have. This whole meeting and mating has been quick. But we were discussing buying some property and building a new house for the three of us. We need to know if that's something you want. We don't know your plans for the future, like are you going to college? Have you already applied and been accepted somewhere? Since I didn't go, I don't know the process, but you've probably got that all figured out."

"First off, I would be devastated if we didn't live together," Nikita admitted. "Ever since you told me about your family, they're all I can think about. And meeting Trenton. From the way you both speak about your dads, I'm ready to meet them both. And Rory. I need a grandma who'll have my back, not stab me in it. As for college, I didn't apply anywhere. Blake discouraged it. I'm pretty sure he was counting on me finding a mate and continuing the dire line. He would never let me go off to school anyway. I've always had shadows everywhere I went."

"If it's something you want to do, Kyllian and I will help you apply. Between us, we have the money to pay for it if it's too late to get scholarships or grants."

"I appreciate the offer. Learning comes easy to me, but I've not found anything that screams 'this is what I want to do with my life.' I'm aces with computers, but Blake monitored everything I did at home. I think he was afraid I'd try to find you. I figure I have plenty of time to figure out what calls to me. What about you? I take it since you stayed home you didn't go either?" she asked Quinn.

"I took online classes and studied psychology. I couldn't get a degree when I wouldn't do the clinical part of the course because that had to be done on site. Since I didn't plan on having patients, I was okay with that. It was more an interest for my line of work."

"Yeah? What is it you do?"

Well, hell. Quinn hadn't thought that through. She didn't know whether she and Kyllian should admit to their careers, but Kyllian took the question.

"I told you I would never lie to you, and this might be hard to hear, but you need to know what it is we do and why if you're going to live with us. Before we get to that, I need to stop for fuel. I think we should grab some snacks and find somewhere to sit and talk. We're close to the Ozarks, and we still need to decide whether or not you stay here to graduate."

"Snacks are always good. I need to pee anyway."

When Kyllian parked, Quinn stopped Nikita from getting out. "Let's wait on Kyllian so he can go in with us. After what happened last time, I'd rather not have a repeat."

"I get it. Safety in numbers and all that." Nikita unbuckled and shifted in her seat, facing Quinn. "Is it wrong of me to be glad Mercy lost her mind? If it wasn't for her wanting revenge, as messed up as her reasons, I wouldn't have met you and Kyllian."

"And I wouldn't have met the two of you either. Kyllian told me a little about his brothers' mates and all the bad things they had to go through to meet. We're just adding our story to theirs. I think sometimes we have to go through a storm to appreciate the sunshine."

"I like that." Nikita let out a little hum. She reached out and brushed her fingers down Quinn's cheek. "Sorry. Just making sure you're really here."

When Nikita went to pull away, Quinn placed her

236

hand atop her daughter's. "I feel the same way. Not a day went by that I didn't think of you." Quinn's eyes misted, but she didn't care. If ever there was a time for happy tears, this was it. "I was your age and scared to death going back home. So many times I tried to tell my dad what happened, but I couldn't stand to hurt him. It was bad enough I ran away for months. He tried to find me. Called the police and everything, but I went far enough from the apartment they didn't consider the distance. I did leave him a note telling him I needed to run so he didn't think I'd been taken. Still, it took a toll on him. I didn't know about his heart condition, and those months…"

Nikita used her thumbs to wipe the tears off Quinn's face. "I can't imagine not being able to take to my fur and run. I'd have gone nuts too. Isn't he a shifter?"

"He's half human, and his family lives as such. They would take a trip once a year somewhere they could shift and let the wolf go. Other than that, they shift in the house for a few minutes and that's it. When my mom was still alive, she tried to explain the need to him, but he either forgot, or he thought I'd take on part of his human genes. He didn't understand how strong dire wolf DNA is. I don't blame him. I have the greatest father in the world. He did what he thought best, raising a toddler, then a child, and eventually a teen with no help from anyone. Not even his family. When I returned and noticed how bad he looked, I vowed to never do anything to cause him pain again. That's why I couldn't tell him what happened."

Nikita lunged at Quinn. She hugged her hard and

scented her neck. Quinn had only known her father's touch for so long, and now she had both her mate and daughter to fill that need. They held each other until Kyllian eased open the door and escorted them inside where they both used the restroom. The trio then snagged all kinds of snacks and soft drinks for the road. Back in the car, Quinn got in the front so she could hold Kyllian's hand. After spending the last hour with her daughter, Quinn was at ease, even if they had some hard topics to cover.

"While you two ladies were in the restroom, I searched for somewhere we could sit. There's a park not too far from here."

Nikita didn't wait to tear into a bag of crunchy treats. "Gah, I was starving."

Kyllian tensed. "Why didn't you say something? I'd have gotten you real food."

"Dude, this is real food. Really good. Cheddar Bugles are like the best thing ever. I would share, but they're all gone. Sorry."

"Guess I know what we'll be stocking up on. What else do you like to eat?" he asked.

"Pizza. Extra cheese with pepperoni. Burgers and fries. Oh, and strawberry shakes. A good rare steak, because wolf. Loaded baked potatoes. Mac 'n' cheese with bacon. Not much of a seafood person, but coconut shrimp is pretty good. No sushi. That's just gross. Do either of you cook? If not, that's okay. I know my way around the kitchen and a grill. Bethany couldn't cook for shi-itake."

"Nice save." Kyllian laughed. There'd been a smile on his face ever since getting Nikita back. "I'm okay in the kitchen, but it sucks cooking for one person, so I either eat with my parents or order in."

"I'm a pretty good cook," Quinn added. "Though lately, I've been fixing healthier dishes. With my dad having heart issues, I'm trying to keep him around as long as possible."

"That sucks. Is it hereditary? Like are you going to have heart problems too?" Nikita asked.

"I have no idea, but I should probably find out. I've never been to a doctor."

Kyllian flipped the turn signal and pulled onto a side road. "One of the Hounds is a doctor, and his mate is a nurse. We can have them check you out if you'd be more comfortable than going to a stranger."

"I think I'd like that."

"Who's gonna cook for your dad? Is he moving in with us too?"

"I'm sure he'll stay in our house. At least for now. It's where our business is."

"We're here." Kyllian parked in the mostly empty lot away from other cars. "Grab the snacks and let's go sit over there." He indicated a stone table and benches under a large tree. Quinn sat next to Nikita, and Kyllian took the bench opposite. He looked around, his Eagle eyes flashing briefly, while Nikita dumped all the snacks in the middle of the table. She chose another bag of Bugles, and Quinn took the white cheddar popcorn. She'd be digging husks out of her teeth, but she'd deal with it since popcorn was her go-to snack. Kyllian grabbed a soda and uncapped it, taking a long drink. After wiping his mouth on the back of his hand, he said, "Okay, Trouble. Time for the truth. Do you know what a mercenary is?"

"Someone who kills people for money."

"Yes. That is what I am. Your mom is my handler, which means she receives the requests for jobs. She researches the mark – the person or people we're supposed to take out – to make sure they deserve to die. My brothers and I put down the worst of humanity. We don't go killing indiscriminately. These are rapists, serial killers, human traffickers. People who the police either can't catch or can't hold them when they do."

Nikita chewed her bottom lip, and Quinn waited her out. After thinking for a bit, she asked Quinn, "You do the research on the computer?"

"Yes. My dad started the company when I was little. When I was old enough, I began helping him with the background checks. That's the main reason I studied psychology, to help me better understand the people I was looking into. Well, that and to understand my own mental issues. I was a mess for a long time."

"Makes sense. If I wanted to learn to do the research, would you teach me?"

"I… I'd want you to think long and hard about it. Delving into these people isn't for the faint of heart. These are the worst of humanity."

"I get that. But why should you have to be the only one seeing that crap?" Nikita took Quinn's hand and rubbed her thumb over Quinn's knuckles. "If you say no, then you say no, but like I said earlier, I'm good with a computer. If not helping you, maybe I could work with Bishop."

Kyllian tilted his head to the side. "You're okay

with what we do?"

"Why wouldn't I be? You're doing the world a favor. Mom killed Stewart all those years ago, and when I was fighting the RC pack, I'd have killed one of them if it came down to it." She reached for a Dr Pepper and twisted the lid off. "There are some beings who don't deserve to walk among us."

Quinn was impressed. She had been afraid their jobs would be a deal breaker. She should have known better; Nikita was her kid.

"You're something else, Trouble. You know that?" Kyllian raised his bottle, and Nikita tapped hers against it.

"Now that we have that out of the way, let's talk about school. I really don't care if I walk across the stage to receive my diploma. With you doing the mind voodoo on the pack, I don't want to have to answer all the questions I'll get about why they aren't there with me. And there will be questions. Besides, Tarryn is the only real friend I have, and I doubt she'll be there either."

"If you're sure, we'll handle it."

"I'm sure. I have a question. What are we going to do about Mercy? You didn't get a chance to work your voodoo on her, and I'm betting she doesn't let this go."

Kyllian leaned his elbow on the table. "It's not voodoo, it's called my Gryphon voice."

Nikita waved her hand in the air. "Voodoo, voice, same diff."

"I save your life, and you give me sass. I see how you are. You don't hear your mom giving me sass, now do you?" Kyllian winked, and Nikita giggled.

241

Quinn let the two of them banter for a few minutes before asking, "What *are* we going to do about Mercy? She knows where I live, which means Dad could be in trouble."

"Well, we can all stay at your house with Trenton for a while. He'll want to meet Nikita and get acquainted with his granddaughter, and you need to pack. I can watch over you all while you take care of that. When you're ready to move, I'll have Ryker send a couple of the younger Hounds to guard him if Mercy hasn't shown her face by then."

"How far do you live from each other? Just asking because you had all my stuff sent to your house, and I'm gonna need some clothes."

"Not that far. About an hour. We can stop and do a little shopping for the time being."

"Really? Can I get whatever I want?" Nikita bounced with excitement.

Kyllian frowned. "Within reason. I've seen what teens try to pass off as decent. No hoochie momma clothes on my watch, Kiddo."

Nikita burst out laughing and fell against Quinn's side. "Hoo-hooch…" She snorted, causing Kyllian and Quinn to laugh with her. "Hoochie momma. Who even says that?"

"Just for that, I'm buying you the frumpiest granny dresses I can find."

"No! No, I take it back. Please, oh please, Kayos. Don't make me wear granny dresses." Nikita linked her fingers under her chin and batted her eyelashes.

"Trouble, I tell ya." Kyllian grinned and stood. "Come on, ladies. Let's hit the road. We still have another eighteen or so hours. We'll need to find somewhere to stop for dinner. Afterward, we can either drive straight through or stop for the night. Up to you two."

Quinn sat in the back with Nikita on the next leg of their trip. The three of them talked about everything and anything that came to mind, getting to know each other. She quickly realized she was in trouble with her little family. Both Kyllian and Nikita were snarky and witty. They bantered back and forth, giving each other shit, and her smile didn't leave Quinn's face. Not even when Nikita asked to listen to the radio. Her daughter couldn't sing a lick either.

During their chat, Nikita told them how her life had been. While Blake doted on her, he was the only one. Her two oldest siblings resented that, and Bethany tried to make up for it by taking their sides. Nikita did most of the cooking, since like she alluded to earlier, Bethany was a shit cook. She loved playing softball, but as she grew older and stronger, she wasn't allowed to play for the school team. Nikita also enjoyed swimming, and Kyllian promised to take her to Lucy's as soon as the weather turned warmer. She loved to read, and Quinn couldn't wait to take her to a book signing. It would be a first for them both. She loved all genres of music, which Kyllian gave a dramatic sigh of relief upon hearing. And like Quinn, the girl could put away the food. Quinn chalked it up to shifter metabolism. When Nikita apologized for eating "like a pig," Quinn oinked at her, smiling.

The more Nikita spoke of her past, the more Quinn realized she had been criticized from those who should have lifted her up. As much as Quinn hated Blake, she was thankful he was the only one who didn't berate Nikita for every little thing. Quinn wanted Kyllian to turn the car around so she could go back and kick all their asses.

After eating dinner, Kyllian asked if they wanted to find somewhere to stop for the night, but it was Nikita who nixed that idea. Holding both their hands outside the restaurant, she smiled and said, "Please, let's just get home."

CHAPTER SEVENTEEN

Kayos

BY THE TIME they got to Quinn's house, Kyllian was beat. Emotionally and physically. If he weren't a shifter, he would have needed to pull over for a nap, but he pushed through, knowing it was what Nikita wanted. Trenton was waiting on the steps, and as soon as Quinn was out of the car, he jogged down to meet her, grabbing her in a fierce hug. He turned her so he could keep one arm around her, and he opened the other one to Nikita.

"Come here and let me hug you," Trenton said. Nikita didn't hesitate. She ran into his embrace, trusting he was as awesome as Quinn said. Kyllian's eyes may have misted a little, but as Sutton always said, there was no shame in a man showing emotion, especially when they were tears of joy. Trenton released Quinn and focused on his granddaughter. "I'm so glad you're here," he whispered against her hair, and Nikita nodded against his chest. Kyllian took advantage and snagged Quinn around the waist from behind so he could both hold her and watch their girl get loved on. Quinn settled her hands on top of his, and the two of them enjoyed the moment.

"Okay, breakfast or sleep?" Trenton asked.

"Food. So much food," Nikita begged, and Trenton laughed. "Although Kayos probably needs sleep first. He didn't get to nap like Mom and I did."

Trenton's eyes widened. It was his first time hearing Nikita claim Quinn as her mother. "Let's head inside, and I'll start on breakfast. I can do eggs and bacon, pancakes, biscuits, whatever you want."

"Yes, please. All the above. I'm a growing girl, and—" Nikita's stomach rumbled. Grinning sheepishly, she pointed at her tummy. "See? Starving."

Trenton wrapped his arm around Nikita's shoulder, leading her inside. "Did they not feed you?" He glanced over his shoulder in a mock scowl. "If this is how you take care of my girl, I'm going to keep her." Nikita beamed at her grandfather.

"Oh, they fed me, but it's been hours since dinner." Once inside the house, Nikita took in her surroundings. "I have a question," she asked as they continued on into the kitchen. Kyllian and Quinn followed, halting at the entrance. Nikita hopped up on a stool at the island as Trenton went to the fridge. "What should I call you? Kyllian's dad is Pops, so I was thinking maybe Grandpa, but you're too young for that." Trenton froze with the door open, and he took a few seconds to not so surreptitiously wipe his eyes. When he turned, the love shining through was thick enough to wrap itself around all of them. Nikita had no idea the gift she was giving the man. She propped her chin on her hand, studying him. "I could call you Shooter, but that might get us some funny looks."

"Shooter?" Trenton frowned, looking to Quinn and Kyllian for help.

"Yeah, because you sniped that bas— that mean uncle who held Mom captive at the cliffs."

"You told her about that?" Trenton asked.

"They tell me everything," Nikita piped in, waving a hand in the air. "I've had enough lies to last a lifetime, and Mom and Kayos promised to never lie to me. Anyway, not Shooter. Hmm. How about Papa T? Unless you prefer Grandpa."

Trenton crossed the few feet and reached across the island, gripping Nikita's hand. "Papa T? I like it because you're right. I'm too young to be called Grandpa. Now, what would you like to drink?"

Nikita slid off the stool and rounded the counter. "How about I help you with breakfast while those two" — Nikita waved her hand in Kyllian and Quinn's direction — "need sleep." She looked at them and said, "Go on, shoo. I need alone time with Papa T," and gave them a wink. Cheeky girl.

"What if I'm hungry?" Kyllian pouted.

Nikita fisted her hips. "Are you?"

"As a matter of fact, I am. And I heard the word biscuits. So if you don't know how to make those, you should let Papa T teach you."

"I see how it is. Gonna use me for slave labor. It's a good thing you're cute."

"Cute? *Cute?*" Kyllian huffed and crossed his arms over his chest. "I am *not* cute." He nudged Quinn. "Tell her."

Quinn laughed, shaking her head. "You are kinda cute in a tatted, badass way."

Kyllian's phone rang. When he saw who was on the other end, he answered it, putting it on speaker. "Mom, please tell my mate and daughter I am not cute." Rory didn't respond, so Kyllian checked to make sure the call hadn't dropped. "Mom?"

After clearing her throat, Rory answered, "I have to agree with your girls. You are being cute."

"Zeus, not you too?"

Rory laughed. "I just called to check in. Make sure you made it to Trenton's safely."

"Yes, ma'am. We got here about fifteen minutes ago."

"Excellent. Your pop and I will hit the road after we stop by your house. Anything else you need?"

"No, thank you. We'll see you in a bit." Kyllian punched the off button and pocketed his phone.

"Your parents are coming?" Nikita asked, her face lit like it was Christmas morning.

"Yep. I talked to them last night while you were snoring. Almost couldn't hear them over the noise."

Nikita glared at him. "I do not snore."

Kyllian, keeping a straight face, nodded. "Do too. In fact, I'm worried about you. Might have to get Rev to check you out. See if there's something wrong up there." He twirled his finger in the direction of her face.

"Mom? You seriously mated this one? He's rude and a lying liar who lies."

Quinn had her lips curled in, but her body was shaking. Trenton's eyes were on Kyllian, something warm shining his direction. Kyllian tugged Quinn's ponytail, then kissed her temple. "I'm going to grab our bags out of the car and take a much-needed shower. I'll leave the three of you to breakfast."

"I don't snore!" Nikita called to Kyllian's back.

"You kind of do, but it's just little snuffles," Quinn said. "It's adorable."

"Thank you. Now, breakfast because starving here."

Kyllian took his time going out to the car. He had spoken to his parents on the drive while Quinn and Nikita slept. Trenton and Sutton were the ones who planned on his parents coming to visit so soon, and Kyllian was glad for it. He didn't want them to have to wait on meeting his girls. He sent Sutton a text requesting they stop and grab a few helmets in different sizes. He wanted to be able to take them out on his bike. He also texted Hayden and put in an order for a sidecar and told him how he wanted it painted. Hayden promised to put everything aside and make it priority. Knowing his mother, Rory would want to take Nikita shopping. Kyllian was okay with that because he hated malls with a passion. He would need to assess Nikita's willingness to go back to a mall so soon, but knowing his girl, she wouldn't think twice about it. Sutton and Trenton could visit while Kyllian took Quinn out for a ride.

As much as he wanted Quinn naked in the shower with him, he left her alone to be with her daughter and dad. Kyllian took his time under the hot water, jerking off while thinking of his mate's mouth wrapped around his dick. She was too enticing, even doing nothing more than breathing, and imagining her on her knees got him off in record time. They really needed to find property and get that large house started ASAP.

249

"Biscuits!" Nikita's mitt-covered hand pulled a pan out of the oven when he walked into the kitchen. "But you don't get any," she added, smirking.

"Yeah? Then you don't get the surprise my parents are bringing."

Nikita dropped the pan on the counter and whirled around. "Did I say no biscuits? I meant all the biscuits. Buttered? Jelly? How would you like them, oh father of mine?" She hugged the mitt to her chest.

Kyllian sucked in a breath. This kid was going to be the death of him. He figured she was joking, but still, he wanted her to call him dad. Wanted her to come to him when she needed guidance. He wanted her to know she was loved for more than her dire genes.

When he didn't answer, Quinn came to the rescue. "Actually, he likes to pile them high with bacon and eggs with blackberry jam on the side." She crossed the kitchen, pushing a mug of coffee into his hands. "Breathe, Baby," she whispered.

Kyllian took the offering in one hand and gripped Quinn's nape in the other. He pressed a quick kiss of thanks to her lips. Nikita helped Trenton get the food on the table with ease proving she hadn't lied about doing the cooking in her old life. Kyllian refused to say "at home" because her home was with him and Quinn. While they dug into their food, Trenton spent most of his time staring at the girl. Kyllian wasn't the only one smitten. Nikita was a charmer. Witty and sassy.

Quinn showed Nikita around while Kyllian helped Trenton clean up from breakfast. "Thank you," Trenton said while loading the dishwasher. "All I've ever wanted was for Quinn to be happy, and you've made that happen. I can't tell you the last time I heard her laugh, and Nikita? Goddess that girl is something. She reminds me of Quinn when she was younger. Before… Well, you know."

"I do know. And I'm the one who's happy. I'm thankful Pop chose me to watch over Quinn when you called. He could have chosen any of the Hounds, but he picked me. If I didn't know better, I'd think he was psychic."

"Or maybe he knows you better than you think. He and I talked at length last night. He said you've been in your head more than usual lately, and he wanted to give you something, or someone, else to focus on. It just worked out you were Quinn's destined mate." Trenton was quiet a few minutes as they finished up setting the kitchen back to rights. When laughter rang out from upstairs, Trenton smiled. "It's funny how life can change on a dime. Talk to me, Son. How are you feeling about going from being a bachelor with no strings to being a mate and father in less than a week?"

Kyllian's heart warmed at the honorific. Trenton Shepherd was a good man, and Kyllian was honored. "I never thought I could be this happy. I've watched all my brothers find their own mates recently, and honestly, I was envious. It wasn't so bad before Hayden found Sadie and Mateo because he and I spent most of our time together. I'm always welcome at their home, but I don't want to encroach when they're still finding their feet. Now I'm the one who gets to come home every night to my mate and child. I know Nikita's practically grown, but…" Kyllian paused when Quinn and Nikita came downstairs.

A monitor beeped, and Nikita looked around. "What's that?"

"That would be your other grandparents at the gate," Trenton said. "Come on, I'll show you." Kyllian and Quinn followed behind and waited while Trenton pointed to the portable screen on the counter. "Always check the monitor to see who's at the gate. If it's someone you don't know, come get one of us."

Nikita stared at the image, grinning. "May I?' Trenton gestured for her to continue, and Nikita pressed the talk button. "Shepherd residence. How may I direct your call?"

Sutton's grin was wide. "You may direct me to my granddaughter. I come bearing gifts."

Nikita bounced on her feet. "Let 'em in!" Trenton pressed the button to open the gate, and Nikita took off toward the front door, not waiting on the rest of them. She rested against the porch rail, leaning over, bouncing on the balls of her feet. When the SUV came into view, she froze.

Kyllian was at her side in a heartbeat. "What's wrong?"

"What if they don't like me?" she whispered.

"Did you not see the smile on Pop's face when you answered the buzzer?" Kyllian set his hands on her shoulders and squeezed. "Trouble, they already love you just as much as your mom, Papa T, and I do. Never doubt that."

"Kyllian Lazlo, you turn her loose. Gram needs a hug," Rory called out. Nikita was off like a shot. Rory wrapped Nikita in her arms, pressing kisses to her hair and whispering in her ear. Nikita nodded furiously at whatever it was Rory said as they rocked side to side. Sutton rounded the vehicle and waited his turn. Quinn stepped up next to Kyllian, watching the scene play out. When Rory passed Nikita off to Sutton, she turned her focus to Quinn. Rory smiled, walking up the steps. Holding out her arms, she told Quinn, "Come here and let me look at you." Quinn placed her hand in Rory's, and Rory brushed a strand of hair off her face. "Welcome to the family."

"Dad, look!" Nikita called out. She was wearing a pair of riding goggles, grinning like a loon.

"Dad?" Rory whispered.

"I told you she was something else." Kyllian laughed as Nikita helped Sutton with their bags, goggles firmly in place.

Nikita bounded up the steps, stopping in front of Kyllian. "Now all I need is a bomber hat, and I'll be set."

"Don't you think you might need a heavy jacket and boots? I know you have your own fur, but you'd look funny riding a motorcycle as a wolf."

"There you go being cute again. Gram said she'd take me shopping for whatever I need." Nikita went from bubbly to serious from one second to the next. "Are those things I really need? I don't want to ask for too much."

"Let me tell you something," Rory interrupted. "We have eighteen years to make up for, so nothing is too much where you're concerned. Besides, if you're going to ride, you need good protective gear. You and your mom both. I was thinking we could visit today and let everyone just chill. You've all had an exciting few days, and Kyllian looks dead on his feet. Tomorrow, we'll head to the mall unless that's too soon. If you don't want to step foot in another mall, we'll go to specialty stores, or heck, we can get everything online and have it delivered."

Kyllian could kiss his mother for being in tune with not only Nikita, but him as well. So he did. He pressed his lips to her temple. "You're not wrong. How about you and Pop visit with Trenton and Trouble while Quinn and I take a nap?"

Nikita snorted, and Kyllian shoved her playfully. "Behave."

With eyes shining behind the goggles, Nikita saluted. "Aye, aye, Captain."

Sutton clapped Kyllian on the shoulder on his way past. Everyone filed into the house, and with Nikita safely with her grandparents, Kyllian led Quinn upstairs. He bypassed the room he stayed in when he first arrived and led her to her bedroom. Closing the door, he leaned against it. "As much as I want to toss you on the bed and do wicked things to you, I do need to sleep."

"Then let's sleep." Quinn turned the bed down, stripped to her underwear, and climbed on, scooting to the far side.

"Not helping, Pretty Lady." Kyllian removed his clothes as well, leaving on his briefs, and lay down beside his mate. He pulled her to him, and Quinn snuggled against his back. "No wiggling," he commanded, and Quinn held still. It didn't matter. Having her against him was temptation enough, but

254

Kyllian willed his dick to stand down. He slid his arm around her, resting his hand on her chest between her breasts and neck. With the steady beats of her heart beneath his fingertips and the scent of her skin in his nose, Kyllian fell right to sleep.

When he woke several hours later, he was in the same position, but he was alone. Kyllian didn't like it. He had planned on spending time with Quinn's bare skin, mapping it with his fingers and tongue. Rolling to his back, he reached out with his senses. The house was quiet, but voices sounded outside the window. Kyllian stood and stretched, then walked over to look out over the backyard. Sutton and Trenton stood off to the side talking, their attention focused on the woods. They didn't appear to be on guard, just alert. Wondering where the females were, Kyllian dressed, ready to get downstairs and join them.

"Good nap, Son?" Sutton asked.

"I would have been better if I didn't wake alone," he groused.

"I understand that, but you'll have to get used to sharing your mate."

"Speaking of…"

Sutton inclined his head toward the woods. "Nikita wanted to see Rory's Lion, and Rory wanted to see the girls' Wolves, so they all took to their fur."

"We should join them," he suggested. Toeing off his boots, he said, "Shall we?"

"We shall, but don't you want to strip in the house?" Sutton asked.

Kyllian engaged his Eagle's eyes, searching the trees. "Nope. They aren't anywhere close. Come on. If

255

you hurry, you both can shift before they see us."

Sutton shrugged and began removing his clothes too. When Trenton didn't move to join them, Kyllian urged the male, "You too, Trenton. This is family playtime."

Trenton appeared stunned, and Sutton prodded his friend. "He's right. You need this too. Come on, old friend." That was all the encouragement he needed. The three of them were naked and shifted in record time. Kyllian didn't wait for them. He turned his Lion loose and bounded for the familiar path. It didn't take him long to find his two dire wolves. Nikita was chasing after her mother, but Rory was nowhere in sight. Quinn skidded to a stop, but Nikita kept running toward him. Kyllian braced for the hit, and when it came, he rolled with the smaller wolf. Nikita yipped, and Kyllian huffed against her muzzle. He shook out his mane, hitting her in the face, and she yipped again, then nipped at his front leg before darting off. Kyllian chased after her. She was quick, but she was no match for his larger size. Just when she was within his reach, a golden body dropped from somewhere blocking his path. Rory's Lion met him head-on, keeping her body between him and Nikita. He growled playfully, and Nikita trotted up beside Rory, leaning into her.

Sutton, on silent feet, snuck up behind Nikita and swiped at her bushy tail with a large paw. Nikita jumped, spinning around, and seeing who tagged her, lunged. Kyllian rarely got to enjoy the playful side of his parents, but they were putting on a show for their new granddaughter. Trenton got in on the action. While Nikita was focused on wrestling with Sutton, he bumped against her, sending her rolling. She shifted within seconds, laughing hard.

When she caught her breath, she called out, "Mom, help. They're ganging up on me." And just as quickly, she was back in her fur. Quinn's mighty animal stalked toward the grandfathers. At the last second, she turned and jumped on Kyllian. He let her roll him. She was strong, but not strong enough to take him down. Within seconds, the smaller dire wolf was nipping at his tail. Kyllian let out a displeased rumble that didn't deter either of his girls. The six of them spent another hour playing and running until Nikita shifted and declared she was starving.

"Since you all can't shift without losing your clothes, why don't you all go get dressed? Mom and I will wait 'til the coast is clear. Wait. Let's think about this. Papa T, you go first. Then you go look out the front window so Gram and Pops can get dressed. Dad can go next. I know we're all shifters and nudity shouldn't be a thing, but yeah... Can't say I wanna see y'all in the buff." When nobody moved, she rolled her eyes. "Papa T? I'm wasting away over here." Trenton's smaller wolf charged Nikita, sliding to a stop, inches from her legs. She jumped back, laughing. He licked her hand, then took off through the woods. As instructed, they took turns heading back to change. Once inside, Nikita went to the fridge and began pulling items out.

Quinn took Kyllian by the hand, leaving the others to sort out dinner. She led him to her office where she sat down behind the computer. "I had an alert come in earlier, but I didn't have the heart to work when she was so excited about playing."

Kyllian sat in the chair opposite the desk and admired his mate as she worked. While she was focused on her laptop, he pulled out his phone and shot a text to Lucy, asking how things were going with the Stone Clan. Not expecting an immediate answer, he went back to staring at Quinn. What a difference a couple weeks made. The last time he sat in that spot, she was stoic and aloof. Never smiling. Sadness rolling off her in waves. Now? She was relaxed while typing away. When she glanced up, she grinned. "What?"

"Just happy." And that was the truth. Before meeting Quinn, Kyllian was content if a little lonely. He had wondered what it would be like having a mate, but he never dreamed how complete he would be.

After dinner, Sutton pulled Kyllian to the side and handed him an envelope. He opened it and pulled out two documents and two cards. The papers were Nikita's new birth certificates. One with the last name Shepherd and the other stating she was a Lazlo. Kyllian knew which one he hoped she chose, but it was her decision. Being shifters, he and Quinn didn't have to get married. They had the mate bond securing their future. But he would be lying to himself and anyone he told if he said he didn't care if she remained a Shepherd. He wanted the three of them to be a true family. With the birth certificate and Social Security cards, he wouldn't need to adopt Nikita. They could skip the formalities and legal hassle.

"Whatcha got here?"

Kyllian had been so in his head he didn't hear her approach. Quinn studied him from across the room.

His Gryphon rumbled, and Kyllian figured it was speaking to her Wolf. Quinn tilted her head to the side, eyes unfocused. She smiled and stood, joining them.

"We have something for you," Quinn said. She took the documents from him, sifted through the options, and handed one certificate and one card back. With the other two, she held them out to their girl. Trenton and Rory looked on as Nikita studied the certificate.

With tears in her eyes, she asked, "Really?"

"If that's what you want." Shaking the envelope, he told her, "You have options. If you'd rather have Shepherd as your last name, that's your choice."

Nikita took a deep breath, and Kyllian held his. "Is this okay with you, Mom?"

Quinn cupped Nikita's cheek, wiping away a stray tear. "I think it's perfect."

"Then we should have a wedding. I know you're mates and all, but if I'm going to be a Lazlo, you should too."

Kyllian couldn't agree more.

CHAPTER EIGHTEEN

Nikita

NIKITA INSISTED ON making cupcakes to celebrate. Papa T was eating healthy, but one cupcake wouldn't hurt. When he told her he didn't have cake mix, she told him she didn't need it. She busied herself in the kitchen with Rory helping. While Nikita mixed, Rory talked about the twins and their antics. Nikita couldn't wait to meet the two rambunctious boys. Hearing about them had her a little melancholy. She missed Jake and his sweet smile. With Kyllian wiping the packs' memories of her, Jake wouldn't miss her. Wouldn't remember all the time they spent together with Nikita reading to him. Shifting and wrestling together. He was the only one not intimidated by her larger animal. She hoped time would lessen the pain, and that somewhere in the back of his mind, he would somehow recall having a big sister who loved him.

Even with that bit of sadness, that day was the best one of Nikita's life. Only riding her dad's Gryphon was more fun. *Her dad*. It was crazy how Kyllian already felt like more of a father than Blake ever did. Blake had loved her, but Kyllian adored her. When it was time for bed, Nikita took her new documents to the room she was staying in and placed them on the dresser. Somehow, Kyllian had made it so she was officially his. She figured her cousin Lucy had something to do with it. He had talked about his niece more than once. Nikita knew there was more to her story than he shared, but what he had said was enough to know Lucy was a brilliant hacker. After taking a shower, Nikita climbed under the covers and imagined what that would be like. She'd mentioned helping her mom with the family business, or learning from Bishop, but now Nikita thought she might like to learn from her new cousin. A cousin who was mated to a Gargoyle.

While eating cupcakes, Lucy called to fill them in on what was happening in New Atlanta. Nikita had listened to a story that could have been a thrilling novel or movie. Rory had cursed without apology when Lucy mentioned being shot at. Then she thanked Zeus that both Lucy and the human who took the bullet were both okay. After the call, both Sutton and Rory answered her million and one questions. Nikita often imagined there were other shifters in the world. Why would there only be wolves? And the past week proved her right. Wolves, Gryphons, and Gargoyles probably weren't the only ones either. And now that her parents were together, surely they would have more kids. Would they be wolves, Gryphons, or a hybrid of the two? Like with Lucy and Tamian. Would their children be a blend? Nikita fell asleep thinking of all the possibilities.

The next week was a little crazy. Gram took Nikita shopping, going overboard with clothes and shoes. Her mom worked when necessary, which meant Papa T did as well. Pops had brought helmets for her and her mom, and with the new boots and thick jacket she got on her shopping spree, Nikita was ready to ride. While Quinn worked, Kyllian took Nikita riding. When it was her mom's turn to go for a spin, Nikita spent time in the kitchen with Rory after she got her schoolwork done. Kyllian had called the school, weaving a tale that allowed her to finish out the year remotely. Nikita and Tarryn talked often and video chatted every night before bed. Nikita couldn't share with her best friend how Kyllian made everything happen, and that sucked.

Gram and Pops stayed with them for a week. Nikita would have been sad about them leaving the next day, but Quinn was ready for them to move to Kyllian's house and begin the next phase of their lives together.

Nikita woke that next morning to her dad cursing loudly. She rolled out of bed and dressed in a new pair of jeans and sweater. She had loved shopping with Rory who let her choose whatever style she wanted. Nikita had been tempted to buy one "hoochie" outfit to tease Kyllian with, but in the end, she didn't want to waste the money. When she got downstairs, Kyllian was hugging Quinn.

"What's wrong? Did something happen?" she asked, approaching them.

"The police are here," Rory answered.

"What? Why?"

"That's what we're waiting to find out," Papa T said, looking out the front window.

When the patrol car parked at the top of the driveway, Papa T opened the door, and everyone else followed him onto the porch. It was brisk outside, and Nikita wished she'd taken the time to put her shoes on. The cop got out, his hand on his pistol.

"Quinn Shepherd?"

Her mom stepped forward. "I'm Quinn."

"You need to come with me for questioning."

Kyllian tugged Quinn behind him. "What's this about?"

"Miss Shepherd is under investigation for kidnapping Nikita Aberdine."

"Kidnapping? How can my mom kidnap me? I'm her child. And my last name is Lazlo, not Aberdine." Nikita closed the distance and grabbed her mom's hand.

It was then Mercy got out of the backseat of the patrol car. "See? I told you. They brainwashed her. Her dad is beside himself. You can call him. He'll tell you."

Rory growled, and if Sutton hadn't grabbed her arm, Nikita had a feeling there would be a fierce lioness ripping Mercy apart.

Kyllian relaxed his stance. "Officer, I can assure you I am Nikita's dad, but if you won't take my word for it, call this man she claims is Nikita's father. Ask him for yourself."

Mercy fisted her hands, her body shaking with rage. "You wiped his mind, didn't you?"

"I have no idea what you're talking about. Nikita, honey, go grab your birth certificate." Nikita did as he asked, grabbing both the paper and her shoes while in her room. She might be a shifter, but Upstate New

263

York was still cold this time of year. When she returned, the second officer had Mercy by the arm, and her eyes were wild, flashing with the yellow of her Wolf. Nikita handed Kyllian the paper, then pulled on her socks and shoes.

Kyllian strode down the steps but stopped a few feet away. The cop was on the phone, his eyes trained on Mercy. "You have one daughter and her name's Carrie? And she's thirteen? I see. Yes, thank you. I'm sorry for the misunderstanding." He thumbed his phone off and took the paper Kyllian offered, proving her parentage. While he looked it over, Mercy became more agitated, yelling about mind manipulation. Nikita's grandparents surrounded her, forming a protective barrier. She wasn't worried, though. Nikita had seen Mercy's animal enough times to know she was no match for a dire wolf, much less two of them and three Gryphons. Papa T would be able to hold his own as well.

"I apologize for the disturbance." The cop handed the certificate back before addressing his partner. "Read this woman her rights for filing false charges."

That was the moment Mercy truly lost it. She jerked away from the officer, shifting and shredding her clothes. "What the fuck?" The cop who'd been holding her stepped back, his eyes filled with fear.

"Oh, hell no." Rory pulled loose from Sutton, shifting and ripping through her own sweater and jeans. Her tawny fur rippled with the change, and within seconds, she was on Mercy, taking her down.

"Rory, no!" Sutton then shifted, going after his mate.

The cops both had their weapons out at that point, and Nikita yelled to Kyllian, "Dad, they have guns. Voodoo them!"

"Everyone freeze," he yelled. "Drop the guns." The officers obeyed, and Mercy stopped thrashing about. Sutton roared, and Rory released the hold she had on Mercy's Wolf. She turned on Sutton, baring her sharp teeth. When he growled, she stalked back toward the house but not before she bumped into him hard. Rory stalked up the steps and sat beside Nikita, nudging her with her big head. Nikita knelt beside the Lioness and wrapped her arm around her thick neck. That was how a grandmother should behave.

"Thank you," Nikita whispered. Rory chuffed in response.

Quinn made her way to where Mercy was sprawled out on the driveway. "Shift, now." Nikita shivered at her mother's alpha voice and wasn't surprised when Mercy obeyed. "Get up," Quinn commanded. Pushing to her feet, Mercy glared, her naked body on display. Sutton's Lion took a step back and sat down, his tail swishing behind him. "I should gut you where you stand, but you're not worth the trouble of cleaning blood off the concrete." Instead of letting her claws out, Quinn punched Mercy in the face, knocking her back to the ground. "That's for Nikita, you bitch."

"Go, Mom!" Nikita jumped up, pumping a fist in the air.

Quinn grinned at her as she walked over to stand with Kyllian. "Voodoo time?"

Kyllian winked at Nikita. "Voodoo time."

After Kyllian wiped the cops' memories, he sent them on their way, keeping Mercy with them. "Now, what to do with you?"

Mercy spat. "Fuck you."

Rory roared, and Sutton growled. Papa T had been silent up until that point, sticking close to Nikita. He patted her on the shoulder, then joined the others on the driveway. "You came to our home under false pretenses. You led my daughter to the RC pack and put her life in jeopardy. You tried to kidnap my grandchild. Tell me why you think we should spare your life?"

"It was supposed to be me." Mercy thumped her chest. "I was supposed to be the Alpha mate and have his kids, but Quinn came along and took everything from me."

Quinn let her claws out. "No, I didn't. Blake was already mated to Bethany, so if anyone should feel slighted, it's me. Stewart's the one who went back on his promise to your parents. You should have left when they did and started over. You've held onto your anger all these years and directed it at me and my daughter when Blake's the one who did you wrong. Did Scott really betray me back at the store, or was that all you?"

Mercy shifted her eyes when she said, "Scott wanted his revenge too."

"She's lying." Nikita rubbed Rory's head before approaching Mercy. "Scott loved Quinn. After all these years, he still loved her. It's why he refused to mate with you."

Mercy's eyes flashed, but Nikita wasn't scared. She was a dire wolf, so she flashed her own, letting her canines elongate. "Or did you forget that Scott is Tarryn's uncle?" Nikita rolled her head side to side and bounced on her feet.

"Easy, Trouble." Kyllian closed the distance between them, standing at her back with his hands on her shoulders. "Regardless of why you lost your fucking mind, the fact remains you did. You messed with the wrong family. If it were up to me, I'd turn my mom loose on you." Rory got to her feet, and Mercy took a step back.

"Keep her away from me."

Kyllian removed his hands from Nikita's shoulders, crossed one arm over his body, resting the opposite elbow on it, and tapping his lips. "I tell you what. I'll let you go, but—"

"But you're going to erase my memories." Mercy jutted her chin. "Get on with it then." She planted her feet and fisted her hands.

"Where's your car?"

"My... It's at the police station."

Kyllian reached for Nikita's hand, and she took it. He looked down at her, searching her eyes for something. She didn't know what, but she trusted him more than anyone in her life. When he smiled, it was soft. "Mercy, you will forget Nikita and Quinn. You will return to your pack where you will watch over Jake. You will make sure he is treated fairly. If it ever seems like his parents, siblings, or grandmother are influencing him in any way that is negative, you will come to New Troy and find any Hound of Zeus. They aren't hard to spot. Just look for a biker with a Hounds patch on their back. You will go forward and live a peaceful existence, striving to make the world a better place. Walk to the end of the driveway. Wait there until a ride share picks you up."

Nikita snickered. "Aren't you forgetting something?" When Kyllian frowned, Nikita rolled her eyes. "She's naked."

"Oh. Well, that could present a problem. Run in the house and grab her some sweats and a T-shirt."

Nikita saluted him and took off jogging inside. The sooner she got Mercy dressed, the sooner they'd be rid of her. She opened the door and allowed Pops and Gram to walk through first. Their clothes were also in tatters outside. Five minutes later, Mercy walked out of sight and out of their lives.

Once everyone was in their skin and dressed, Nikita plopped down on the sofa and blew out a breath. "I don't know about y'all, but I've had all the excitement I can handle. I'm going to sit right here and veg, if that's okay with everyone."

Rory and Sutton sat on either side of her. "Can we veg with you?" Gram asked.

Nikita rolled her head to look at her grandmother. "I thought you had to go back home today?"

"Nah. Tomorrow is soon enough." Rory patted her leg, and Nikita leaned against her arm.

"Sounds good to me."

Quinn

QUINN AND TRENTON sat in the office talking business while Kyllian took Nikita for a ride. Her girl was born to be on the back of a motorcycle. Hayden sent updates on the sidecar he was designing, and Quinn couldn't wait for Nikita to see it. Quinn was excited for it to be finished so the three of them could ride together. Kyllian promised as soon as it was done, they would go on a family ride. She was looking forward to meeting his brothers and their mates and kids as well as spending more time with Rory. Kyllian's mom had stepped in the last week, basking Quinn in her love.

"I'm going to sell the house," Trenton said, bringing her back to the business at hand. They had been discussing how they were going to work separately with Quinn moving to Kyllian's until they could build a house.

"Really?" She had hoped he would move to New Troy instead of staying in their huge house alone.

"I have no reason to stay here with you moving. I'm not going to be over an hour away from my girls. I was thinking I'd get something similar so you have an office and Nikita has her own bedroom for when she visits."

"Dad, that's a great idea. Nikita is adamant she learns more about computers so she can help me out. Kyllian offered to turn one of his spare bedrooms into a temporary spot while our house is being built, but I like the thought of still having an office wherever you are."

"Did you decide on the property?"

"Yes. It's not too far from Ryker's. We'll have

almost thirty acres, most of it wooded. It's not as much as we have here, but there's enough for us to be able to shift when we want. I'm so happy you're coming with us."

"Me too. It also puts me closer to Sutton. I've missed my friend all these years. We talk on the phone, but I'd like to start getting out more."

"I'm sorry."

"Quinn, I didn't mean—"

"No, I know you didn't, but I'm the reason you don't have any close friends. I'm the reason you stayed holed up in this huge house. You have no idea how much I appreciate you. And goddess, I love you." Quinn stood and rounded the desk, kneeling next to his chair. She took his hand in hers. "You are the best father in the world. You deserved better than a punk teenager who lost her shit. And before you go blaming yourself for that, don't. You were a single father doing the best he could, and it really was enough. I just didn't realize it. I want to be the best mother to my daughter. Although Nikita's an adult, I still want to be there for her. I want to make up for lost time, so I'm happy she wants to learn the business. Instead of going off to college, she'll be with me. I know it's selfish, but I want that so badly. Having you close will be the icing on the cake. It's been you and me for so long, and I'm not ready to give that up."

Trenton pressed his palm to her cheek. "I'm not either. Having Nikita in the business is a great idea. She can learn what you do, and in turn, you can start helping me in the field. I will want to retire at some point, and when that day comes, I will turn the whole thing over to the two of you."

"And I'll gladly take over at that point. You deserve to live for yourself now. Who knows? Maybe you'll meet a lovely lady to spend time with."

Trenton shook his head. "No. Your mother was my destined mate."

Quinn rose and returned to her chair. "I get that, Dad. You'll never have another one, but that doesn't mean you can't find a companion to go to dinner with. Take in shows or travel with. If Mom hadn't been gone almost twenty years, then yes, I would say it's too soon. But it has been that long. Too long to be alone."

"I haven't been alone. I've had you."

Quinn smiled softly. "We both know it's not the same. I want you to promise me you'll at least think about it."

Trenton sighed. "I promise, but please don't push. Things will be hectic over the next few months with both of us moving and setting up a new place. I also plan on spending as much time with Trouble as possible." Trenton had adopted Kyllian's nickname for Nikita.

"She is kind of smitten with her Papa T." With Nikita's prior home life being ingrained, it took time for her to realize she wasn't expected to be the cook and maid. Nikita had taken over cooking, promising she didn't feel it was what they expected. She truly enjoyed being in the kitchen, especially when Trenton acted as her sous chef. They made a wonderful team. Quinn appreciated not having the responsibility. It gave her more time with her mate. So far, everything was perfect. The only issue Quinn hadn't addressed

271

fully was Kyllian returning to Dominion. He hadn't brought it up, but she had overheard a couple of phone conversations when he thought she was out of earshot. One was from his buddy Gunnar who had stepped in when Kyllian needed the time off. The other was from the owner of the club asking when he was coming back. Kyllian told them both he needed more time and explained he had a new mate and daughter to focus on.

Quinn didn't want him to resent her. She didn't want to take away something he felt was a service to others. That was another reason she was ready to move. She needed to meet Charlie and Wynter. Find out how they handled their males being part of the lifestyle. Charlie did scenes with Spyder, but Quinn wasn't a sub. She wasn't into pain other than spankings as she'd recently discovered. Living with her father and Nikita didn't offer much privacy, so they hadn't been able to really explore things in the bedroom. If Quinn joined him at the club, they could use one of the back rooms and get as loud as they wanted. That alone was reason enough for her to at least see what it was all about. As soon as they got her things moved, she was going to offer to go with him.

The gate alarm beeped, and Quinn's heart sped as it did every time she saw her mate and daughter together. Nikita adored Kyllian. If she didn't know how special he was, Quinn might be a little jealous of their bond. For all she'd been through, Nikita was a light in the darkest of times. She drew everyone into her orbit, but no one loved her as fiercely as Kyllian did. For that, Quinn was grateful. She needed a father who wanted her for the snarky, brilliant teen she was, not what was in her DNA.

The last couple weeks had been a learning curve for all of them. As per Nikita's wish, Kyllian called the school, explained how she needed to finish the school year online, and they accommodated her. She was still on course to graduate top of her class but refused to return and walk across the stage with her classmates.

The front door opened, and Nikita bounded into the office, her cheeks flush from the crisp air. She wore the aviator cap Kyllian had found to go under her helmet, her goggles perched on top. Nikita removed her heavy leather jacket and draped it over the empty chair, settling on Trenton's lap.

"What's the skinny?" she asked.

"Your bony butt," Trenton responded.

"Ha!" Nikita squirmed, digging said butt on his thighs, and he promptly dumped her off onto the floor.

Kyllian entered the office, one eyebrow raised. "Trouble, why are you on the floor?" He continued past the two of them and took his place behind Quinn's chair, leaning over to kiss her temple.

Nikita scrambled to her feet, taking the chair next to Trenton. She pointed at him. "Ask Papa T. It's all his fault."

"Right." Kyllian pulled at Quinn's ponytail, carding his fingers through it. "Pop called while we were out. He and Mom will be here in about an hour with the truck." Quinn wasn't taking much with her, but it was enough they needed a rental van. Sutton offered to bring it so they wouldn't have to return it to New Utica afterward.

"Oh, I need to grab our clothes out of the dryer."

Nikita popped up and took off, snagging her jacket as she went. That was another thing the girl insisted on helping with. She didn't mind doing laundry, but she hated dusting with a passion. Kyllian, for whatever reason, didn't mind the task. He said it was soothing. Quinn had a feeling he did it so she and Nikita didn't have to.

Everything okay? Kyllian asked through their bond.

"Dad has decided to move with us. Well not in with us, but he's looking for a house close to your parents'."

"That's wonderful, Trenton. I know Pop will enjoy having you closer, not to mention the three of us will as well."

"It makes sense. I was telling Quinn I'll find something similar to this house. That way we can still have the business set up the same."

"And that sounds even better. With all the changes, some things need to remain the same. I'm going to go help Trouble with the laundry so we're ready to pack the truck when it gets here." Kyllian tugged Quinn's ponytail before he strode from the room. Quinn eyed his firm backside as he left, and Trenton cleared his throat.

"What? He has a nice ass."

"TMI, Quinnlyn. TMI."

CHAPTER NINETEEN

Kayos

THE GATE ALARM beeped, and before Kyllian could check the monitor, Nikita yelled, "I got it." Quinn and Trenton had disappeared upstairs to go through a few of Finola's things Trenton wanted her to have, so Kyllian and Nikita had offered to clean up after lunch.

"Uncle Ryker's with them," Nikita announced, surprising Kyllian. Nikita and Quinn had met most of the family via video calls. Hayden, Sadie, and Mateo had made the trip to meet them in person, but everyone else had decided to wait until they got moved.

Kyllian followed Nikita outside, and as soon as the vehicle stopped, she was pulling open Rory's door. "Gram! I missed you." She didn't let Rory get out. Instead, she leaned in to hug her grandmother.

Sutton angled out of the van and sidled up to Kyllian. "That will never get old."

Kyllian had to agree. Seeing his girl so excited was a joy to behold. Ryker and Mac got out of the SUV and joined them. "Mac, this is a pleasant surprise." Kyllian opened his arms, and his niece walked into his embrace. She was still finding her place in the world, but she was no longer hesitant with all the touchy-feeliness of family.

"You're different," she muttered against his chest.

"Yeah? How so?"

Mac stepped back and angled her head, studying his face. "You're smiling."

"I smile," he scoffed.

"No, you don't. Not unless the twins are around. Or you're antagonizing Uncle Hay. This is a real, honest-to-Zeus, not fake smile."

Nikita, hand-in-hand with Rory, joined them. "Hey, Mac. It's good to finally meet you in person."

Mac pointed at Nikita. "And this is why. Oh, and her." She looked over Kyllian's shoulder. He already knew Quinn was there. He could feel her in their mate bond. That had taken some getting used to. Some of the couples had stronger bonds than others, but he and Quinn could mind-speak. The first time he heard her voice in his head, he thought it was his Gryphon, but the words weren't any his beast would have said. When he mentioned it, she explained that wolves could communicate in their shifted form, so she figured it was a byproduct of being destined mates, shifted or not.

Kyllian held out his hand for Quinn. When she and Trenton joined them, he made the official introductions. Mac was a few years older than Nikita, but his girl latched on to her new cousin. Being wolfkind, Nikita was tactile, and she didn't hesitate to hug Mac. When she pulled away, she touched the strand of red in Mac's hair.

"This is so cool. Mom, I want to streak my hair."

Quinn rolled with it. "It's your hair."

"Yes! Mac, where did you have this done? You have to go with me. Make sure I get the right color. Red looks great with your skin tone, but I think I want something different. Maybe purple." Nikita hooked her arm through Mac's and led her toward the house asking a million and one questions. If that had been a few months ago, Mac would probably be mortified, but the mates had been spending more time with the young woman, bringing her out of her shell. Elijah's love helped too.

"What just happened?" Ryker asked.

"Trouble," all the others answered in unison.

With six adults loading the van, it didn't take long to be packed and ready to hit the road. Nikita opted to ride with Mac and Ryker instead of with Sutton and Rory like originally planned. Quinn hugged her dad, the two of them shedding a few tears.

"I'll be fine, Sweetheart. I'm going to be busy packing. I want to be ready as soon as I find a new place."

"Promise you'll eat healthy," Quinn begged.

"I promise. Nikita left several meals in the freezer, and I do know how to look up recipes. I'll be fine."

Nikita rolled down her window and leaned out. "Mom, chop-chop. Daylight's burning."

Quinn shook her head and hugged Trenton one last time. He brushed a kiss over her temple. "You heard the girl. Chop-chop."

Kyllian handed Quinn her helmet before strapping on his own. They had ridden together several times over the past couple of weeks, and she was a pro at that point. While his bike had a small backrest, it wasn't meant to double someone for long hauls. Hayden had already found Kyllian a larger Harley with a deluxe passenger seat. It had a tour pack as well as hard saddlebags for storage. He planned on taking his girls on many road trips, and they would need the space. Nikita's sidecar was complete and attached to the new bike. Quinn didn't know it was finished. He couldn't wait to surprise them both.

As much as he loved riding with Quinn's arms wrapped around his middle, he was happy when they arrived at his house. Their house. At least for the time being. The property he found was perfect for their need to shift and run. The three of them had pored over house plans similar to what Ryker built for his family. It was larger than they needed, but Kyllian planned on giving Nikita siblings at some point in the future. She admitted to missing Jake. On the rare occasions his girl's mood turned melancholy, it was when she thought about her little brother. If Kyllian could get away with it, he'd kidnap the boy and make him part of their family.

Nikita was the first one out of the car, bouncing on her feet. Kyllian rolled to a stop beside the van and killed the engine. Quinn climbed off first, removing her helmet. She waited with their girl while Kyllian did the same.

"Come on, Dad. I want to see my new room." Rory had let it slip that she had redone one of the rooms for Nikita. Not only that, but his mom, with Kyllian's permission, had enlisted the help of the other mates

278

and turned his bachelor pad into a warm, inviting space for his new family. Rory sent photos by text afterwards, and he was just as excited to see the changes.

"Come on, Trouble. I'll show you and your mom around while the men start unloading the van." Rory led the way, unlocking the door and ushering them and Mac inside. Kyllian took Quinn's helmet before she followed. He placed it on the bike, then went to help his dad and brother.

"Welcome home, Son," Sutton said, opening the door to the van.

"It's good to be home. It'll be even better when we get our new house built."

Kyllian and Ryker compared notes on the house plans and contractors while they hauled boxes and the few pieces of furniture Quinn wanted to bring. The changes to his house were subtle, mostly pops of color added throughout. The one item he noticed right off was the new living room suite. His sofa had seen better days, but it had been good enough for him and Hayden to kick back on and play video games. It had been replaced with a sofa and matching love seat. His leather recliner was off to the side with a quilt draped over the back.

Nikita was on her knees in front of the entertainment center, rifling through the various gaming systems. He stopped and nudged her with his boot. "You like to play?"

"I only got to when I was over at Tarryn's, so I'm not that good."

Kyllian handed the box he was holding to his dad

so he could squat beside her. "Then you'll just have to practice." He tugged on her braid to get her attention. When she looked at him, the tears surprised him. "Hey, come here." When he opened his arms, Nikita lunged at him, sobbing into his chest. Kyllian sat down and settled his girl over his lap, rubbing circles on her back. Quinn rushed into the room and sat down beside them. Rory stared at Nikita's bent head and cursed under her breath. With the exception of when she was thinking of Jake, Nikita hadn't indicated she was anything but happy in the short time she'd been with them. Kyllian had been expecting it to hit her, but it still broke his heart.

"I'm happy." Nikita pulled back and swiped at her face. "I'm so fricking happy, you know? I don't miss my old life. I do miss Tarryn and Jake, but how is it that I'm okay without all the people I grew up around? What does that say about me? About them? I feel guilty that I have this new life. This perfect existence. I was envious of Tarryn and her parents, but then I would feel ashamed of myself. I had a nice house, plenty of food, new clothes even if they weren't the style I would choose for myself. I never went without, but I still wanted something else. Something more. And now I have it. But to get it, Mom was taken, and you were shot. Hell, people died because of me." Nikita tucked her head under Kyllian's chin, and the sobs returned.

Kyllian didn't bother trying to stop his own tears. "No, Sweetheart. People died because of Mercy's need for revenge. Because Blake and his father wanted your mom's dire bloodline. Because Dennis was an asshole. None of what happened was your fault. You never would have run away to find Quinn if Blake had been honest. If his mother hadn't wanted her own revenge. How you turned out so good, so loving, so smart is beyond me. This life you have now is the one you deserved all along. You deserve this and so much more, and I vow to you now, I will do everything in my power to ensure you have it all."

"I love you. You don't know how much I love you and Mom."

"I think I have a pretty good idea because, Trouble? We love you that much more. You are the daughter I never knew I wanted. You have brought so much joy to my world in such a short time."

Quinn leaned in. "You are the daughter I thought about every day for eighteen years but was too afraid to go back for. I loved you from the first moment I held you and I never stopped. If anyone is undeserving, it's me. But I'm grateful for you. So very thankful you did run away. I hate what you went through. Not just after you left the pack, but how you were treated over the years. If I could go back and tell my younger self anything, it would be to stay and fight. Stay until I found you. We can't change the past, and regrets cause nothing but heartache. You're here now. We're a family. Not just the three of us, but Papa T and all the Lazlos. I'm going to thank the goddess every day for this gift. The gift of my mate and my beautiful baby girl." Nikita released Kyllian and turned to her mother. The three of them sat quietly afterwards, letting all the words sink in.

When the tears dried and they climbed to their feet, Nikita nodded to herself as though she had made a decision. "We need to have a party with all the Lazlos and Papa T too. Mom and I need to officially meet our family." She patted Kyllian on the chest. "And you need to make that happen. I'm going to wash my face now, and Mom? You need to come with me. You look like a raccoon." Not waiting on Quinn, Nikita headed down the hallway to the half bath. Quinn thumped her head on Kyllian's chest. Her body was shaking, and Kyllian worried she was crying again. Then she snorted. Kyllian hugged her tightly and laughed along with her, muttering, "That's our Trouble."

Quinn

THE MEETING-THE-LAZLOS PARTY was in full swing. Lucy's home was utter chaos, and Quinn had never been happier. When Kyllian called to thank his niece for getting Nikita's paperwork handled so quickly, he mentioned the get-together, and Lucy insisted they hold the gathering at her place. She and her mate, Tamian, flew in from New Atlanta to be there, and Nikita was smitten with her cousin, sticking close and peppering her with all kinds of questions regarding computer infiltration as she'd begun calling hacking.

When they first arrived at Lucy's manor, Natalia was there with her boys. The twins ran to the door, and upon seeing Quinn and Nikita together, they froze.

"Look, Marsh! They're twins like us!" Major

exclaimed.

Kyllian dropped to his knees and poked Major in the belly, setting the boy off in the most adorable giggles. "Not twins. This is Quinn, and this is our daughter, Nikita."

"Nikita," Marshall said softy.

"Chiquita," Major added. They looked at each other grinning and proclaimed, "Banana!" The boys fell against each other laughing. "Hey, Lollipop, we have a banana in the family!" Major yelled.

Quinn had met Natalia and Maveryck via video chat, but every time they spoke, the boys had either been asleep or off visiting Rory and Sutton. Still, Quinn knew which one was which by their demeanor. The lavender-haired woman with her slight Russian accent joined them by the door. She ruffled both their blond heads, her eyes filled with the same love Quinn held for Nikita.

"Speaking of bananas, Grammy Rose has a treat for you two in the kitchen."

"Is it pizza?" Major asked, rubbing his tummy.

"You'll have to go see."

"Come on, Marsh!" Major grabbed his twin's hand, and the two boys took off at full speed. Natalia followed the boys more sedately.

"You weren't kidding," Quinn said. Kyllian had regaled her and Nikita with stories of the twins, and meeting them in person didn't disappoint.

The manor was filled with Lazlos, and after all the introductions were out of the way, the males went off to the game room to shoot pool and drink beer. Before he walked away, Quinn reminded Kyllian not to bet against his youngest brother, earning her a swat to the ass.

Kerrigan had mixed batches of what Maveryck called her world-famous margaritas, and Quinn had to agree they were delicious. Mac and Elijah were on kid duty, keeping the twins and Mateo occupied. Trenton, who had driven in the day before, sat with Sutton outside where they could sip whiskey in peace. When Rory shooed everyone out of the kitchen, the mates took Quinn to the den. They welcomed her as though they'd been lifelong friends. Each one took turns telling how they met their respective mate and what they endured. Quinn didn't have friends or siblings, but in each of these amazing women, she formed an instant bond.

The day was absolutely perfect, from the twins keeping everyone entertained, to the brothers being together on a rare occasion, to the fabulous food Rory single-handedly prepared. Having spent so many years with only her father for company, Quinn worried she would get overwhelmed, but instead, it was like coming home. It *was* coming home. This family of bikers, mercenaries, and Gryphons accepted Quinn, Nikita, and Trenton with open arms and all the love they had to give. This was what family was about.

After the food had been demolished and Kerrigan and Rhiannon helped Rory clean up the kitchen, Lucy found Quinn and asked her to go for a walk. When they were outside, Lucy dove right in. "Nikita is amazing. I'm sure you know this, but I'm talking about with a computer. She has a natural gift, and I would be honored to teach her more. Now that things in New

Atlanta are calm, Tamian and I plan to be here for a while. His father is ready to hand over the crown, so Tamian will be spending time with Xavier over the next few weeks, which leaves me with some downtime. If you and Kyllian agree, I'd love to have Nikita over and begin her training. I didn't say anything to her until I spoke to you first."

"That's very kind of you, and if you're sure you don't mind, I know she would love it. Kyllian and I talked it over already. Nikita wants to join me in the business, and with you teaching her what you know, that will give me time to focus on the aspects Dad handles. He said he eventually wants to retire, and the sooner that happens, the better. He deserves it."

"Not only don't I mind, I'm looking forward to it. I was good at what I did, but after spending time with Julian and Henry, I now know so much more, and I want to pay it forward, if you will."

"Then I'll tell Nikita the good news. She—"

"Major Lazlo, get your butt back in this house!" Natalia yelled after her son who ran out the back door, buck naked.

"But I'm a polar bear, Lolly!" Major dashed past Quinn and Lucy, headed for the swimming pool. He didn't stop until he did a cannonball in the deep end.

"Do either of you want a child? Because I have one for a couple thousand," Natalia asked, glaring at her son.

Lucy grinned. "I'd pay double that to keep him."

"Pay?" Natalia crossed her arms over her chest and tapped her foot on the concrete. "I'm offering that amount for someone to take him off my hands."

Major climbed out of the pool, stomped over to his mom, and shook his hair out like a dog. "You'd miss me, Lolly." When Natalia grabbed at him, he shrieked and took off running to the door where Hayden was waiting with a towel.

"If anyone's buying this little dude, it's me," Hayden said, wrapping Major up before tossing him over his shoulder.

Mercedes stuck her head out the door. "Yeah, what he said." Sadie was a gorgeous, curvy Latina. Her son, Mateo, was a little older than the twins, but he followed them everywhere they went. It was evident the boys spent a lot of time together.

Natalia pointed a finger at Sadie. "You remember that the next time Mateo comes home with permanent marker on his face."

Sadie just shrugged. "It came off. Eventually." Natalia rattled off something in Russian, and Sadie cackled.

When they returned inside, Quinn went to find Nikita to tell her the good news, but Kyllian intercepted her. "I have a surprise for you both."

About that time, a sharp whistle filled the air, and Sutton said, "Everyone out front."

"What's going on?" Nikita asked.

"You'll see," Kyllian told her. Nikita looked at Quinn, and she shook her head. She had no idea what was going on.

When they walked out the front door, everyone was gathered around. Kyllian took Quinn and Nikita by the hands and led them to the front of the group. "Less than two months ago, I was a lonely Hound. My brothers had found their mates, and while I was happy for them, I was also a little jealous. Then Pop sent me on what I considered a babysitting job, and my life changed forever. Not only did I find my own mate but also an amazing daughter. The Lazlos are about family, and as a family we ride together." Kyllian nodded to Hayden, who disappeared around the side of the house. A motorcycle revved to life, the garage door motored up, and a few seconds later, Hayden rolled down the driveway on a sleek, black Harley, complete with a sidecar.

"Dad! You did it!" Nikita squealed before jumping into his arms.

"I promised you I would, and I couldn't have my other best girl riding on something that wasn't comfortable." He put Nikita down and held out his hand for Quinn. "Come on. Let's take a look."

"Dad!" Nikita gasped when she rounded the bike. Quinn joined her and knelt to admire the paint job.

"What's it say?" Major asked, squirming in his dad's arms. "I wanna see."

Nikita beamed with joy. "It says, 'Here comes Trouble,' and it has a wolf on it."

Hayden was beyond talented. Quinn could see why he won awards for his creations. The wolf was an exact depiction of Nikita in her shifted form. Kyllian pointed to the gas tank, and Quinn gasped. A smaller version of her Wolf adorned the tank.

"Oh, Kyll, it's gorgeous. And that seat?" Quinn loved riding, but she had to admit the wrap-around seat would make the trip so much more enjoyable. Quinn grabbed Kyllian and kissed him, tongue and all, not caring his family was watching. Everyone gathered around, admiring Hayden's artistry.

"You gots a wolf, and we gots a Hulk," Marshall said softly to Nikita.

"We sure do." Nikita brushed her fingers through his hair, then went to Hayden. "This is absolutely amazing, Uncle Hay. Thank you."

"You're most welcome, Nik."

Nikita skipped over to her dad. "When can we ride? If I'd known this, I'd have brought my goggles."

Kyllian pointed to the sidecar. "Look in there." Nikita did, and she pulled out her goggles, waving them in the air. "Does this mean…?"

"It does." He turned and called out, "Everyone ready?"

Quinn was confused until the brothers, Tamian, and Elijah walked around the house to the garage and all returned on their own bikes. There was a flurry of activity as all the females and kids went inside to bundle up. Since Trenton didn't ride, Sutton and Rory were staying behind to keep him company.

Major ran through the house, yelling, "Wait for me, Lolly. I gotta pee!"

Nikita was grinning like a loon as she and Quinn put on their coats. "This is why Dad told me to bring my cap. Did you know?"

"I knew he had Hayden working on the sidecar, and I saw pictures of it in stages, but I didn't know it was finished or that he bought a new bike."

Nikita sighed. "He's the best."

Quinn tugged on one of the flaps of Nikita's cap. "He sure is."

Everyone was bundled up and climbing on their respective bikes when Major came bounding down the steps, his little helmet bobbing on his head. "Someone help me strap this thing on."

Warryck knelt in front of the boy. "I got you, Little Man."

Quinn grinned up at Kyllian. "I want one."

Natalia passed by holding Marshall's hand and muttered, "Two thousand, and he's yours."

"Sold," Kyllian called after her.

"Princess, stop trying to sell off my son," Maveryck said, slapping Natalia's ass as she passed.

Quinn waited to see what the Russian would do. Instead of scowling, she arched her eyebrow and mouthed, "Later." She got the twins situated in their sidecar with ease. Before climbing behind her mate, Natalia grabbed his beard and laid a passionate kiss on him. Maveryck was smirking as she climbed behind him and put her helmet on.

Nikita was seated in her personalized sidecar, a grin plastered on her face. Her earflaps stuck out from beneath her helmet, and her goggles were secure over her eyes. "This is gonna be so much fun."

When everyone was ready, Ryker raised a fist and announced, "Hounds, let's ride."

There were whoops and hollers all around as they pulled down Lucy's driveway. The deep rumble of the motors sent a thrill through Quinn's core, and she let out her own "woohoo." Nikita held out her hand for a high five, and Quinn smacked her gently before propping her triceps over her armrests. As much as she liked riding wrapped around Kyllian's waist, her cushioned seat was much more comfortable. The seven bikes rode not side by side but staggered. Ryker took the lead with War next in line, followed by Tamian and Elijah. The three bikes with sidecars went last.

As Quinn took in the scenery, she couldn't help but thank the goddess one more time for the gift or her mate, her daughter, and their family.

CHAPTER TWENTY

Quinn

"MOM, I'M HEADED to Lucy's."

Quinn stood from her desk chair and stretched, then met Nikita by the office door. "Okay, honey. I'll see you tomorrow at Rhi's shower."

"You still going early to help Kerrigan set up?"

"Yes. I'm picking up the flowers from Charlotte's shop first."

"Perfect. I'm grabbing the cupcakes on my way. Love you. Tell Dad I love him too." Nikita kissed Quinn's cheek and headed through the house to the garage where her new car waited. Like everything else she did, Nikita learned to drive with ease. When she passed her test, Kyllian took her to buy a cute little four-door with one of the highest safety ratings available. And, as Lucy suspected, Nikita was a whiz with computers. Nikita was with Lucy almost every day while Tamian was visiting his father, giving Quinn and Kyllian plenty of alone time.

Their new house was close to being finished, so between packing and all the sex, Quinn had been busy. Things had been close to perfect with the exception of

Kyllian's job at Dominion. The first time Quinn went with him, she walked in the door and froze. Men and women strolled through the club in various stages of dress, some completely naked. Kyllian offered to take her home then and there. She almost took him up on it until Charlotte and Wynter came over and took pity on her. Kyllian had one sub he needed to "work with" that night, and Kyllian promised she could go in the back room and watch. The sub, Brandon, was a young man who'd been in an abusive relationship. Kyllian didn't share his background without getting the man's permission first.

Charlotte and Wynter were best friends, and they bantered much the way Kyllian and Nikita did. They snipped and teased each other, but it was friendly and full of love. After sitting with them for five minutes, Quinn relaxed. Kyllian admitted later to asking Spyder to have Charlotte speak to Quinn about the club and what went on there.

"How do you handle Jude doing scenes with other females?" Quinn asked her once they were seated at a booth. Kyllian was on guard duty that night, and he promised to check in with her often.

"I don't. If he wants to do a demo, I'm his willing participant."

"That makes sense, but Shibari is beautiful. Even I could do that. Kyllian inflicts pain."

Wynter propped her chin on her palm and asked, "Has he explained why he does it?"

Quinn nodded. "He says he's providing a service. Before we mated, he had a dedicated sub he had sex with afterward. He promised he would no longer do

292

that, but if his subs get off on the pain, it's still sexual in nature."

"Would you be okay with it if all his clients were men?" Charlotte asked.

"Yes." They had discussed that too. "But only one of his subs are men. I feel like I'm being petty. He's my destined mate. I know in my soul he would never do anything to disrespect me. This is my hang-up, and I'll learn to deal with it."

Charlotte grabbed Quinn's hand. "I think if it really bothers you, Kyllian will stop doing it. That's part of being a mate, making sure your other half is always happy."

"But I don't want him to make all the sacrifices."

"Uh oh," Wynter muttered.

Quinn followed the other woman's eyes. A young man stalked through the door and right up to Kyllian. Even with her shifter hearing she couldn't hear what was being said. The man's head was bent, and Kyllian had his hand on the guy's shoulder.

"That's Brandon," Charlotte said. "Poor guy. He hasn't done well with Gunnar. Silas is ready to kick him out."

"Kick him out? Why?"

"From what Spyder said, Kyllian's way of Domming is different than Gunnar's. Both know how to wield the various pain implements, but Kyllian has a way of knowing exactly what they need. Like last time Kyllian dealt with Brandon, all they did was talk."

It was that moment, that statement, that changed everything. Quinn studied psychology to understand how the mind worked. Kyllian instinctually understood what his clients needed without having taken a single class. When Kyllian looked over at her, she nodded. *Go take care of him. I'm fine with Charlotte and Wynter.*

Do you want to come watch?

No. He needs your undivided attention.

Thank you, Pretty Lady.

Quinn turned back to the two females, and Wynter was watching her closely. "Can you and Kyllian mind-speak?"

"Yes. When we first met, our animals chatted with each other, but after we were mated and things settled down, well, it just happened."

"I'm so jealous," Charlotte huffed. "You two are" — she looked around — "you know. It's so not fair."

A man with long hair and lots of ink strolled over to their table. He wore tight leather pants and nothing else. He leaned down, getting in Charlotte's face. "What's not fair is my mate sitting here with way too many clothes on."

Charlotte put her hand on his face and gently pushed him away. "Go away. We're having girl talk."

"Hi, Quinn. I'm Spyder." He didn't offer to shake her hand; instead, he bowed his head slightly.

"It's nice to finally meet you. Kyllian's told me all about you."

Jude did a little dance move, shaking his ass and twirling around. "All good stuff. Am I right?"

"Don't you have someone to tie up?" Wynter asked.

"Yes, you if you don't behave. Don't make me go get Hawk."

"Oh, please. Go get Hawk," Wynter sassed.

"Nope. He's busy. Speaking of getting busy, how about we do a scene, Sweetness?"

"I thought you were on the floor tonight?"

"I am, but Silas has a new client who is interested in Shibari. He asked if we would demonstrate."

"Sure." Charlie turned to Quinn. "Will you be okay with Wynter?"

"Yes. I'd love to see what the two of you do as well."

Charlotte took Jude's offered hand, and the two walked toward the back of the club.

Wynter sighed. "Those two doing a scene is amazing. But now that I have you to myself, please tell me about your pack."

"I don't actually have one." Quinn leaned in and told Wynter about what happened to her after her mother died, the Ozark pack, and how she ended up meeting Kyllian and finding Nikita.

"Wow, your dad's family sounds like mine." Wynter told Quinn about her ancestors coming down from Canada several generations prior, and even though Wynter could shift without stripping, she assured Quinn there was no dire DNA in her lineage. Wynter didn't expound on what magic she did have, and Quinn understood the need to keep some things secret. It did make her curious though.

That night had been life-changing. Quinn was awed by Jude and Charlotte's scene. Then, after seeing the change in Brandon after he and Kyllian went to a back room, she knew Kyllian was needed there for more than watching the floor. She trusted her mate, and once they were in the car on their way home, she told him as much.

Now, almost two months later, she was waiting on him to get home from a job. It had been a two-person hit, and Kyllian, Ace, and Ripper had taken the contract down in Massachusetts. Nikita researched the marks with little input from Quinn, proving she was capable of helping with the family business.

The garage door opening had Quinn checking the monitor out of habit. Not having a long driveway took some getting used to, but as far as they knew, all threats to their family had been taken care of. Quinn rose from the desk to go meet her mate. He strode through the door and stalked to her, not stopping until he grabbed her ponytail, wrenched her head back, and devoured her mouth. Kyllian was always intense after a job, and Quinn reaped the rewards.

"Where's Trouble?" he asked, nipping at her neck.

"At Lucy's. Why?" Quinn already knew why, but she wanted him to say the words.

"Because I'm going to fuck you hard, and I don't want to scar our daughter." Kyllian grabbed her hand, practically dragging her to their bedroom. "Strip. Now. This is going to be hard and fast. I do not like being away from you for so long."

"It was only two nights," Quinn reminded him as she undressed.

"That's two too many." When she was bare, Kyllian pushed her onto the bed, dragged her ass to the edge, and spread her legs, burying his face there. He didn't tease this time. He licked and sucked and plunged until she was writhing against his wicked mouth. Once she caught her orgasm, he rose and slid his hard cock home in the slickness. As he pounded into her heat, Kyllian leaned over and took her mouth in a near-bruising kiss, her release evident on his whiskers. The first time she tried to wipe it off, he grabbed her wrist and told her his beard was his "flavor saver", and he wanted to smell her as long as possible.

As promised, Kyllian gave it to her hard. She loved sex with her mate. When he came home from jobs, it was always a hard fuck. When he caught her during the day, he would kneel between her legs as she sat at her desk and eat her out. If he woke her in the middle of the night, it was slow, lazy lovemaking. Sometimes she woke him in the early morning with a blowjob. It was never the same but always satisfying.

Kyllian got his nut, screaming the house down when he came. This time when he pulled out, he knelt between her legs and sucked and lapped at their combined releases. She knew what was next, so when he stood and leaned down, she opened for him. Kyllian licked inside her mouth, sharing their spend with her.

"Shower, Pretty Lady. Then we need to talk." Kyllian rose and pulled her off the bed, leading her to his massive walk-in shower. He released her hair from the band as the water heated. Before meeting her mate, Quinn washed her hair every three or four days, but showers with Kyllian usually ended in more sex and her hair getting wet. Plus, he loved to lather her long strands and massage her scalp. Quinn didn't hate it. It was one of her favorite things he did for her.

"Don't we need to get ready for the club?"

"Talk later." Kyllian was in a mood, and when he was, she let him be. He pushed her under the hot spray, tipping her head back. Quinn closed her eyes and let him have his way with her. Kyllian lathered her hair, massaging her scalp, before rinsing the foam from it. He wrung it out and applied conditioner, moving her so he could bathe her body. His tone had been gruff, but his callused hands were gentle as he applied her favorite body wash. Silent Kyllian was unusual, so Quinn worried about what was on his mind.

Kyllian scrubbed his body quickly, then he rinsed the conditioner from her hair. After shutting the water off, he grabbed a towel and wrapped it around her hair before taking another and drying her off. Using the same towel, he swiped at his body only enough that he wasn't dripping. Kyllian removed the towel from her hair and squeezed the excess water out. Knowing she hated leaving it tangled, he opened the top drawer, grabbed her brush, and gently set about running it through until her hair was sleek. Quinn studied his reflection in the mirror. His brow was furrowed as he contemplated whatever it was bothering him.

When he was satisfied with her hair, Kyllian put the brush away. He picked her up and carried her back to the bedroom, placing her on her feet long enough to pull the covers down. "Bed, Pretty Lady." Quinn climbed onto the mattress and scooted over to her side. Once Kyllian was lying next to her, he pulled the sheet up to their waists, rolled to his back, and settled Quinn on top of him.

Like flipping a switch, Kyllian went from intense to tender. "Brandon moved to California."

"Does that bother you?" Quinn had met the young sub on a couple occasions. She understood Kyllian's need to help the man. Hell, Quinn wanted to adopt him, bring him home, and smother him with love.

"It did until he promised to find a good Dom to continue his therapy." That's what Kyllian called what he did for the man. Not a scene. Not kink. Therapy. Quinn got it. It took her seeing Brandon that night at Dominion go from sad to smiling after spending time in the back with Kyllian. He ran his fingers through her damp hair. "He was the last one. I turned all the others over to Gunnar."

Quinn tried to push herself up to sitting, but Kyllian banded a strong arm around her, keeping her against his chest. "But why? I told you I was okay with it."

"You did, and I believe you, but I need something else, Pretty Lady. Yes, I'm good at what I do, but I was no longer getting anything out of it. When I became a Dom, I needed that release. Not the sexual part but the part where I expended the energy. Whipping, flogging, caning, it all allowed me to release the tension of the day. It was an outlet for my frustrations." Kyllian trailed his fingertips down her cheek. "I no longer need that. Spending any time away from you with someone else, even if it isn't sexual, no longer sits well with me. You're my mate. You deserve that time, even if it's thirty minutes. I deserve my time to belong to me, and I want every spare moment with you I can get. We have enough in our lives taking us away from one another."

Kyllian framed Quinn's face with both hands, his

eyes soft and shining with so much love. "Besides, I think it's time we give Nikita a brother or sister. I know you said you wanted to get to know one another first, but I don't want to wait, Quinn. The house will be done soon, and we can turn one of the bedrooms into a nursery. I want to see you round with my child. I want to add to our little family of three. Trouble's growing up. She won't live with us forever, and I don't want to wait any longer. Please tell me you want that."

Quinn was stunned. She had been so worried about the secret she was keeping, surprised Kyllian hadn't caught on. "Stay right there," she said, slipping from the bed.

Kyllian pushed up to rest on his elbows. "Where are you going?"

Quinn opened the top drawer of her dresser and pulled out what she now felt would be a welcomed surprise. Handing the plastic stick over, she waited.

"This... You... Quinn?"

"I wasn't sure how to tell you."

Kyllian threw the sheet off, tossed the positive pregnancy test on the bed, and grabbed her up in his arms. "You open that pretty mouth and say, 'Kyll, we're having a baby.'"

"Kyll, we're having a baby," Quinn whispered.

Kyllian grinned, then slid to his knees. He pressed soft kisses to her belly and whispered, "Hey, Little One. This is your papa. I can't wait to meet you. You already have the best momma in the world carrying you around, and you have the most awesome big sister. She's trouble, but in a good way. I hope you're just like her." Kyllian hugged Quinn's legs and pressed his ear to her stomach. Quinn knew what he would hear because she'd already discovered that faint, rapid heartbeat. Her Wolf had alerted her to the fact that she was pregnant, and once she really paid attention, Quinn detected the little life growing inside. He looked up at her, tears glistening.

"Thank you, Pretty Lady. For loving me. For giving me a daughter, and now for giving me what I never imagined I would be blessed with."

"I'm the one who's grateful. Before you walked through my front door, I was a shell. You gave me my life back, made me whole. You've given me everything."

Kyllian stood and held up a finger. "Not everything." He went to his own dresser, and when he turned around, he held out a stunning platinum ring topped with a sapphire surrounded by diamonds. Quinn held out her hand, and as he slipped the ring on her finger, he said, "As mates, we don't need the ceremony to be bound to one another, but I want it anyway. Quinn Shepherd, will you marry me?"

"Yes."

Kyllian kissed her until she couldn't breathe. When he stepped back, he walked over to where he dropped his jeans earlier and pulled out his phone. A few seconds later, it rang.

"Hey, Dad. What's up?"

"She said yes."

"Woohoo! Best day ever. Well, best day after you saving me. Ooh, and after getting my sidecar. And maybe after—"

"Yeah, yeah, I get it. It's up there in the top ten."

Nikita laughed. "I'm happy for you both. Now you need to get busy and have me a little brother or sister. *That* will be the best day ever."

Kyllian grinned. "About that…"

The End

A NOTE FROM THE AUTHOR

Thank you for reading Kyllian's story. If you have a moment, a review would be much appreciated. It doesn't have to be long, just heartfelt. This book has been too long in the making. If you follow me on social media, you've probably seen me talk about my mom who is battling dementia. On top of helping out with her, I lost my step-father-in-law. Papa John was like a father to me, and his passing hit me hard. I know everyone has something they deal with every day, but when you're an author and you can't focus, the words are hard to come by, so thank you for your patience.

As always, Candy, Jen, Kerstin, Nikki, and Katie are my cheerleaders, my confidants, and my sanity. My readers are my lifeline too. Without you all, I wouldn't need to put the words to paper. I also have to give a shout out to "the man." His love for me never wavers, even when I don't want to leave the house, ever.

Next up in this series is Ripper and Glory. The leading female's background comes from real life. I am also starting the second-generation series where Major and Marshall will be adults. The series title is Rebel Moon Shifters.

CAST OF CHARACTERS

Sutton Lazlo – Patriarch, former cop, former Pres of the Hounds MC
Aurora Rose "Rory" Lazlo – Matriarch

Ryker "Ryot" Lazlo – MC Pres, Leader of Mercs
Rhiannon Spencer – Witch
    McKenzie "Mac" Colins – Ryker's daughter
    Elijah McLean – Mac's boyfriend

Warryck "War" Lazlo – former Professor, current Merc
Kerrigan O'Shea – Bartender
    Lucy Ball – War's daughter, Computer Hacker
    Tamian St. Claire – Lucy's mate, Gargoyle

Maveryck "Mayhem" Lazlo – MC Vice Pres, Merc
Tatiana Volkova/Natalia Jones – Russian Mafia Princess
    Major Lazlo – Mav's son
    Marshall Lazlo – Mav's son

Kyllian "Kayos" Lazlo – Merc
Quinn Shepherd – Handler
    Nikita – Quinn's daughter

Hayden "Havyk" Lazlo – Bike Designer, Merc
Sadie Rodriguez – Mom
    Mateo Rodriguez – Sadie's son

"The Girls"

Poppy & Daniel Ellis
    Devon (son) & Nora
    Theo (son)
    Jericho - grandson

Holly & Alexander Carter
Aster & Dylan Roberts
Laurel & Tucker Williams
Dahlia & Linus Parks
Iris & Brooks Nelson

The Hounds

Zareck "The Reverend" West
Patrick "Tank" Murphy
Roman "Hawk" Hayes
Ripley "Ripper" Davidson
Asher "Ace" McMurray
Sultan
King
Judge
Shadow
Legend
Brick
Maximus
Locke
Storm

ABOUT THE AUTHOR

Multi-genre author Faith Gibson began writing in high school, and through the years, penned many stories and poems. As her dreams continued getting crazier than the one before, she decided to keep a dream journal. Many of these nighttime escapades have led to a line, a chapter, or even a complete story.

"Love is love, and there's not enough love in the world." This belief she holds strongly, and it's the prevailing theme in her works, all of which come with a happy ending.

Faith believes her purpose in life is to entertain the masses, even if it's one person at a time. Living just outside of Nashville, Tennessee, with the love of her life and her pit bull pup, when she's not hard at work writing her next adventure, she can often be found playing trivia while enjoying craft beer, listening to live music, or off on an adventure of her own.